MURDER'S MADNESS

Other books by

Alex Matthews

MURDER'S MADNESS

by

Alex Matthews

VEILED INTENT

PRESS

Library of Congress Control Number: 2007938467

ISBN 978-0-9794756-0-3

10 9 8 7 6 5 4 3 2 1

Dedication

For my husband Allen, who makes all things possible.

Acknowledgements

Many thanks to all the people who helped in the birthing of this book: my husband, Allen Matthews, whose fourth career has become book promotion; my editor, Chris Roerden, who would not accept less than my best; my fellow critique group members, Nancy Carleton, Carol Hauswald, and Ginny Skweres, who faithfully refused to let me get away with anything; my publicist, Barbara Young, who applied her vast energy and enthusiasm to book promotion; Deputy Chief Robert Scianna of the Oak Park Police Department, who explained the finer points of police procedure; and Chicago Tribune reporters, Maurice Possley and Ray Gibson, who increased my knowledge of journalistic ethics and the process of investigative reporting.

Chapter 1

AUGUST

Cassidy McCabe was standing in the kitchen reading the directions on a box of pasta when she heard the back door close. *If Zach's home, it's later than you thought. Did you perhaps procrastinate a bit in getting your butt downstairs to start dinner?* He came around the short wall that divided her client waiting room from the kitchen, his sturdy broad-shouldered presence making the large space seem smaller. She felt the stirring of warmth his arrival usually triggered.

"Hey," he said, "I'm glad you haven't started dinner yet. I'm meeting a woman at seven who's interested in the condo."

"I don't have any clients, so I can come with you and meet the potential tenant. How'd she sound on the phone?"

"A little strange."

"Strange how?"

"Evasive. And there was something else, but I can't put my finger on it."

"Now I really want to go."

They drove to Marina City, a landmark building in Chicago with two round corncob-shaped towers. People often referred to it as the twin towers, although the building bore no resemblance to the obliterated World Trade Center. Zach had lived in a Marina City condo before moving into Cassidy's Oak Park house and afterward had kept it for rental income.

He drove up the ramp onto the concrete plaza between the two towers. Then he handed his

Subaru over to a car-parker, who, for eleven dollars, would allow his car to sit two hours in the garage that occupied the first nineteen floors of both towers. They crossed the plaza, entered a glass-domed structure, and rode the escalator down to the below-ground lobby.

A short, plump woman was pacing in front of the glass doors at the entrance to the West Tower. She was clad in a stylish skirt and jacket, each a different shade of blue, the colors uncoordinated. When she turned, Cassidy noticed that although she'd arranged her light brown hair in a tidy bob, she'd used a heavy hand with her blush, resulting in garish red patches on her cheeks. *Good hair, nice clothes, but mismatched colors and clownish makeup. She forgot to look in the mirror before she went out?*

Zach asked, "Are you Delia Schiff?"

Staring between them, the woman responded with a meek yes.

"I'm Zach Moran, and this is my wife Cassidy."

He led the two women into a room where a uniformed guard made sure only those who belonged got past the security system. Zach held his key card in front of a red electronic eye and a second glass door slid open, admitting them to the elevator lobby.

They rode to the forty-first floor, then stepped out into a donut-shaped corridor with ten pie-shaped condos fanning out from the center. Zach opened the door to his unit and took them through the entry hall into the living room.

Cassidy's breath caught slightly as she took in the view: high-rises to the east, a small slice of Lake Michigan visible between the buildings, a plumy cloud riding high in the lavender-tinted sky. Although she'd gazed through the glass wall countless times, the changing light made the view appear slightly different each time she saw it.

Delia turned her head to the side and stared into the middle distance, a distracted look on her face.

Cassidy wondered if the woman had even noticed the view. "What do you think of it?" she asked.

Delia showed no sign of having heard Cassidy's question.

Maybe a little deaf?

Cassidy put her hand on Delia's arm. The woman started, then focused on Cassidy's face.

"Does this seem to be what you're looking for?"

"It's very nice." A tremor passed through a muscle on her cheek. "I'd, um...I'd like to rent it."

Cassidy exchanged a look with Zach, a thought passing between them. *Something isn't right. Well, you knew that when you first looked at her. But it could be something simple. She's a social isolate...always lived with her mother...out of her element here.*

Zach rested his hands on his belt. "You haven't seen the bedroom or the bath yet."

"Yes, I should do that."

Trying to act normal. That's what makes her seem so strange.

Zach showed Delia the other two rooms.

When they returned, she began twisting her hands together. "What do I have to do to rent it? I know I'd be happy here."

Cassidy asked, "Why this particular condo?"

"Well, um, it's the right size...the kitchen is nice."

What's she not saying? "What else?"

"It has a good security system." Then, in a barely audible tone, "Nobody could bother me here."

"Is someone bothering you in the place you live now?"

Delia fished a tissue out of her shoulder bag, dabbed at her nose, then twisted it around her finger. "I didn't mean to say that."

"Someone *is* bothering you."

Delia shook her head.

"Tell me about it," Cassidy said in a gentle voice.

"It, um...it really isn't anything. Just this person who moved in across the hall. He stares at me when I go out."

"Where do you live now?"

"This dump in Uptown. But I don't want to talk about it." Then, a note of despair creeping into her voice, "People never believe me anyway."

Cassidy felt herself softening. "I'm a therapist. I'm not going to judge you."

The woman moistened her upper lip. "This guy's been watching me since the day he moved in. Sometimes he calls me names. He tried to grab me a couple days ago but I ran back inside my apartment and locked the door. I've reported him to the landlord but he won't do anything."

"You must be scared to death," Cassidy said. "I can see why you'd be desperate to get out of that building."

"That's why I'd like to rent this unit as soon as I can."

Zach moved closer to Cassidy, grasped her upper arm, and gave it a not exactly tender squeeze. She read it as a don't-get-sucked-in gesture.

She asked, "But why this one? There are lots of buildings with good security."

Looking at the floor, Delia twisted her hands again. A few seconds passed before she started speaking. "I've been turned down at some other places because I don't have any credit history. I pay for everything in cash. You see, I have a trust fund so I've never held a job." She pulled a brown envelope out of her purse. "I brought a copy of my financial statement to show that I can easily afford the rent. And I do volunteer. You could talk to the Volunteer Coordinator at the Chicago Food Depository and she'll tell you how reliable I am."

Zach said, "I'm sorry, but I have to see a credit history just like everyone else. You could try Logan Square. Some of those buildings might be easier to get into."

Sympathy welled in Cassidy's chest. *Delia's obviously got problems, but that doesn't mean we should just brush her off.* She looked into her husband's face, which had gone from congenial to remote.

"There's no reason we have to be rigid about this. If Delia's landlord will vouch for her, I think that should be good enough."

Zach replied, "We can talk about it later."

To Delia, Cassidy said, "So what would your landlord tell us about you?"

"I always pay my rent on time. I'm clean and quiet and never make any trouble."

"And he'll verify this?"

"I think so." Delia caught her lip between her teeth. "But he doesn't, uh...he doesn't want me to leave so he might not tell the truth. He wants me to stay so the other tenants will have someone to, um...torment. Someone has to be tormented, and if I'm gone they'll have to pick on one of their own."

Oh shit. Way worse than I thought. "How do they torment you?"

"They talk about me. I can hear them through the walls. It's gotten so bad the last few nights I could hardly get any sleep."

Auditory hallucinations. Probably schizophrenic. But lots of schizophrenics do okay as long as they take their meds. Although—if she's hearing voices— she probably isn't. Or she could be on her meds but decompensating because of stress.

Cassidy said, "I think you hear voices."

"No! No I don't!"

"But that doesn't necessarily rule you out. If we knew you'd been stable for a while, if we knew you were taking your meds and consistent about it, we'd give you serious consideration."

"I'm not on meds."

"If you don't tell the truth, we can't possibly rent to you."

A short silence. "All right, I am." Delia's eyes shifted to Zach. "But he won't let you anyway."

"Zach's nicer than he seems."

"No I'm not."

"*Are* you taking your meds?" Cassidy asked.

"I haven't skipped a pill in over three years."

"The other thing is, we'd have to talk to your doctor."

"Could you talk to my therapist instead? My doctor's hard to reach but my therapist returns calls right away."

"Sure."

Delia took out a business card, wrote something on it, and handed it to Cassidy. The therapist's name was Sue Bolas and Delia had added the woman's cell number.

She asked in a whispery voice, "You think there's a chance?"

"I do," Cassidy replied.

"I wouldn't get your hopes up," Zach countered.

* * *

Going out into the humid August air, they headed toward the Smith and Wollensky steak house, a part of the Marina City complex.

"I know you feel sorry for her," Zach said, after they were seated. "Hell, I do too. But I'm not renting to a wacko."

"She's not a wacko. She's a schizophrenic. At least I think that's what she is."

"Isn't calling her *a* schizophrenic almost as bad as calling her a wacko?"

Cassidy gave an exasperated huff. "All right, a person with schizophrenia."

A waiter arrived at their table, a professional smile on his chiseled face. "Can I get you something to drink?"

Zach ordered a bourbon and soda. Since he usually limited himself to wine with dinner, Cassidy took this as a cue. *But you already knew he was aggravated. More than aggravated—afraid you'll back him into a corner and pressure him into doing something he absolutely doesn't want to do.*

"She says she's taking her meds," Cassidy said. "Lots of schizophrenics are able to function fairly well when properly medicated." *As if you had any experience with schizophrenics. Well, you did go to a seminar once.*

"You believe her? She sounded crazy as hell to me."

"I admit she was a little off, but for the most part she was able to hold it together. She showed up on time, knew what she wanted, presented her case in a reasonable way. I think it's just the stress of being threatened by her neighbor that's caused her symptoms to flare up."

"Even if she's taking her meds now, that doesn't mean diddly about what she'll do in the future. Nutcases are famous for going off their meds."

"She says she's been stable for three years. Come on, Zach, we can't discriminate against her because she's mentally ill."

"What if she busts up the furniture? Or throws herself off the balcony? Or attacks one of the other residents?"

"If she sees her therapist, stays on her meds, and lives in a safe environment like Marina City, there's no reason to think she'd make any trouble."

"A lot of ifs."

The waiter brought Zach's drink. "Are you ready to order?"

An intense pang in Cassidy's stomach alerted her to the fact that she was ravenous. "Uh ... just a minute." *You let him go, it'll be another half hour.* She hastily opened her menu.

"I'll be back in a few."

"No, wait, I know what I want," she lied, restraining herself from grabbing his jacket. Seconds ticked by as she scanned the entries.

The waiter's smile stiffened.

Three beats later, she looked up to make sure he hadn't succeeded in scuttling off. "I'll take the salmon."

Zach said, "The sirloin, rare, and a bottle of Oregon Pinot Noir."

After the waiter left, Zach continued. "If you won't listen to me, why don't you ask that woman you know—the one on the condo board—what she thinks of renting to a schizophrenic?"

"A person who has schizophrenia."

"So why don't you ask her? Maybe she'll have more influence than I do."

"I don't really know her. She's a friend of Gran's. But she's very nice and I'm sure she'd disapprove of discrimination on the basis of an illness."

"You just make things up as you go along, don't you?"

"It doesn't matter what Joan thinks. Delia needs to be in a safe place, and we're in a position to help someone whose life is harder than we can even imagine."

"You didn't buy that shit about people tormenting her, did you? That was obviously pure paranoia."

"Yeah, I know it was. But it could be true that some guy in the building's harassing her. Bullies tend to look for people like Delia. If her therapist says she's off her meds, then I agree, we shouldn't rent to her. But if Sue Bolas tells us Delia is compliant and stable, I think we have to let her have the condo."

Deep ridges appeared on Zach's brow. "You're going into your do-or-die mode, aren't you?"

"I've been doing my best not to be so controlling."

Zach gave her a hard stare. Then his body softened and he reached across the table to take her hand. "Yeah, I know you have. Sometimes you get this look on your face like it's nearly killing you to keep your mouth shut, but you do."

"Only this time I can't. Delia's desperate to get into Marina City and I feel it would be just plain wrong to deny her if she's capable of living independently."

Later that evening Cassidy was sitting on the waterbed, her calico cat bundled on her chest, the two engaged in a heartfelt petting session, when the phone rang. Cassidy tried to pick up the cordless from her nightstand without moving her torso, but Starshine, who resented the slightest interruption in their lovefest, abandoned Cassidy's chest and went to sleep at the foot of the bed.

"I'm Sue Bolas, returning your call," the woman on the other end said. "Delia gave me permission to tell you anything you want to know."

"I'm a therapist myself," Cassidy said, "but I've never worked with ... people who have schizophrenia. I guess the first thing I need to know is whether she's taking her meds."

"I'm certain she is. She's quite intelligent and has a clear understanding of how bad it can be if she doesn't."

"Um...she talked about the neighbors tormenting her. I had the impression she was paranoid and hearing voices."

"It's the stress. Did she tell you about the thug who tried to assault her?"

"You think that really happened?"

"Considering she was fine before he started harassing her, I have no reason to doubt what she said. But then, as he continued to terrorize her, her stress level went up and she started having auditory hallucinations. This can happen to anybody with schizophrenia. Their voices almost never completely disappear. During low stress periods, the voices are like a radio playing softly in the background and the person can pretty much ignore them. But when there's an increase in stress, the voices get louder and nastier, and the person starts to believe them. The thing that's encouraging here is that even though Delia's been going through an extremely frightening period, she hasn't had a full-blown episode."

"So what do you think she'd be like if we let her move into our condo?"

"Her symptoms would probably abate and she'd be stable again. She's thoughtful, kind, a great sense of humor. I really like her."

Cassidy reported to Zach what the therapist had said.

His mouth tightened. "All right, I give. If her landlord is similarly enthusiastic, I'll let her move in."

Chapter 2

FEBRUARY

A Sunday morning, temperatures below freezing, a leaden sky threatening to drop more bucketfuls of snow onto Oak Park. Cassidy was staring into her closet trying to cull out the most disreputable articles of clothing when the phone rang. Happy to be interrupted from one of her least favorite tasks, she crossed to her desk on the opposite side of the bedroom and picked up.

"It's Delia."

"Oh hi," Cassidy said. Once her tenant's symptoms had subsided, she and Delia had started doing things together on occasion.

"Something bad's happened. You have to come down here right away."

"What?" A flutter of anxiety in Cassidy's stomach. "What is it? What happened?"

"I can't tell you over the phone."

"Why not?"

Delia whispered, "People are listening."

Oh no! Her symptoms kicking up again.

"What exactly do you need me to do?"

"I just said I can't talk on the phone. I'm afraid, I'm afraid. There are bad things happening. You're the only one who can help."

What are you going to do? You have no experience with this kind of thing.

"Look, Delia, I think it would be better if you called your therapist."

"It has to be you! You have to come!"

She's in crisis. You have to do something.

"I know you're upset, but I doubt I'd be able to do anything for you. Maybe you could call 9-1-1."

"Didn't you hear me?" Delia's voice climbed to a higher octave. "You're the only one who can help."

Cassidy tried to think of a way out and couldn't.

"I'll be there in a little while. In the meantime, is there anything you can do to keep yourself safe?"

"I could lock myself in the bathroom. But locks won't keep them out."

"The bathroom sounds good to me. I'll let myself in, then tell you I'm there so you'll know it's okay to come out."

Delia's voice implored, "Please come soon."

Cassidy gazed out the window at a thick maze of snow-covered branches. Her hands shaking, she shuffled through the clutter in her top desk drawer and found Sue Bolas's card. She dialed the therapist's cell number and Sue answered.

"This is Cass McCabe. I talked to you back in the summer about renting to Delia Schiff."

"Have you heard from her?"

"She just called. Said she needed me to come to Marina City. She sounded pretty delusional."

"I'm not surprised. She quit taking her meds about a month ago."

"She quit? I thought you said she wouldn't do that."

The therapist sighed. "Ordinarily she wouldn't. But her former psychiatrist left her managed care company and she started seeing this new doctor who changed her medication. The drug he gave her made her nauseated, but when she tried to get him to put her back on the old one, he kept telling her to give it more time. She couldn't take the nausea so she quit. Personally, I think her doctor's getting a kickback from the drug company."

"That's so outrageous! I hate when doctors get away with things like that."

"Don't we all."

"So what's the treatment plan?"

"She needs to be hospitalized. When I saw her two weeks ago, I tried to convince her to go voluntarily, but she wouldn't hear of it. Then she blew off her next appointment and now she's screening my calls. She's avoiding me because she knows I'd have the cops take her in if I could just get her into my office."

"Is that what I should do? Call the police once I get inside the condo?"

"That wouldn't be my first choice. Being manhandled by the cops is pretty traumatic. If you can get her to trust you, you might be able to persuade her to go voluntarily. There were a couple of times I was able to convince her to let me take her to the ER."

"But how do I do it?"

"You have to join in her delusion. Get her to talk and act like you believe what she's saying."

"If she won't go voluntarily, should I call the cops?"

"Yes."

"Is there any chance she'd get violent if she knows I'm doing it?"

"I don't think so." A pause. "But it would be better if she didn't know."

Hanging up, Cassidy sucked in air. She knew she should get going but couldn't bring herself to move. She wished Zach were his old self and that she could tell him about Delia's call and he would feel protective and insist on driving her to Marina City.

But he isn't and you can't and he won't. Left the house a couple of hours ago without a word to you and he probably has his cell turned off. And even if you could reach him, he probably wouldn't say what you want him to.

Having taken a moment to feel sorry for herself, she was ready to leave. She put the Marina City key card and the condo key into her purse, bundled herself in a heavy coat, punched numbers on the security system panel, and went out the back door.

Cassidy used her key to open the condo door, releasing a cloud of noxious air, the stink of over-ripe garbage. The galley kitchen to her left was heaped with take-out cartons. The dressing-room mirror to her right was scrawled with words in red marker: *Mother Mary, My Rosary,* and *Help Me.* The bathroom door was closed.

Another step brought her into view of the living room. Thick layers of newspaper covered the glass wall overlooking the balcony. Feeling claustrophobic, she clutched her arms across her chest, then punched a button to turn on the track lights.

She went back into the dressing room and knocked on the bathroom door. "It's me, Cass. I'm here."

Delia came out into the dressing room. Large purplish bags hung beneath her bloodshot eyes and her light brown hair was matted to her scalp. The flowered blouse and striped cotton pants attiring her ample body looked as if they'd been slept in.

"Let's go sit in the living room," Cassidy said.

"Are you sure it's safe?"

"Yes, really, I am."

Delia sat in the middle of the sofa, legs pressed together, arms folded across her midsection. Cassidy placed a dining room chair opposite Delia so they could face each other.

"What is it you need me to do?" Cassidy asked.

"Go with me to get my rosary. My mother said it would protect me. She gave it to me just before the car crash. But I forgot it. I left it up there. I was bad, so bad." Delia's voice turned vicious. "They keep telling me I'm a bitch, disgusting, vile."

Cassidy wiped her palms on her jeans. Her chest was tight and the duct-taped newspapers gave her the creeps.

"Your voices are saying that?"

"They won't give me any peace. I can't even sleep at night."

"So where did you leave your rosary?"

"In that room on the top floor. I was going to go back and get it myself but I was too scared." Delia covered her face with her outstretched hands. "It was horrible! So horrible!"

"What was?"

"The Angel of Death. I saw him. He was all glistening and shiny. There was blood on the tarp. And he had this naked person hanging in the closet."

The hair rose on the back of Cassidy's neck. *Not true. Just a delusion. But sometimes killers do hang bodies to drain the blood.*

"You saw the Angel of Death on the top floor of this tower? And that's where you left your rosary?"

"I had to go up there. The Dark Angels were after me. They could see me through the glass, even after I put the newspapers up. So I went into the stairwell. They couldn't find me there and people hardly ever use the stairs. But then I heard a door close down below, and footsteps, so I had to go all the way up."

"You climbed from here to the top? That's twenty stories."

"It was hard to keep going but I had to."

"And that's when you saw the Angel of Death?"

"Not right away. I went into that room up there. You know, the room with the door that lets you onto the roof. I've been there before but this time there was a tarp spread on the floor and a package of trash bags in the corner. I tried to go out on the roof. The voices were screaming at me to jump and I thought maybe this time I'd give in to them. But the door was locked so I couldn't get out. Then I hung my rosary on the handle and sat down on the floor. The Dark Angels hadn't found me yet so I thought I'd just stay where I was. Then the elevator dinged and I forgot my rosary and ran back into the stairwell. But I left the door open a crack and I heard sounds." Delia fell silent.

"What kind of sounds?"

She clamped her hands over her ears. "Bad sounds. Horrible sounds."

"Then what?"

"I listened for a long time, and I couldn't understand what was happening so I opened the door a little wider and peeked inside."

"What did you see?"

She covered her face again. "I told you already."

"The Angel of Death?"

Delia turned her face away from Cassidy.

"What did you do after that?"

"I came back here and waited until it was light. Then I tried to make myself go get the rosary. I tried and tried but I couldn't get myself to go, so I called you."

"And I'm the only person who can help you?"

"You have white magic. You got your husband to let me move in."

Why would she want to live here if this is where the Angel of Death hangs out?

"So you and I are going to retrieve your rosary and then maybe we can think about finding you some help to turn down the volume on your voices."

Delia sat up straight. "What are you talking about?"

"Getting you some help."

"I'm not going in the hospital!" Delia screamed. She rose and advanced on Cassidy, her hands raised in front of her like the paws of an attacking bear, her stocky frame appearing to swell with each step. Thrusting her face close to Cassidy's, she screamed again. "You stupid bitch! You filthy whore! Don't you even think about trying to hospitalize me!"

Panic sweeping through her, Cassidy pressed her spine against the back of the chair. Her mouth went dry and her words came out thin and raspy. "I'm sorry. I shouldn't have said that. I won't do anything you don't want me to."

Delia stalked back to the sofa and sat down.

Boy, did you ever screw that up. You didn't join in her delusion. You didn't get her to trust you.

Cassidy cleared her throat. "Would this be a good time to get your rosary?"

"It's so hard to go back. But I can't leave it there. Mom said it would protect me, that I should always keep it with me." Delia's chest rose and fell in a deep sigh. "All right. I'm ready."

Delia opened the door, then stopped and said, "I have to get my key."

That's good. Coherent enough to keep track of things.

Cassidy's tenant took her purse from the hall closet, set it on the breakfast bar, and shoved her key in her pants pocket.

Chapter 3

When the elevator doors slid open, Delia turned away, covered her face with her hands, and pressed herself against the back wall of the elevator.

"I shouldn't have brought you up here," Cassidy said. "You go back to the condo and I'll get your rosary and be down in a jiff."

Pulling her hands away from her face, Delia looked at Cassidy. "How do I know you won't take it?"

"Because I have white magic. People with white magic don't steal." *That was good. You're getting the hang of this delusion thing.*

Delia buried her face again.

Cassidy stepped halfway out of the elevator and scanned the small, brightly lit room. "There's no one here." *Not that you think any murderous person ever did inhabit this space. You do know the Angel of Death is nothing more than an auditory hallucination created by the misfiring of electrons in Delia's brain, don't you?*

"I'm going to get the rosary," Cassidy said. "You can come with me or stay here."

Facing forward, Delia began sidling around the edge of the elevator. "I guess I'll go with you."

They entered a narrow room with three elevators at one end and a door leading out onto the rooftop at the other. Zach had taken Cassidy up to the roof to see the view a couple of times when they were dating. She knew the door was locked during the winter.

The two women crossed to the door, where the rosary dangled from its handle. As Cassidy reached for it, Delia pushed her hand away.

"It's mine. Nobody can touch it but me." She hung the rosary around her neck and began fingering the beads. "Let's go down now."

"I want to look around first."

"No! This is a bad place. We have to get out of here."

Cassidy gazed straight at Delia. "I have white magic, remember? That means it's safe to stay as long as we like." *What are you doing? Joining Delia's delusion doesn't mean actually believing it.*

"But I don't like it here."

Cassidy held Delia's gaze.

"I'm going to wait in the stairwell. But hurry up, won't you?" Delia headed through a doorway on their right.

A second door stood directly across from the stairwell. Cassidy opened it and discovered a deep janitor's closet, with a floor drain inside a concrete trough, a faucet a couple of feet off the floor, thin vertical pipes on the left-hand side, thicker horizontal pipes overhead, and a water heater behind the drain. She shuddered as pictures began to form in her mind.

The fact that the closet exists is not evidence of a crime. You should leave now before your own electrons start misfiring.

She bent over to inspect the drain but saw no traces of blood or hair. Then she noticed a few specks of something that looked like rust on the chrome faucet. She picked one up. It was definitely rust, and she thought it had to have fallen from the pipes above. Lifting her eyes, she could see rust on the horizontal pipes. Only one of them appeared high enough to hang a body from.

A rope thrown over a pipe would dislodge some rust.

But neither Delia's delusion nor flecks of rust on a faucet were grounds for calling the police. *Unless you could show them something approximating evidence, they'd pat you on the head and tell you to stop watching horror movies.* Cassidy located a large bucket in the back of the closet, turned it upside down, and climbed on it. When she stood on tiptoe, she could see that the rust had been disturbed on the pipe closest to the ceiling. She proceeded to inspect the rest of the closet but found nothing out of the ordinary.

She moved on to scrutinize the white walls outside the closet, then went down on one knee to examine the speckled asphalt tiles. At first she thought the floor was so dirty she'd never be able to find anything, but after considerable searching, she came across a small brown spot near the place where the door was attached to the frame. She touched it with one finger. Something stuck on the floor, not part of the pattern. She thought it resembled dried blood. *That's just what you want to believe so you can justify calling the police.*

She stood. *Actually, you don't have any choice. If there's a chance it might be blood, you have to call them.*

Her hand automatically started digging in her purse for her cell. She thought about how she could frame her story so it would sound believable and whether she should wait until Delia was back in her condo before she made the call.

Not that easy to lie to the cops. Better do it now before you lose your nerve.

She was punching numbers into her cell phone when Delia came back into the room.

"Who are you calling?"

"The police. About that person you saw hanging in the closet."

"No you're not. You're going to have the cops take me to the hospital."

"No, really, I'm calling about the murder."

Delia's face darkened. The cords stood out on her neck. "You lying piece of shit. I know what you're up to. You can call the cops all you want—they aren't going to get me." Turning on her heel, she plunged back through the doorway.

Could be suicidal. Last night her voices were telling her to jump off the roof. You have to stop her. Cassidy went running after her tenant. As she started down the stairs, she could see Delia hit the landing below, then disappear around a corner. By the time Cassidy made the same turn, Delia was nowhere to be seen. Cassidy pounded down two more flights, then stopped to listen. At first, all she could hear was the thudding of her heart and her own heavy breathing. Then, as her body quieted, she became aware of the silence. A silence so palpable it seemed inconceivable that anyone else could be in the stairwell with her.

Cassidy opened the fire door to the circular hall, took the elevator to the forty-first floor, and went inside Delia's unit. Delia wasn't there. Cassidy, her legs quivering from the run, sat on the sofa and called the non-emergency police number.

"I want to report possible evidence of a murder." Cassidy waited while the operator transferred her call. Several seconds later, a female voice came on the line. Cassidy repeated her request.

"Your name?"

"Cassidy McCabe. My husband and I own a condo at Marina City which is currently rented out. Our tenant is the one who thinks she witnessed a murder."

"Can you put your tenant on the line?"

"She doesn't want to get involved. When I told her I was going to call the police, she left the building."

"So you didn't see anything yourself? You're just passing on what your tenant told you?"

"Yes."

"All right, go ahead."

"The incident occurred in the room on the top floor of the West Tower, which is pretty isolated this time of year. My tenant got a brief look into the room from the stairwell. She said she saw a tarp on the floor with blood on it, a person standing in front of the janitor's closet, and a body hanging inside the closet over the drain. This all happened last night. She was afraid to notify the police so she called me. I went up to the roof and found what looks like a blood splatter just outside the closet."

The voice asked Cassidy where she was calling from and instructed her to remain in the condo until the police arrived.

When the bell rang, Cassidy opened the door a few inches, slid out, and closed the door behind her. *Seeing Delia's living quarters would not make the cops more inclined to believe your story.*

"I can't let you into my tenant's apartment," she explained to the two uniforms standing in front of her. "It would be a breach of her privacy."

The older cop—white skin, lumpy features, an expanded waistline— frowned suspiciously. The younger cop—brown skin, patrician face, trim frame—stood behind his partner and looked bored.

Cassidy reiterated her tidied-up version of Delia's account.

"Okay, let's go see what you got," the older cop said.

They went to the top floor and Cassidy pointed out the specks of rust on the faucet and the brown spot on the floor. Watching the cops exchange a skeptical look, Cassidy felt like an idiot. *Whole thing sounds nuts even without the Angel of Death.*

The older cop said, "We're gonna have to call in the dicks. You gotta wait in the squad till one of 'em's ready to take your statement."

Cassidy knew the drill. *All the hours you've spent in the backseat of a cop car, you could've taken a nice vacation in Hawaii.* The uniforms escorted her to a blue-and-white parked on the Marina City ramp. As she started to get inside, the stench of greasy hamburgers and smoke caused her to rear back from the car.

"What's the matter?" the older cop demanded.

"Um...I guess you two must practically live in your car."

"It's the stink," the younger guy asserted. "Same thing I keep telling you, only she's too polite to say it. That fucking second-hand smoke is gonna be the death of me."

"You don't like it, get yourself a new partner." To Cassidy, he said, "Sorry if it offends you, but that's where you gotta stay."

"I'll get used to it."

Settling into the backseat, she took shallow breaths until her olfactories adjusted. As the odors faded from her consciousness, she debated whether to tell the detectives she was married to Zach Moran. He'd been a crime reporter at the *Post* for more than a dozen years. Most Chicago cops were familiar with his name, and many had had personal contact with him. Unfortunately, because he'd written a number of police exposés, quite a few considered him the enemy.

On one hand, they might try to get revenge on Zach by giving you a hard time. On the other hand,

*they might not overtly ridicule you if they knew it
was going to get back to him.*

A short time later, a nicely dressed woman
approached and rapped on the window. Rolling it
down, Cassidy gazed into a finely molded mahogany
face that looked familiar.

"I'm head of the condo board security committee
and I need to know what's going on here, but I can't
pry a word out of the police."

"This is probably just a false alarm." Cassidy
climbed out of the car so they could talk at eye
level. Only five foot two herself, she noted that the
window rapper was at least an inch shorter than
she was.

The woman squinted at Cassidy. "Don't I know
you?"

"You must be Joan. I met you at Gran's house.
I'm Cassidy McCabe, Mary's granddaughter."

"Oh, of course." A smile lit up the woman's face.
"It was at that brunch Mary had last summer."
Joan was a petite woman clad in a wool coat, A-line
skirt, pantyhose, and low-heeled pumps. She
looked to be in her fifties.

"It's nice to see you again," Cassidy said. "I wish
I could be more help, but I can't really talk about
what's going on."

"Yes you can," Joan said sternly, sounding like
the Oak Park school principal she used to be.
"You're obviously involved or you wouldn't be sitting
in this police car. Now I want to know why the cops
are here and what they're doing up on the sixtieth
floor."

Cassidy hesitated. She didn't want to be an
alarmist, but she couldn't think of any way to avoid
answering Joan's question without being rude.

"Zach and I have our condo rented out and our tenant called this morning to tell me she thought she'd seen something going on in that rooftop room." Cassidy paused. "She said it looked to her like someone had been murdered."

"Murdered?" Joan's coffee-colored eyes widened. She pressed her hand against her chest.

"My tenant only got a glimpse. She wasn't really sure what she saw, but I thought I should report it just to be on the safe side."

Joan's gaze pinned Cassidy. "You're not telling me everything, are you?"

"I've already said more than I should. The police don't want me talking about this."

"All right, I'll leave you alone for now. But you haven't heard the last of me."

That was stupid! Shouldn't have mentioned your tenant. If the killer—assuming there is one—finds out who the witness was, Delia could be in danger. Even more than she is already from her illness.

Cassidy, who considered waiting a subtle form of torture, sat hugging herself in the cold car for almost half an hour. *Brought this on yourself. Nobody but you would go hunting for evidence at the scene of a delusion.*

She was checking her watch for the fifth time when two men in overcoats walked up to the squad. One of them opened the door and asked her to step out.

"You Ms. McCabe?"

She nodded.

"Detective Roloff. And this is Detective Sapko." Roloff had a clean-cut boyish face, with brown hair falling over his forehead and an amiable, straightforward gaze. His partner appeared tougher, grimmer, more tight-lipped.

Cassidy made a quick decision. "You might know my husband, Zach Moran. He covers the police beat for the *Post.*"

"Sure, I know Zach. Good reporter."

Sapko made a less friendly noise.

Cassidy retold her story, then the detectives moved her from the squad to their unmarked car. After another wait, they drove her to the district station that housed Area Three, the detective unit assigned to the northeast section of Chicago.

Chapter 4

The tension in Cassidy's stomach eased slightly when Roloff came into the interview room and seated himself across the table from her. *Thank goodness it's the one who at least looks nice.* She knew it was time to admit that she'd fudged her story. She also knew that cops were not particularly forgiving of people who lied to them. She'd been down this road before and absolutely hated being the brunt of cop sarcasm.

Roloff flipped through his notepad. "You say your tenant was in the sixtieth floor stairwell last night. What was she doing there?"

"Were you able to tell whether that spot was blood? I guess you must think it could be or you wouldn't have brought me down here."

"Could you please answer the question?" he asked in a polite tone. "And this time, how about the truth?"

Cassidy grimaced. "How did you know?"

"Your story has some holes in it. Like why would anybody be in a stairwell late at night? And why would she run away when you called to report the crime? Sounds to me like your tenant was in on the murder and you're trying to protect her. Are you two lovers or what?"

He said "murder." Oh God, maybe your loony suspicions weren't as loony as you thought.

"I think you should know that I'm a therapist—but not Delia's therapist—and she has schizophrenia. She was doing fine until a few weeks ago when she went off her meds. Now she's having a psychotic episode, and her voices are telling her that there are Dark Angels out to get her. The reason she was in the stairwell is she thought they couldn't find her there."

Cassidy glanced at the detective. His face was impassive. *Every bit as good at maintaining a neutral expression as you are with clients.*

She went on to repeat Delia's story. "It sounded enough like a real murder that I wanted to take a look at the janitor's closet, and then when I found that brown spot I knew I had to call the police. But I didn't think anyone would take me seriously if I told them about the Angel of Death."

Roloff pinched his lower lip. "You got that right."

"Why aren't you yelling at me for lying?"

He shrugged. "If I got pissed every time somebody embellished their story, I'd be living on Maalox. Besides, we've uncovered a probable murder that might not have surfaced for a while if you hadn't doctored your story."

"A probable murder? You wouldn't call it that if all you had was a blood spot. You must've come up with some other evidence. Where did you find it? In the drain?"

He smiled blandly.

"Oh, that's right. Cops never tell civilians anything."

"I did tell you we're calling it a 'probable murder.'" He pushed his hair back from his forehead. "What kind of relationship did you have with your tenant? Why did she call you?"

"She said it was because I have 'white magic' but I think the real reason was that we'd formed a friendship of sorts. When she first moved into the condo, she wasn't doing so well, but then she calmed down and was able to lead a fairly normal life. About a month after that, Zach and I had tickets to a play, then at the last minute he couldn't go and none of my friends were available, so I invited Delia. It turned out we got along really well. Then she invited me to a couple of other things and that's how we got to know each other. I wasn't her only friend. She knew some people from her day program and her halfway house, but I was the only one who didn't remind her of her illness."

"So where do you think we ought to look for her?"

"I have no idea." Cassidy narrowed her eyes. "Is she a suspect?"

"Cops never tell civilians anything, remember?"

"This was a premeditated, highly organized murder. People with schizophrenia aren't able to commit crimes like this. They just act out impulsively."

"We'll take that into account."

Shouldn't have lectured him. That never endears you to anyone.

Cassidy gripped her hands together on the table. "I'm really worried about her. She's definitely a danger to herself"—Cassidy flashed an image of Delia coming at her with her hands raised—"and possibly to other people. What will you do if you find her?"

"Interview her. Let her go if we don't have enough evidence to charge her. Same thing we do with everybody."

"Couldn't you have someone take her to the hospital?"

"Only if she's suicidal or homicidal."

"Could you call me?" *As if you could do anything.*

"That's not going to happen."

When Roloff finished, a beat cop drove Cassidy back to Marina City. Delia wasn't there, not that Cassidy had expected to find her at the condo. Given her tenant's level of panic, Cassidy thought that Delia would put as much distance as possible between herself and the twin towers. Delia's purse still sat on the breakfast bar, indicating that she hadn't stopped to pick anything up before leaving the building. *Outside in the cold with no coat or plastic or money.*

Cassidy wondered if Delia might be in danger from the killer. If he knew she'd seen him, she probably would be, but Cassidy couldn't imagine any way he could have found out.

She stood in the living room, not sure what to do next. The stench from the kitchen and the oppressive look of the newspapers on the glass wall made her feel as though she'd stepped inside an alien psychotic world. She wanted to tear the papers off the glass but feared that if Delia returned and found her protective shield missing, she'd take it to mean her home had been invaded.

You could take out the garbage. She couldn't possibly see that as sinister.

You have no idea what she might see as sinister, but the garbage has to go.

After tossing the spoiled food and scrubbing the counter, Cassidy paid her parking fee, collected her Toyota, and drove west toward Oak Park. Twenty minutes later she hit Austin Boulevard, the boundary between a gang-infested Chicago neighborhood and her own middle-class progressive suburb.

She walked in the back door and saw Starshine sitting tall in one of the two fan-backed wicker chairs that flanked the window in her client waiting room. Fixing a translucent green-eyed gaze on her human, the diminutive calico uttered a friendly *mwat.*

"It's nice to be greeted," Cassidy replied. "I certainly could use a warm mooshy cuddle about now. And considering that my two-legged companion is likely not to be in the best of moods, I'm glad to see you're awake and willing to acknowledge my existence."

Cassidy hung her coat in the free-standing oak closet that served as a divider between her waiting room and the kitchen. Jumping down from the chair, Starshine displayed considerable interest in sniffing Cassidy's pant legs and tennis shoes.

"You won't come near me if I'm wearing perfume, but I suppose you *like* the smell of rotten food, greasy hamburgers, and smoke."

As Cassidy crossed her large, newly redecorated kitchen, Starshine raced ahead of her to spring onto the counter and sit next to her food bowl. *Mwat*, the cat said again, coaxing Cassidy to break the diet rules and give her an extra meal. Now that the calico had shed her extra pounds, Cassidy had relaxed the strict food regimen she'd instituted a few months earlier. Today, however, the metal bowl contained what appeared to be an untouched serving of wet food that was beginning to crust over.

"So you talked Zach into feeding you, then turned up your little pink nose at this tuna glop you adored yesterday. You aren't really interested in eating, are you? You just want to prove your dominance over your humans."

Mwat, Starshine repeated, bumping her head against Cassidy's arm.

"I'm not giving you any new food to snub."

Zach had left a mayo-covered knife, a plate, and a pile of crumbs on the counter. While Cassidy was straightening up, Starshine crossed from the right side of the sink to the left, moving out of Cassidy's line of vision. Cassidy had just closed the dishwasher when she heard an explosive crash behind her. Whirling around, she saw a broken coffee grinder on the floor, beans scattered everywhere. Starshine sat on the edge of the counter and surveyed the wreckage, a look of innocence on her face.

"How could you do this to me? I just finished cleaning up Delia's horrible mess and now I have my own horrible mess to contend with."

Starshine's tail swished. Her eyes turned wild and black. She leapt halfway across the kitchen, then raced out of the room.

Unrepentant little brat!

Cassidy could hear television voices from the den as she hit the L in the stairway to the second floor. Once she reached the hall at the top, she could see Zach through the open doorway.

"Hey, where were you?" he asked.

Plunking down in the comfy leather chair next to his, she gazed at an image of a World War II warship on the screen. "I didn't think you cared." *Ohhh, that sounds so pathetic.* "Wait, I take that back. I didn't mean to say it that way."

"Look, you know this isn't about you."

"Maybe not, but I sure am getting the fallout."

"Did you come in here just to rag on me?"

"I came in here to talk to you, but I'm not about to compete with the TV."

He clicked it off.

"Delia called this morning." Cassidy hesitated, not wanting to admit that Zach had been right when he said Delia was likely to go off her meds. "She's delusional and hearing voices." Cassidy went on to tell him everything that had happened since she left the house.

"Delia certainly called the right person. I doubt there's anyone else on the planet who would've gone looking for evidence."

Cassidy gazed into his bronze-skinned face, trying to ascertain whether he was making fun of her. He appeared serious and concerned, so she decided he wasn't.

"I guess the forensic guys were able to determine that my brown spot was blood without sending it to the lab."

"Yeah, they can prove a substance is blood in the field, but they can't tell if it's animal or human without running a lab test. However, once they knew it was blood, they did exactly what you said. They cleaned out the trap beneath the drain and must have come up with hair, flesh and more blood. With evidence like that, they know they've got a homicide on their hands but they can't say it straight out until they establish who the victim was or find a body with matching DNA."

"Given how tight security is, I suppose both the victim and the killer would have to live at Marina City."

"The victim definitely. There'd be no point bringing someone in from the outside just to kill him in that rooftop room, which is, after all, a public space. But it's possible the killer wasn't a resident. He could've come in with the vic or had the victim buzz him in." Zach scratched his jaw. "But probably not. Most people wouldn't want to expose themselves to the security camera. Although, if he really knew what he was doing, he could've gotten through without his face showing up on tape."

"One of the things I can't figure out is why the killer would pick a place all the residents have access to. I assume he drained the blood, cut up the body, and carried it out in those trash bags Delia saw." Cassidy winced as pictures crowded into her mind. "It must've taken hours, which would make it a pretty risky proposition."

"Maybe not. I'd guess he staked the place out over a period of time and never saw anyone there. Why would anyone visit that room when the door to the roof is locked? Besides, if he wanted to kill the guy inside the tower, where else would he find a janitor's closet big enough to accommodate a hanging body?"

"Must be a sociopath. They're grandiose and big on risk taking."

"Another thing you need to keep in mind, he never expected anyone to find out a murder'd been committed there. He intended for the victim to simply disappear. If you ever want to get rid of someone, a disappearance is the way to go."

"Even I know that. If you can't produce a body, the police don't want to talk to you." She paused. "I suppose that means the body may never be found."

"Depends on how good the killer is. Even with a dismembered body, it's surprisingly hard to keep the parts from showing up eventually. But if the guy's an experienced hit man, the victim will simply disappear."

She picked up a pen from the table next to her chair and started pushing the clicker in and out.

"Something else on your mind?"

"I'm worried about Delia. She ran off with nothing but her key."

"When she gets cold enough, she'll show up back at the condo."

"I don't think so. In her mind, Marina City's become a very unsafe place."

"If she doesn't go back to her condo, she's likely to wind up on the street."

"Don't think I haven't been obsessing about that. I keep picturing her frozen body on a park bench."

"They have shelters all over the city. Besides, schizophrenics seem to be pretty savvy about making it on their own."

"We just assume that because we never hear any statistics on how many die."

"I hope you're not planning to go look for her."

"I wouldn't know where to start."

Zach's gaze drifted back to the TV screen. Cassidy replaced the pen on the table. She had more to say but didn't know where to begin.

After about three beats, Zach asked, "We done now?" He turned the TV on.

Cassidy stood, grabbed the remote out of his hand, and turned it off. "You left this morning without a word to me. I looked all over the house for you, then I finally checked the garage and saw that your car was gone."

"Sorry, I forgot to tell you."

"This isn't the first time."

Zach ran a hand over his face. "I've got a lot on my mind."

"You're depressed."

"Not this again."

"Of course you're depressed. Up until two months ago you loved your job. You had an editor who thought you walked on water and let you investigate anything you wanted. Then he retired and they promoted this jerk who's got a grudge against you. So now you're stuck with an editor who keeps sending you out on these piddly little stories that usually don't even make it into the paper. This has to be a huge loss."

"Would you please not tell me things I already know?"

"There must be something you could do to win McCready over. Maybe say you were wrong when you fired him. Remind him it was the only time you ever took on an editorial position. Say you didn't know what you were doing, that it was a big mistake on your part. Maybe he just needs to see you grovel before he'll let go of his grudge."

"He'll see me grovel when hell freezes over. Besides, it wasn't a mistake. His stories were sloppy. He didn't have his facts straight. I had to can his ass."

"How did a guy like that get to be editor at a big-league paper like the *Post*?"

"He improved over time. Plus he wanted the promotion and I didn't."

"Okay, I can understand why you wouldn't want to grovel. I doubt that I could make myself do it either. But maybe you could just go one-down a little, stroke his ego. Say you were in over your head when you took that editing job."

"I wasn't in over my head, I just didn't like it," Zach said, an edge to his voice. "And if I went one-down, he'd see it as a sign of weakness and give me an even harder time."

"Your job used to be the most important thing—"

"No, you're the most important thing."

"Now you hate it."

"These things happen. I had a good ride, now I've hit a snag. Everybody runs into some shit in the course of their career."

"Maybe. But in the meantime, I'm pretty unhappy with the way you're acting."

"Pretend I'm a client and be empathic."

"You're drinking more."

"Not that much. I never go over three drinks a day."

"You disappear for hours and your cell is usually turned off. Even when you're here, you're emotionally absent. It seems like you aren't interested in anything I have to say unless I have a murder to report." *Some women might think he was having an affair, but I'm certain he wouldn't do that, and even if he would, he doesn't have the energy for it.*

"You keep telling me I'm depressed. Doesn't that give me a free pass for being a little shut down?"

"Not if you won't do anything about it."

"We've had this argument several times already."

"Yes, but I still haven't gotten through to you. I can't understand why you refuse to take antidepressants. You've always used chemicals to alter your mood. Drugs when you were younger, alcohol now. If medication would make you feel better, why not take it?"

"You want me to take something that could lower my libido, make me blimp out, and drain what little energy I have left?"

"You haven't had any libido since McCready took over."

Zach's face darkened in anger.

"I'm sorry. I shouldn't have said that."

"I wish you'd get off my case about this medication thing. I realize I haven't exactly been a pleasure to live with, but give me some time and I'll pull it together. I just need you to leave me alone."

Chapter 5

Cassidy headed toward the waterbed, her favorite place to sit when dark clouds wrapped themselves around her. Then she remembered she needed to report in to Delia's therapist.

Calling on her desk phone, she told Sue Bolas what had happened.

"That poor woman! Out in the cold without a cent to her name. Here's hoping she creates enough of a disturbance that the police pick her up and take her to the hospital."

"Does she have any family she could go to?"

"She has a cousin but I doubt Delia'd go anywhere near her."

"They're not on good terms?"

"Delia had wealthy parents who stood by her through everything, but they died in a car crash when she was in her twenties. After that, her cousin took her in and it was a disaster. They lived together for several months, then Delia's condition deteriorated and I guess the cousin got scared or something. She threw Delia out without giving her a chance to pack her clothes or get her medications or anything. To this day, Delia goes into a rage when she talks about what her cousin did."

"Has Delia ever been homeless before?"

"For a few weeks before she started seeing me. She's a real survivor, you know. One way or another, I'm sure she'll get back on her feet."

Just saying that because she's a therapist and needs to create a sense of optimism. Sort of thing you might say.

Cassidy thanked Sue for filling her in and signed off

Digging a half-empty bag of peanut butter cups out from under the mess on her desk, she parked herself on the waterbed with pillows behind her back. She wished Starshine would come sit on her chest, but the calico was in some other part of the house or had gone out through her cat door to keep watch over her yard.

Cassidy opened a Reese's, stuck the wrapper back in the bag, and bit the candy in two. Her mind bounced from one bad thought to another. She doubted that Zach would simply pull himself together on his own. Delia was missing and Cassidy had failed to get her tenant into the hospital. On top of that, Cassidy had uncovered evidence of a grisly murder but had no way to find out what was happening. *God, I hate not knowing things.*

Unwrapping another peanut butter cup, she looked at the clock on the bureau. Four-twenty. Too many hours until bedtime. She had no idea what to do with herself.

Some time later, when the Reese's were gone and the bag was stuffed with wrappers, the phone rang. Since the cordless was missing from Cassidy's nightstand, she went to her desk to answer.

"This is Joan Frasier. I'm the one who made you talk to me this afternoon at Marina City."

"Oh hi, Joan. What can I do for you?"

"Your grandmother tells me you know something about criminal investigations."

"Um...I guess you could say that." Cassidy was embarrassed about getting involved in so many homicides. It wasn't the sort of thing therapists were supposed to do.

"After I talked to you, the cops went around and knocked on everybody's door, and it looks like they've identified the victim. Well, we won't know for sure until the DNA results come back, but we think it was Miles Gerlinsky. He seems to be the only one who's missing."

"I'm glad to hear the cops are making progress. Hope he wasn't a friend of yours."

"Not Miles so much as his wife, Tessa. She's worked herself into a real state. Afraid the cops will think she killed him. Which is ridiculous, of course. Tessa's far too good-hearted to hurt anybody. I'm sure the police won't arrest her, but I can't get her to listen to me. And that brings me to the reason I called. Your grandmother says you know all about police procedure. And you're a therapist to boot, so you must know how to calm people down. I thought maybe you could come talk to Tessa and convince her she doesn't have anything to worry about."

Cassidy could feel herself brighten. *Something useful to do. Even better, a chance to find out about the victim.*

"I'll be there in twenty minutes."

She went out into the hall, glanced at Zach in the den, and started down the stairs. *No you don't. Tit-for-tat is not a therapeutically approved way to deal with resentment.* She turned around and told him where she was going

"Thanks for coming," Joan said, standing in her condo doorway.

Cassidy was surprised to note that the petite, dark-skinned woman still wore the skirt, hose, and heels she'd had on earlier, not to mention a shimmery cashmere sweater and a pendant on a gold chain. *Can't stand pantyhose. Except for*

*weddings and funerals, you've completely liberated
yourself from those waistline stranglers.*

"I'm glad you called. I had all these questions
about the murder, and now at least one of them's
been answered."

"Come on inside. I have to get my keys, then we
can scoot on over to Tessa's. She's just three doors
down."

Cassidy waited in the entryway while Joan
searched inside her purse. "Did you and Tessa get
to know each other because you're neighbors? I
don't think Zach made a single friend the whole
time he was here."

"It's just my busybody nature. When I was
principal at Percy Julian, I considered it my duty to
know the name of every kid in school—particularly
the at-risk kids." Joan pulled out her key ring and
slipped it into her skirt pocket. "Then, when I
moved here, I felt like I needed to know all the
people who lived in my building, at least to speak
to."

Leaving the condo, the women followed the
circular hall. "Of course there are always some
holdouts—people who slam the door on me—but I
can put names to faces for most of the residents.
And a few, like Tessa, became good friends."

They arrived at Tessa's door. The woman who
opened it was in her mid-thirties, several inches
taller than Cassidy and Joan, with a willowy figure,
jaw-length golden hair, and enormous gray eyes.
Her face was drawn and her lids were puffy, but the
delicately sculpted angles and hollows of her bone
structure indicated that beneath the ravages of
loss, she was a beautiful woman.

"This is Cassidy McCabe," Joan said. "She
should be able to tell you what the police are likely
to do."

Cassidy raised her hands in protest. "I'm really not an expert. I've just picked up some tips from my husband, who covers the crime beat for the *Post*." *Or used to, before he got demoted to fender-bender journos.*

"You're too modest," Joan said. Then, to Tessa, "What she's not telling you is that she's solved a couple of crimes by herself."

"Not really. Zach and I almost always work together."

"It's so...so nice of you to make another trip to Marina City." Tessa stood back so they could come inside. "I've been a wreck since the police took me in for questioning. Or I should say, since Miles"— she took in a breath—"didn't come home last night. I thought about calling missing persons, but I've always heard they won't do anything until someone's been gone at least twenty-four hours. Now I'm afraid they'll think I killed him because I didn't report him missing."

"No they won't." Joan put a comforting hand on Tessa's arm. "Of course they had to question you. They always question the spouse. But I'm sure they'll understand why you didn't call missing persons."

Tessa's luminous eyes moistened. "Joan's been wonderful but neither of us knows a thing about police procedure. We don't even watch cop shows."

They went into the living room. An emerald-green sofa stood against the wall facing the balcony and beyond the balcony, a view of the East Tower. Round tables covered with floor-length emerald skirts, shorter cherry-red skirts atop the green ones, stood at either end of the sofa. A large, square coffee table held a number of plants in small red pots. Two emerald easy chairs faced the sofa, and a large polished wood desk stood against one wall.

Abstract paintings hung above the sofa and the desk.

"Um...why don't we sit down?"

After Joan and Cassidy were ensconced in the easy chairs, Tessa spoke again. "I almost forgot. I was planning to ask you what you wanted to drink. I have fresh decaf. Or wine or bottled water."

All three opted for coffee. When they were settled with red-flowered mugs in their hands, Cassidy said, "I'd like you to tell me about last night."

Putting her mug on the wooden table, Tessa clenched her hands together in her lap. "Miles got a call from Henry—what time was it?—oh, yeah, about nine-thirty. Henry, he's an older guy, lives five floors up from us. He and Miles always have their heads together. Talking computers. Miles said Henry needed help with some sort of glitch. Then he left."

Joan turned toward Cassidy. "Last time she saw him."

"I didn't think anything about it," Tessa continued, "until I woke up at one and realized...realized he wasn't home. I assumed they'd just lost track of time. I called Henry but his machine picked up. Then I called his cell. It rang a long time. Finally he answered. He said he was asleep and I should call back in the morning. When...when I found out Miles wasn't there, I could just feel my stomach drop. I knew something had to be wrong, so I called Henry back and this time he woke up enough to tell me that Miles had left...he'd left around eleven."

Tessa started taking short, shallow breaths. "I had no idea what to do. I kept trying to think of some explanation, but all I could come up with was that Miles'd had a stroke or heart attack or something and collapsed on his way back here." She shook her head. "He's in such good health that didn't seem likely, but since I couldn't think of anything else, I checked out our hallway, Henry's hallway, the elevators, the stairs. Of course he wasn't there. So then I sat on the sofa and waited until morning."

"What a long night that must've been," Cassidy said.

"The longest I've ever lived through." Tessa pressed her hands against both sides of her face. "The phone rang a little after six and my heart did a flip-flop...but it was only Henry. He wanted to know if Miles had shown up yet. Said he'd taken a sleeping pill and that was why he'd been so groggy. The phone woke Amy—that's our four-year-old. She came and snuggled with me on the couch. Didn't say anything for a while, then asked where her daddy was." Tessa sucked in air. "I told her he hadn't come home. I wanted to reassure her but I had this sinking feeling that something terrible had happened and I couldn't make myself say that everything was going to be all right."

Cassidy dug a small spiral pad out of her purse. "Do you mind if I take a few notes?"

Tessa's brows drew together. "Why would you want to do that?"

"Um..." Cassidy skittered around inside her head trying to figure out for herself why she wanted to do it. "I'm sure I'll be thinking about this later and I'm afraid I'll forget something important if I don't write it down."

Tessa took a moment to consider. "I guess it'll be all right."

"Where's your daughter now?" Cassidy asked.

"My mother came and got her this morning."

Cassidy looked at Joan, then Tessa. "We don't know for sure that Miles was the victim. Maybe he wasn't the only one who went missing last night."

Joan shook her head. "I made dozens of phone calls. Everyone else is accounted for."

"But there have to be some reclusive residents nobody ever sees."

"You don't know what Joan's network is like," Tessa said. "She had neighbors knocking on each other's doors all over the building. I don't think anybody escaped her reach."

"Then I guess we have to accept it was Miles in that rooftop room."

A grim look came over Tessa's face. "And the only two suspects are Henry and me."

"Well, not exactly. The police will have to consider the possibility that Miles stopped off at someone else's condo after he left Henry's." Cassidy took a sip of coffee, giving herself time to consider how she would phrase the next question. "For instance, are there any women in the West Tower Miles might have been interested in visiting?"

"If you're asking whether he's having an affair, I don't think so. Not that he never did. He's had two since we were married. In both cases, he didn't bother to hide them. Which is why I don't think he's having one now. If he were, he would've made sure I knew about it."

Studying Tessa's face, Cassidy saw no sign that the young widow was disturbed by her husband's behavior. "That sounds pretty heartless. Or maybe abusive would be a better word."

"Heartless will do. He's cold, but he doesn't have any particular agenda to hurt me. He's more indifferent than anything else. When he let me know about his affairs, he wasn't rubbing my nose in it so much as keeping me apprised of his activities. It doesn't really matter that much anyway."

Cassidy, who had been deeply affected by her first husband's infidelities, suddenly realized that Tessa might not be the grieving widow she'd assumed her to be.

To Tessa, Joan said, "He may have been indifferent about your happiness, but he sure wasn't indifferent about whether you stayed married to him."

Chapter 6

Tessa glared at her friend.

"You need to tell her," Joan said. "Cassidy's a therapist. If anybody can keep a secret, she can."

Tessa gave Cassidy a long look. "You promise to keep what I'm about to tell you confidential?"

She hesitated. *What if she incriminates herself? You wouldn't want to have to keep that a secret, would you?*

Yes, but if you don't promise, she won't tell you, and you can't stand not knowing things. Besides, she's not a client so you can break your promise if you have to.

"Okay, I promise."

"I wanted out of my marriage. I was desperate to get out. But when I told Miles I was going to divorce him, he threatened to make Amy pay for what I'd done. He has a mean streak to him. It usually isn't directed at Amy or me, but if I'd left, it would've been. So I stayed." Her voice dropped to a whisper. "And sometimes I fantasized that a truck would run over him and solve the problem for me."

"Why wouldn't he let you go?"

"He can't handle rejection. It just does him in. One of the reasons he started his own business was that he'd go absolutely bonkers whenever his boss criticized him. After each of his affairs, he made a big point of telling me he'd dumped them, not the other way around."

"When you told me about his disappearance, you sounded genuinely distraught. Is that how you feel? Or are you actually glad he's gone?"

"Of course I'm distraught. Or at least I was last night. It was agony not having any idea where he was or why he didn't come home. Besides, he's

Amy's dad and she adores him. I don't know how I'm going to tell her."

No one spoke for several seconds, then Cassidy asked, "Is there any way the cops could find out about your marital situation?"

Clearing her throat, Tessa stared at the floor. "Joan threw a party a few months back. Miles and I were fighting before we went. Then, after we got there, I had too much to drink. I got kind of loud and argumentative. I don't remember exactly what I said, but I think the word 'divorce' came up a few times."

"So someone may pass that on to the cops."

Joan ran her hand down one of her cashmere sleeves. "What we want to know is whether the police would consider this a sufficient reason to arrest her."

Cassidy thought it through. "As far as I know, the police never make an arrest unless the state's attorney is confident he has a winnable case. I'm not turn up any forensic evidence—you know, something that would put you at the scene of the crime. And if you weren't there, of course they won't find anything. The other is whether they locate the body." *Not a body—parts. But she doesn't need to know that.*

"I think it's pretty rare for cops to make an arrest without a body, although if the DNA results are positive, they'll have evidence that Miles was murdered." Cassidy paused, wondering if she should stop there. *You need to tell her all of it.* "If they find out you felt trapped in your marriage, they'll have motive and opportunity. But without a confession or forensic evidence, the case would be entirely circumstantial. I have the impression prosecutors are sometimes able to win on circumstance alone, but they have to have a tremendous amount of it, and in this instance I don't think they'd have nearly enough to build a compelling case."

By the time Cassidy finished talking, Tessa's face had lost its color.

Joan picked up her friend's hand and squeezed it. "I don't know why you're looking so scared. From what Cassidy says, there's almost no chance you'd get arrested."

Tessa managed a feeble smile. "I know you're right, but I just keep thinking what if they do find a body? What if they do find evidence that makes it look like I did it?" She drew in a breath, then looked at Cassidy. "There's one other thing I should tell you. The police wanted to search the condo, but I was in such a panic after they questioned me, I wouldn't let them. I guess they can't use that against me, though."

So the police haven't searched yet. Cassidy could feel her antennae begin to vibrate. *Who knows what leads we might find if we get in ahead of the cops?*

In case you haven't noticed, no one's asked you to investigate.

But they might not mind if you did. It'd make life more interesting. Keep you from obsessing about Zach.

Cassidy said to the other two women, "How would you feel about it if I did some poking around? Talked to some of the people Miles knew. Checked out some things."

"You mean you want to try to find out who the killer is?" Joan asked, her voice ringing with enthusiasm.

Tessa frowned. "I don't like that idea at all."

"Why not?" Joan demanded. "Don't you want to dig up everything you can? Personally, I'd love to try my hand at a little detective work."

"We should leave it to the police," Tessa asserted. "They have authority, technology, experience—everything we don't."

"Cass knows quite a bit about investigating. And I'm head of security, which means I have the authority to look into any crime that occurs in the building."

"That's ridiculous," Tessa said. "You don't have authority to 'look into' a murder."

"You may know that, and I may know that—and some others may know it too. But if I stand face to face with one of the residents and say I'm head of security, there aren't many who'd refuse to answer my questions." Joan gave Tessa the kind of hardball stare she'd undoubtedly used on recalcitrant students. "And I expect you to back us up as much as we need you to."

Tessa's shoulders slumped, her resistance clearly melting under Joan's challenging gaze.

Cassidy looked into Tessa's blurry gray eyes. "You're right, the police can do a lot we can't. But it's been my experience that people often tell things to an ordinary person they wouldn't tell a cop."

"Where do we start?" Joan wanted to know.

"We search the condo."

Panic flashed across Tessa's face. "I can't let you go through our things."

Wouldn't let the cops search. Won't let us. What's she got to hide?

Cassidy rubbed one finger against the smooth green fabric of the armrest. "I hope you understand that the cops'll be back with a search warrant as soon as they have proof that Miles was the victim."

Her voice shaky, Tessa said, "You mean, when they get the DNA results. I gave them his toothbrush. Now I almost wish I hadn't, except I really need to know for sure that Miles is dead."

"You didn't have a choice," Cassidy said. "They would've gotten a court order." *And been suspicious as hell.* "But the cops won't be able to get a subpoena for quite a while. The police lab is really backed up and it takes a long time to get DNA tested."

"Getting back to *our* search," Joan said, "we need to look at Miles' email, his financial records, everything."

"As much as I love you," Tessa said to her friend, "I'm not letting you paw through our stuff. Privacy is too important to me. I'll do the search myself and if I find anything that seems even remotely related to what happened to Miles, I'll let you see it."

Joan brought out her intimidating stare, but before she could back Tessa down, Cassidy intervened. "Actually, I think that might be better. Tessa can take her time and be more thorough." *Never a good idea to coerce people. Just makes 'em resistant and passive aggressive.*

"So if we're not going to search, I suppose the first thing we need to do is talk to Henry," Joan said.

Cassidy asked, "What can you tell me about him?"

"He's retired. Elderly."

"Younger than me," Joan stated.

"Yes, but you've obviously sold your soul to the devil in exchange for eternal youth," Tessa said, a hint of suppressed laughter in her voice.

Joan jabbed her finger at her friend. "I'm seventy-two."

And here I thought she was in her fifties!

"But nobody would take you for more than thirty-nine," Tessa insisted.

Joan said, "Getting back to Henry—"

"He and Miles are—I mean were—such good friends. I know Henry's the obvious suspect—well, I guess I'm the most obvious and he's the second—but I can't come up with a single reason he'd want to harm Miles."

Cassidy asked, "What about other friends in the building? Somebody Miles might have stopped off to see after he left Henry?"

"Miles doesn't have many friends. In fact, I was surprised when he took up with Henry. He started meeting Henry for lunch not long after he went into business for himself. Later they added a couple of other people. They call it the Lunch Bunch."

"I didn't even think to ask what kind of work Miles does," Cassidy said.

"He's an I.T. consultant. Went out on his own over six years ago."

"What about you? Do you work outside the home?"

"I'm an architect. But I scaled back to half time after Amy was born."

Cassidy looked at her notes. "Who else is in this Lunch Bunch?"

"I never paid much attention. Henry could tell you."

Cassidy checked her watch. A few minutes after eight. "It shouldn't be too late to interview Henry tonight. Do you think we'll have any problem getting him to talk to us?"

"He's not real approachable," Tessa said. "He was always friendly with Miles but there were times when he barely spoke to me. I have the impression he doesn't think I'm interesting enough to bother with."

"He'll bother with me," Joan said. Getting his number from Tessa, she went to the phone in the kitchen.

To Henry, Joan said, "I guess you know by now it looks like Miles was murdered." She paused. "I'm here with Cass McCabe—she's the one who notified the police—and we're trying to piece together what happened. She's had some experience investigating murders, so I've asked her to help me interview people." She paused again. "I'm head of the security committee, remember? I have to write up a report. So, why don't we take care of this while it's still fresh in your mind. Cass and I can be at your door in a matter of minutes."

Chapter 7

Henry, clad in a velour navy blue robe and striped pajamas, motioned them into his condo. He was well over six feet, a little on the thin side, shoulders squared, body perfectly straight, thick white hair combed up and back.

"I apologize for my attire. I seem to be preparing for bed earlier and earlier these days."

"I wouldn't have called so late," Joan said, "except that I wanted Cass to have a chance to talk to you before she went home tonight."

Cassidy sank into a massive chair, too deep for her to lean back in, too high off the ground for her feet to rest solidly on the floor. Joan's small frame was swallowed up by a matching chair, while Henry took the sofa. A cherry wood table stood between the chairs and the sofa. Three pieces of colored glass sculpture and a glossy book on art museums around the world sat on the table's surface.

A tall glass case displaying pieces of pottery stood against one wall. The pieces, all a similar shade of gray-green, rested on meticulously placed shelves, each with its own accent light. *Art museums around the world, a lighted display case. Henry must have culture up the wazoo.*

"I guess I should start by introducing you two," Joan said, providing Cassidy and Henry with each other's full names.

As Henry turned his gaze on Cassidy, she detected a subtle gleam of amusement in his faded eyes. "Did Tessa hire a P.I?"

Cassidy smiled and shook her head. "Actually, I'm a psychotherapist, but my husband is the crime reporter for the *Post* and I've learned some things about investigating from him. Joan's a friend of mine, so I offered to help her gather information."

"I assume you've already talked to Tessa. Since she and I are the only viable suspects, and since she's a more sympathetic person than I am, I'd venture to guess you've already made up your minds that I'm the guilty party."

"What makes you say Tessa's more sympathetic?" *He's right, but I want to hear how he got there.*

Henry propped his elbows on his knees and steepled his hands under his chin. "Tessa's more transparent. Her personality falls within the normal range and mine doesn't. I keep my feelings to myself, and that leads people to think I don't have any. For instance, I'm experiencing a real sense of loss over Miles' death, but I'm not about to make a public display of it. So people are likely to assume he didn't mean anything to me."

"What *did* he mean to you?"

"He was my only friend. The only person I've met in a good many years whom I viewed as an equal."

Joan scooted closer to the edge of her seat, resting her low heeled pumps more comfortably on the carpet. "You said you thought we'd already made up our minds, but I can assure you I'm not jumping to any conclusions. We're just gathering information, and what we need from you is an account of what happened last night."

"I was reading my email when my computer locked up and refused to do anything. I rebooted and tried to restart my browser, but I got that damn blue screen of death, so I asked Miles if he could come down and help me. He thought I'd picked up a virus, and it took him, oh, about forty-five minutes to get my computer running again. When

he finished, I invited him to have a drink. I believe
he left around eleven. Then I took my sleeping pill
and went to bed. The next morning I vaguely
remembered what Tessa had told me, so I called her
back to see if Miles had come home. When I heard
he hadn't, I didn't know what to make of it."

"So how do you think he ended up in that
rooftop room?"

Henry stared at the brightly lit skyline beyond
his balcony. "I've been asking myself that same
question ever since the police informed me of his
probable fate. I realize it appears that Tessa and I
are the only two people who could have killed him,
but I know I didn't, and I can't imagine Tessa doing
it either."

"Do you know of anyone who might've had a
motive?" Joan rested her chin between her thumb
and forefinger.

Henry shook his head. "Miles was difficult in
some of the same ways I am, which is why we
understood each other. I expect he occasionally
stepped on some toes, but I'm not aware of anyone
with a reason to kill him."

Cassidy asked, "How are you and Miles
difficult?"

"That's a good question." Henry gave her an
approving smile. "We know what we want and we're
willing to do whatever it takes to get it."

"Two people with that kind of drive usually don't
get along."

"If we'd been competitors, we wouldn't have. But
since we weren't, we could admire each other's
skill."

"Who was in the Lunch Bunch?" Joan asked.

"Just the two of us at first. Then we ran into a
couple of other people here in the tower who had
flexible hours—Sandra Brown and Andy Gearen.

After a while, Andy dropped out." Henry cocked his head to the side, a thoughtful look coming over his face. "Here's something strange. Miles told me that one of Sandra's relatives disappeared. I don't know any details, just that he said it happened. Now isn't that an odd coincidence?"

Almost too freaky to be a coincidence.

"How did Miles find this out?"

"I assume she told him in private conversation."

"Is there any reason Sandra and Miles would be having private conversations?"

"Not that I know of. I didn't mean to imply anything. It was just a stray thought."

Standing in the hallway outside his door, Joan said, "Sounds like Sandra's next on our list. Any chance you'd be available tomorrow?"

"I have clients in the morning, but I could be here anytime after one."

They began moving toward the elevator lobby in the middle of the circular hallway. Cassidy drew her purse strap higher on her shoulder. "After what Tessa said, I was expecting Henry to be more aloof. But he seemed pretty open to me."

"You and I have more forceful personalities than Tessa. I expect he takes people like us more seriously."

Where's that coming from? You don't push people around like Joan does.

Cassidy pushed the down button. "The other thing is, as much as Henry appears calm on the outside, he has to be emotionally reeling. Maybe he was happy to have a chance to talk about what happened to him."

Although Cassidy doubted that Delia would return to her condo, she checked just to make sure, then paid her second parking fee of the day and drove home.

* * *

Cassidy came upstairs to find Zach where she'd left him, in front of the TV. A glass of bourbon and soda sat on the table beside him. She leaned against the doorframe waiting for him to tear his eyes from the screen. She hated the changes she saw in him: the long hours spent watching TV, a loss of interest in the things that used to matter to him, the increased amount of alcohol he consumed. *But at least he's set a limit for himself and seems to be sticking to it.*

He looked up. "You want something?"

"I thought you'd like to hear what I found out."

"Need help with it?"

"Not really." *He used to be fascinated with every little detail regarding crimes.*

"Maybe we could talk tomorrow. You know how I am on Sunday nights."

Sunday nights were so hard for him the only way he could get through them was to zone out. One part of her understood, but another was frustrated that he wouldn't do anything to ameliorate the situation.

Retreating to her place on the waterbed, she drew her knees up tight and wrapped her arms around them.

This is your job! This is what you do! You treat people with depression. He should pay attention to what you say.

You know you're not allowed to be his therapist. He's right in telling you to back off. Maybe he just needs to withdraw and lick his wounds for a while. Lots of people recover without professional help.

She picked up a mystery from her nightstand and forced herself to concentrate on the story until it was late enough to go to sleep. Then she went into the hall, stopping to look at Zach, who seemed unaware of her presence. She wanted to ask him to come to bed with her, to let him know she needed to feel his body next to hers. *You can't do that. If you break his frame, he'll lose all those comforting layers of insulation he's built up.*

She realized she would have to make do with Starshine. Having the calico curl up next to her head was the next best thing to spooning with Zach. Starshine had purred her to sleep countless times when her husband wasn't available.

It hit her that Starshine hadn't greeted her at the door, or run into the kitchen to beg for food, or joined her for a cuddle-in. She'd done none of the things she normally did when Cassidy returned. She hadn't even come padding into the room to settle for the night the way she customarily did at bedtime. *You know how unpredictable felines are. Soon as you think you've got their routines down pat, they do something different.*

Cassidy went through the house checking all of Starshine's usual sleeping places: the closet in the computer room, the sofa, the credenza beneath the dining room window, the box of rags in the basement. After a thorough search of the house, she put on her coat and went outside. Standing on her back stoop, she called "kitty, kitty," but the calico didn't respond. A lamppost across the street cast a pale sheen over her snow-covered yard, the light so soft the gritty layer of dirt on its surface was undetectable, the snow looking as clean and glistening as when it was new.

Cassidy crossed Briar and peered beneath her neighbor's bushes, calling as she went. She walked from the corner of Hazel and Briar to the end of the block and returned by way of the alley. As she trudged toward the back door, a prickly sensation started in her chest.

*Everybody said you shouldn't let her out. But
you were such a wuss, you couldn't say no. You
even had to give her her own cat door so she could
come and go as she pleased. Now she's gone and
you have no idea what's happened to her.*

Cassidy had almost reached the porch steps
when Zach opened the door. "Where were you?"

"I went looking for Starshine. I couldn't find her
in the house so I went up and down the block."
Cassidy could hear the tension in her voice.

"Why didn't you tell me?"

"You've got enough to deal with." She came
inside and hung her coat in the closet.

"You should have told me. I have to go look for
her."

"No, really, there's nothing you can do I haven't
done already."

Gathering her in his arms, he nestled his chin
against her curly cinnamon-colored hair. "I'm sorry
to be so out of it. I came downstairs to fix my final
drink of the night and that's when I realized you
were gone. How 'bout we snuggle on the couch and
have a drink together. If you don't do something to
take the edge off, you'll be tossing and turning all
night."

*Tranquilizing yourself with alcohol sounds like a
great idea. In fact, there are times you can
understand why he drinks.*

When the alarm buzzed, Zach turned it off but
made no move to get out of bed. In the past he'd
been the one to jump up and go downstairs while
Cassidy continued to snooze until he brought her
coffee. But now that his start button wasn't
working, Cassidy had been forced to take the up-
and-at-'em role.

As her brain cells slowly lit up, she seized on a hopeful thought: *Maybe Starshine's back.* But the cat wasn't on the bed, where they usually found her in the morning. Her spirits sagging, Cassidy went down to the kitchen, searched the pantry for a package of pre-ground beans, and stared numbly out the window while the coffeemaker gurgled. She was filling her purple mug when the cat door whapped.

She's home!

Hastening to the basement door, Cassidy almost collided with the calico bounding up the stairs. A well-trained cat-owner, Cassidy resisted the urge to grab the calico and clutch her to her bosom. Instead, she stood back and waited for Starshine to make her wishes known. *Breakfast, of course.* The calico leapt onto the counter, sat next to her bowl, and began scrubbing her face. She did not say *mwat.*

"Aren't you hungry?"

Purring raucously, Starshine bestowed a benevolent gaze on her human.

Cassidy took a can out of the cupboard, snapped off the lid, and thrust the food under the calico's nose. Retracting her whiskers, Starshine turned her head away. When Cassidy tried again, the cat hopped to the top of the refrigerator and continued grooming herself.

"What's the matter? Are you sick? You don't like pureed shrimp? What?"

Starshine twisted around to wash the base of her tail.

Cassidy gazed at her for a long moment. "Or did you eat elsewhere?"

Shortly after Zach left for work, Joan called to inform Cassidy that she'd set up two appointments:

the first with Sandra Brown at two, the second with Andy Gearen at four-thirty.

"How'd they react when you said you wanted to talk to them?"

"Andy's a good guy. He may think we're crazy but he'd never say so. Sandra, on the other hand, required some persuading. Every attempt I've made to win her over has fallen flat. I don't think she cares much for her own gender."

Chapter 8

Cassidy had finished her morning sessions and just opened a can of tuna for lunch when the phone rang.

"Hi, Cass, how you doing?" The voice belonged to Bryce, Zach's college-aged son.

Cassidy smiled inwardly. She had strong motherly feelings for the boy, which he seldom allowed her to act on.

"I'm okay," she said, recognizing after the fact that her voice sounded unusually subdued.

"Just okay?"

"How 'bout yourself?" Cradling the phone between her shoulder and neck, she drained the tuna-water into Starshine's bowl.

"So how come you're only okay? Does it have anything to do with Zach's not answering his cell?"

"He's preoccupied."

"Haven't you lectured me more than once on the topic of not keeping secrets?"

"I was wrong."

Bryce laughed. "People in healthy families don't need to hide things from each other," he said, paraphrasing Cassidy's words to him. "Family secrets are a sign of deeper problems. Since you're obviously holding something back, does that mean we have deeper problems?"

"You should drop your logic class today." She mixed mayonnaise and pickle relish into the tuna.

"So why is he preoccupied? And why do you not sound like your usual spirited self?"

"Zach has a new editor. The guy has a grudge against him and is refusing to let him work on anything but the most trivial of stories."

"Zach's not letting this dude get over on him, is he?"

"There's nothing he can do. The truth is, he's pretty withdrawn. He keeps his cell off a lot and just wants to be left alone."

"I didn't think he ever let anything get him down—except maybe you."

"Nobody's bulletproof." She spread tuna on a slice of bread and added lettuce.

"I don't get it, Cass. I thought you wanted Zach and me to get closer. Why are you making me pry it out of you?"

Because I forgot everything I know about relationships.

"Letting people know about his problems has never been Zach's strong point. But I shouldn't have tried to keep it from you. You need to see that your father has weaknesses just like everybody else and you don't have to try to live up to him."

"Don't you know by now how much I hate being talked down to? I never did think I had to live up to him."

Cassidy met Joan at Marina City and the two self-appointed sleuths took the elevator to Sandra's condo. As they approached her unit, high-pitched doggie yips erupted from inside.

When the door swung inward, two small fluffy canines burst out and planted their paws as high as they could on their visitors' legs. *Another reason to wear jeans instead of pantyhose.*

"I'm having second thoughts," Sandra said.

Cassidy stared at the statuesque figure in the doorway. *Breasts the size of melons. Not just cantaloupes, giant honeydews. Couldn't possibly have come with the original model. Those bee-stung lips and diamond-edged cheekbones had to be bought and paid for as well.*

"Would it be possible to get the dogs to back off a little?" Cassidy asked in the nicest tone she could muster. *As a cat person, you'd obviously rather be the pursuer than the pursued.*

"They're just being friendly," Sandra replied.

Too bad the same can't be said of the owner.

"You agreed to let us interview you," Joan said firmly.

"You caught me off guard. Now that I've had some time to think about it, I can't see any reason to let you and this woman I've never heard of before grill me about Miles."

"I told you, I need to interview everyone in the Lunch Bunch in order to round out my report. The president wants everything in writing as soon as possible."

What's this about a report? Joan obviously made that up. She lies as glibly as you do.

"I don't blame you for being leery," Cassidy said. "After all, you don't know a thing about me. I'm Cass McCabe. Joan and I are friends, and I've had some experience with this kind of thing so I offered to help her with her report."

Sandra scowled briefly, then allowed them to enter. "Oh hell, I might as well get it over with."

Joan went first, then Cassidy, the dogs bouncing joyfully at their feet. Cassidy tread carefully to avoid inflicting injury on any small doggy parts.

Sandra's living room was in perfect order, not a trace of canine hair on the carpet or the furniture. A streamlined neon-blue sofa and loveseat formed an L, vivid paintings hung on one wall, and a mirror covered another. Cassidy wondered if the mirror theme extended to the ceiling above Sandra's bed.

Sandra waved toward the loveseat, waited until her guests were seated, then sat on the sofa, her back rigid. The dogs continued their enthusiastic display.

"Okay, boys, that's enough," Sandra snapped. "Come over here and sit."

They obeyed instantly.

Their hostess's ice-blue gaze rested on Joan, then Cassidy. "What do you want to know?"

"Well, to begin with," Cassidy said, "I'd like to hear about your work. How is it that you're free to go to lunch during the day?"

"I teach classes at a health club and do a little modeling and personal training on the side." She surveyed Cassidy's slender but untoned body. "You know, you'd look a lot better if you had some muscle definition. I'd recommend a weight training program."

Cassidy's mouth tightened. *I'd be so much better off if I were narcissistic you instead of slack-muscled me.*

"I'll think about it. Now, could you please tell us about the Lunch Bunch?"

"I believe Henry's already covered that."

"You've talked to him?"

"Of course I have. He called right after you left."

"We'd still like to get your take on it," Joan said.

"My take. Three of us used to meet for lunch on a weekly basis. At Harry Caray's around the corner. Now one of us is dead." A look of pain swept across her face. She paused, then went on. "There were four of us when I started but Andy quit."

Joan asked, "Who invited you to join?"

"Miles."

"How did you and Miles meet?" Cassidy asked.

"In the elevator. Or maybe the laundry room. It's been a while. I don't really remember."

Miles doing laundry? Can't quite picture it. And when do people exchange more than three words in an elevator?

"So how long since you two met?"

"Let's see." Sandra rubbed the fingers of one hand back and forth across her thumb. "I've been at Marina City five years. I think I met Miles about six months after I moved in."

"What was your relationship like?"

Sandra shrugged. "We ate lunch together. With Henry."

"Were there times the two of you got together by yourselves?"

"Not really."

"Henry told us you had a relative who disappeared. He said you told Miles and Miles told him."

Sandra's expression registered shock. "Henry said that?"

"He did," Joan affirmed.

Shaking her head, Sandra replied, "He must be losing it."

"Did one of your relatives disappear?" Cassidy pressed.

"No. And Miles and I weren't having any private tête-à-têtes either. Henry must be confusing his soaps with reality."

Cassidy could not envision the astute elderly man sitting in front of daytime melodramas. Softening her voice, she said, "You looked pretty sad when you talked about Miles' death."

Sandra turned her face away.

"He must've been important to you."

"Not really." Then, after several beats, "We did sort of click. Not in a sexual way, you understand.

Just platonic. I don't have a lot of friends but I really care about the ones I have." Another prolonged silence. "Henry filled me in on what happened. It's so spooky to think there's a murderer living right here in the West Tower." A vein started to pulse near her temple.

"You sound frightened," Cassidy said.

"Well, I am a little."

"I've been assuming Miles was the only target and no one else had anything to worry about." Cassidy cupped her elbow in one hand.

"I'm probably overreacting."

"The obvious suspects are Henry and Tessa."

Sandra didn't respond.

"What do you think?" Cassidy persisted. "You think one of them did it?"

Sandra's gaze turned icy again. "I think it would be stupid to even speculate."

As Cassidy and Joan walked toward the elevator, Joan said, "It's nearly two hours till we see Andy, but it seems like a bother for you to drive back and forth. Why don't we kill some time at my place? I can scrounge up some milk and cookies. Or should I make that white wine and brie?"

"White wine and brie?"

"Isn't that the Oak Park food of choice? I think it was served at every function I attended. I'm more of a scotch-and-mixed-nuts girl myself, but I was able to adapt."

"Did you consider yourself an Oak Parker when you worked there?"

"Not exactly. And the problem wasn't tokenism. It was that some village leaders were almost desperate for me to succeed so I could stand as living proof that they were making integration work."

Cassidy glanced at Joan's attire. "You don't dress like an Oak Parker."

"You mean the skirt and heels?"

"And pantyhose. I don't know anyone who wears pantyhose if they can avoid it. Oak Parkers tend to dress down in a reverse snobbery kind of way."

Stepping into the elevator, Joan said, "Almost everybody dresses down these days. It's part of the decline of civilization. I've always been a lady and I don't intend to lower my standards anytime soon. Although I have to admit, I did give up corsets and white gloves a few decades back."

They went into Joan's condo and sat on a high-backed navy sofa with walnut trim. A matching walnut table, Ebony magazines fanned out on its surface, stood in front of them. Joan served pecan crescents on a bone china plate and milk in crystal glasses.

"So, do you think Sandra and Miles were lovers?" Joan asked.

Cassidy held her fingers in front of her lips to indicate that her mouth was full. She swallowed and said, "Did you notice how vague she got when I asked how they met? And it looks like she's taking his death pretty hard. If they were lovers, he certainly could've made a side trip to her condo after he left Henry's."

"Why kill him if his death was going to tear her up?" Joan's mahogany brow wrinkled. "That wasn't very smart of me, was it? I guess people do in the object of their affections all the time. Remember what Tessa said about Miles' always leaving first? Maybe he was trying to end the affair and Sandra couldn't handle the rejection any better than he could."

Cassidy wiped crumbs from the corners of her mouth with her napkin, then reached for another cookie. "I have a problem with the logistics, though. Delia said she saw a tarp and a package of trash bags when she first went into the room. Then the elevator dinged and she hid in the stairwell. Later on, when she peeked inside, she saw a body hanging in the closet. If Miles'd just dropped by Sandra's condo, she wouldn't have had a chance to bring up the tarp and trash bags."

"Maybe he called her after he left his condo and said he'd come by later. Or she knocked him out when he walked in the door, took her supplies up to the room, then brought him up after everything was ready."

"Whether he was conscious or unconscious, she'd have to find some way to get him to the sixtieth floor." Cassidy cocked her head and thought about it. "I suppose she could've used one of those drugs that make people compliant."

"That'd work." Joan took a glug of milk, leaving a white mustache on her dark upper lip. She quickly wiped it off.

"I realize I'm not the most spontaneous person in the world, but if I were going to commit such an elaborate crime, I'd want more time to prepare."

"Henry was the only one who could have known ahead of time that Miles was likely to leave his condo when he did."

"Yeah, and that puts me in a bind because I can't picture Henry as the killer. He's so refined, so lacking in motivation, so old." Cassidy suddenly remembered that Joan outranked Henry in years. Her cheeks growing warm, she added, "Well, he's not really that old."

Joan beamed. "I love it when people can't remember I'm not a spring chicken any more.

Henry looks older because of his health problems. He used to be pretty robust, but he had cancer a few years back and hasn't been the same since."

"You know, the more I think about it, the more I'm inclined to agree with you. The killer could've had his equipment ready and just been waiting for the right opportunity. Which makes Sandra—or anybody else Miles might have stopped in to visit— a suspect." Cassidy drained her glass of milk.

"You want a refill?"

"I'm fine. In fact, I'm going to make every effort not to put another bite of food into my mouth until dinner." *Except for peanut butter cups, which fall into the category of comfort, not food.*

"Then I'll just put these things away." Joan carried the glasses into the kitchen and Cassidy followed with the cookies.

The phone rang. "I'm screening my calls," Joan said. "Everybody's trying to pump me for information."

After the ringing stopped, Cassidy heard Joan's outgoing message, then a rapid-fire male voice: "Hey, babe, Danno here. Heard you're asking around about Miles. Got something for you."

Joan hurried to a small roll-top desk in the living room and picked up the receiver. "You have information about Miles?" She paused to listen. "We'll be right down." To Cassidy, she said, "He's leaving in fifteen minutes."

"This Danno a friend of yours?" Cassidy asked as they dashed along the hall.

"Oddly enough, he is. I suspect he's somewhat of a shady character, but he seems to have taken a liking to me and I have to admit, I kind of get a kick out of him."

Chapter 9

Nine floors down, Danno threw his door open. "Hey, doll face, good to see you." He looked at Cassidy. "And you there. Glad to make your acquaintance. Come on in, I only got a minute." A yard wide, almost as short as Joan, he moved as fast as he talked. He was in his early forties, bald on top, a round face, bushy eyebrows and bright beady eyes.

He gave Joan a quick hug, then bounced back a couple of steps. "Okay, here's the skinny. This thing went down two, three weeks ago. I was sittin' in the lobby when Miles gets off the elevator and heads toward the West Tower. Then this big muscular kid comes up behind him and yells his name and Miles turns around and goes, 'Whaddaya want?' And the kid goes, 'Do you know who I am?' and Miles doesn't, so the kid says his name and Miles just stares at him. Then the kid goes, 'You fucker!'" Danno grimaced in embarrassment. "Sorry, Joan, don't mean no offense."

"I was a school principal, remember?"

"So, anyway, Miles tries to leave but the kid gets in front of him and goes, 'You're not just walking away this time.' Then Miles goes, 'I don't owe you nothing,' and the kid starts yelling, 'You ruined my mother's life, you never paid a cent, you owe thousands in child support.'"

"Child support?" Cassidy said. "You mean this was Miles' son?"

"That's what it sounded like. But wait—you haven't heard it all. Miles starts walking toward the West Tower and then the kid yells, 'You're gonna pay for what you did,' and jumps him. Had Miles on the floor and was beatin' the shit out of him when three security guards came in and yanked the kid off. Two of the guards hauled the kid's ass outta the lobby and the third stayed to talk to Miles. They kept their voices down but I was close enough to hear some of it. Miles said he didn't wanna press charges, then handed the guard some bills. My guess, he was payin' to make it go away." Danno began herding Cassidy and Joan toward the door.

"Those guards have some explaining to do," Joan asserted.

Cassidy asked, "Did you tell this to the police?"

"I don't talk to no cops."

After Danno disappeared, Cassidy asked Joan, "Did you know Miles had a son?"

She shook her head. "We'll have to check it out with Tessa. Since she took the week off, she's probably home now."

"How's Amy taking it?" Joan asked, after Tessa had settled her daughter in the bedroom with a video.

"She doesn't understand." The tall, willowy woman dropped into one of the emerald chairs. "How could she? She's only four. But I am seeing signs of stress. She insisted on sleeping with me last night and she's been pretty whiny today. I hate to think what it'll be like for her when I have to go back to work, and I can't afford to take too much time off. In fact, I'll probably have to go full-time."

"This has to be really tough on both of you," Cassidy said. *She used to wish he'd disappear. Now he has, and it's not all champagne and roses.*

Twisting her wedding ring, Tessa heaved a large sigh.

"We have some new information." Joan repeated what Danno had witnessed. "Did you know about this other child?"

"Right after we brought Amy home from the hospital, he told me he had a son. That the boy was around fourteen and he didn't have any contact with him."

Cassidy said, "So that means he'd be about eighteen now."

Joan leaned forward. "That's all he said?"

"I kept after him for days but he wouldn't say another word. I think it just slipped out. That he never intended for me to know. I finally gave up on Miles and asked his mother, but he hadn't told her anything either. Which isn't surprising. He was famous for keeping secrets from her."

"That was one weird relationship," Joan remarked. "You should tell Cass."

"Miles didn't like his mother. When he was younger, he'd go for long periods without speaking to her. But she has money, and after she had a mild heart attack, it occurred to him that if he wasn't at least a little nice to her, she'd probably leave her fortune to her cats. So he started calling and taking her out to dinner a few times a year. Even though he acted begrudging—you know, a real ass about it—she put up with him because she didn't have anybody else." Tessa shook her head. "That poor woman. Now she doesn't even have him." Blinking back tears, Tessa added, "I had to tell her yesterday. It was awful. We both ended up sobbing on the phone."

Cassidy shifted in her chair. "Are the two of you close?"

"I guess you could say that. We were both frustrated with Miles, so that made us allies. We'd get on the phone and commiserate. You know, the enemy of my enemy is my friend."

"You said she doesn't have anybody, but she has you."

"Once I start working full-time, hand holding my mother-in-law will drop to the bottom of my list. To tell the truth, I don't like her that much myself. I mean, I do feel sorry for her. She had a hard life. But there are times when I get sick of her complaining."

"Wait a minute," Joan said. "How could her life have been so hard if she has all that money?"

"She was living on a pretty meager salary until about ten years ago when her uncle died and left her a sizable inheritance. But the really hard part was that her husband moved her to Chicago, then, about a year later, left her for another woman. So she got walked out on, forced into the work world, and had to raise her child as a single parent, all without help from family or friends."

"You think that's hard?" Joan responded. "God only knows how many women have a passel of kids to support on a minimum wage."

Tessa smiled. "According to her it was. She definitely isn't into making lemonade. If you ever hear me start to whine, please slap me out of it."

"Sometimes people need to whine," Cassidy said.

Both women looked at her as if she were nuts.

Nobody wants to partake of your therapeutic wisdom unless they're sitting in your office paying for it.

"Looks like we've run into a dead end where Miles' son is concerned," Joan said, her voice brimming with frustration. "Here we have somebody with a vendetta against Miles, somebody who actually threatened him and was big enough to beat him up—which isn't true of either you or Henry—and there's no way to find him."

"Would the killer have to be physically strong"—Tessa shuddered—"to do what he did?"

"I'm not sure," Cassidy answered, "but it wouldn't hurt."

Tessa said, "I suppose the son could've gotten through security."

"People sometimes do. They start chatting with one of the residents and the guard assumes they're together." Joan fingered her gold pendant. "He would've had to bring a tarp and a roll of trash bags in with him, but I suppose they'd fit in a backpack."

"And plastic rain gear," Cassidy added. "Delia said the Angel of Death was glistening and shiny, and I just realized I've been picturing him in a plastic rain suit. You know, to make sure he didn't leave any DNA."

Tessa lowered her head onto the heel of her hand, her golden hair falling forward. "But how could he have known Miles was going to leave the condo that night?"

"Maybe he got hold of Miles' cell number and called him," Joan said irritably. "Maybe he was working with Henry. We don't have to understand everything to recognize that this is the best lead we've come across so far."

"We should report this to the police," Tessa said. "They'd probably be able to run him down."

"I'll do it," Joan volunteered.

"There's one other thing we haven't touched on," Cassidy said. "That's how the killer removed the body from the building." *Assuming it isn't sitting in somebody's condo.* Cassidy looked at Joan. "Could you talk to the security guards and get someone to check the surveillance tapes to see if any resident carried out several trash bags? Or something else large enough to hold a body?"

"I'll get right on it."

As they were preparing to leave, Cassidy asked Tessa, "Have you had a chance to search the condo yet?"

Tessa let out another sigh. "I've had so many things on my mind. I did go through Miles' email but I didn't see anything out of the ordinary. I'll have to get a locksmith to open up the file drawer in his desk."

"You can't find the key?"

"He kept it hidden. I'm really curious to see what he thought he had to keep locked away from my prying eyes."

And you complain when Zach doesn't tell you he's leaving the house.

Chapter 10

"Have you heard anything about Miles?" Andy Gearen rested his forearms on his legs, his gaze fixed on Joan. He had a lean, athletic body, ginger-colored hair, and a sprinkling of pale freckles across the bridge of his nose. His features were finely honed, his expression earnest.

"How did you find out about Miles?" Cassidy interjected, wanting to get a read on the Marina City grapevine.

"Of course I knew something was up yesterday when a cop knocked on my door, but she wouldn't answer any questions. Later in the evening, I heard some women saying Miles had disappeared, so I called Henry. He told me what he'd learned from the police when they took him down to the station. The whole thing sounds so bizarre. I keep thinking it must be a mistake."

"I wish it were," Joan said.

"I don't understand. Why talk to me? You obviously know more about it than I do."

"We're talking to all the members of the Lunch Bunch and anyone else who lives here and knew Miles. I realize you dropped out, but you were in it for a while."

"It's been a couple of years. Anything I could tell you would be old news." He raised his hands palms out. "Not that I'm trying to get out of talking to you. I just don't want to waste your time."

"Whatever you say, I'm sure it'll help us fill in the big picture."

"Okay, shoot. My life's an open book."

Cassidy's eyes narrowed. *People who really are open seldom feel a need to proclaim it.*

Joan asked, "How did you get started with the Lunch Bunch?"

"It wasn't the Lunch Bunch back then. It was just Henry and Miles. I was the one who came up with the name."

"So how did you get started with Henry and Miles?" Cassidy wanted to know.

"Henry mentioned that he had lunch with Miles on a regular basis and I showed some interest so he invited me to join them."

"And how did you get to know Henry?"

Andy cracked a smile. "I feel like I'm being grilled."

"I'm sorry. It's just that I'm a therapist and I'm so used to questioning clients I sometimes forget I'm not in my office."

"How did I get to know Henry? He was retired. I was working out of my condo. We just, you know, bumped into each other."

A tad vague. "Um...I don't mean to be picky, but could you be a little more specific about that?"

Andy looked at the ceiling, then at the floor, then back at Cassidy. "I'd rather not. It makes me sound like such a loser." He blew out air. "Oh well, that period of my life is over and done with so I guess it won't matter if I let you know how pathetic I was back then."

"I'd like to hear about it," Cassidy said in a low voice, her therapist part coming to the fore.

Andy cleared his throat. "It all started with my divorce. Dianne and I had a home in Naperville, and she was really into house beautiful. She wanted the windows to sparkle...the grass to be cut just so...every weed pulled the instant it appeared. But she didn't want to ruin her manicure, so that left all the work up to me. By the time we split, I couldn't wait to move to the city. I expected to be Highrise

Man, on the go all the time, date all these chicks, have this glamorous lifestyle." He grimaced in embarrassment.

"But once I was here, I discovered I didn't like bars, I wasn't any good at flirting, I hated meeting women over the Net. I tried dating, but it was such a disaster I quit after a few months. Then my company closed its Chicago office and I had to work out of my house. So here I was stuck in a one-bedroom condo with practically no people in my life outside of business contacts." He looked at Joan. "You have no idea how much I appreciated your efforts to get to know me."

"It was nice to find somebody who didn't assume I was trying to pull something over on them every time I knocked on their door."

Andy gazed at the glass wall. "I started hanging out at the mailboxes and in the store, striking up conversations with anybody who'd talk to me. We have a lot of retired people here who are happy to stand around and shoot the breeze, but most of them don't have anything to say." A self-deprecating smile. "As if I did."

"You always have interesting things to talk about," Joan protested. "You don't think I'd waste my time on you if you didn't?"

"Well, the main exception was Henry. He never told me what he'd had for breakfast or complained about the cost of medication. He'd discuss the article he read in the *New York Times* or the lecture he attended. So I started suggesting things we could do together, but I was careful not to make a pest of myself."

"Was he looking for companionship too?"

"Henry comes as close to being self-sufficient as anybody I know. Besides, he was already meeting Miles for lunch. Those two really hit it off. As unsentimental as Henry is, I expect he's going to shed a few private tears for his lunch buddy. But Henry tolerated my company as long as I didn't expect too much of him, and I was even able to wangle an invitation to their lunches."

"So why did you quit?" Cassidy asked.

"I got over being pathetic. I read an article about the Red Cross needing volunteers and realized I could be doing something useful with my time instead of just hanging out. Once I got into it I liked it so much I added a couple of other organizations. Before long I reached the point where there weren't enough hours in the day."

Cassidy tilted her head to one side. "But people can usually squeeze in time for lunch with their friends."

"They weren't really friends. I always felt like Henry and Miles were just putting up with me. Then Sandra joined and it seemed like the three of them shared an inside joke. After I got to know some people at PADS, I was happy not to be a Lunch Buncher any more."

"You have any idea what that inside joke might be?" Joan asked.

Andy squinted in thought. "Could've been my imagination. That wasn't a period of time when I was feeling particularly good about myself."

"Anything else you can tell us about the Lunch Bunch?"

"There was this one other thing, but it might not've been real either. When Miles brought Sandra into the group, he said they'd just met, but they didn't act like new acquaintances. They seemed more like two people who had some history."

Joan traced a finger across the back of her hand. "Like two people who were having an affair?"

"I couldn't say for sure. I just had the sense they'd known each other for a while."

A beat of silence. Then Cassidy said, "I've heard volunteering is a great way to meet other singles. Did you find anybody to date in those groups you joined?"

"I met some wonderful women but by then I was too busy to date."

Guy's in his thirties—a time most men are horny as hell. Why wouldn't he be looking for someone to sleep with?

"Well, I guess we're done." Joan put her hands on the arms of her chair and pushed herself to her feet.

"I forgot to ask what kind of work you do," Cassidy said, standing also.

"Manufacturer's rep for a company that produces customized grillwork."

"Grillwork? You mean those ornate pieces of metal they put on buildings?"

"Yeah, those."

"Who do you sell to? Builders? Architects?"

"Architects, usually."

"Do any business with Tessa's firm?"

"I did some networking with her but it didn't land me a contract."

In the hall outside Andy's condo, Cassidy said to Joan, "Do you think Andy's gay?"

"Where did that come from?"

"He seems so likable and he's not even dating. I'd expect women to be all over him."

Joan frowned at Cassidy as if she'd just given a stupid answer on a test. "A lot of guys stay away from women after getting burned in a divorce."

But not a lot of guys stay away from sex. Although not dating doesn't mean he isn't getting any.

"Did Andy go through a bad divorce?"

"I never asked. It wasn't any of my business."

Cassidy touched Joan's arm. "I doubt that stops you from asking any more than it stops me. If Andy were gay, he and Miles might have been lovers. Then the rejection theory would apply to him as well as Sandra."

"But there'd be no reason for Andy to stay in the closet. After all, we're right here in the heart of River North. You see openly gay people all over the place."

"I guess I shouldn't jump to conclusions. It's just that so many of my clients have secrets, I start thinking everybody does." *Well, don't they?*

By the time a car parker handed over Cassidy's Toyota, rush hour was in full swing, which meant it would take twice as long to drive out of the city as it had to drive in. She was sitting in a left turn lane behind five cars, watching the light make its second change from green to red, when her cell phone beeped.

"I can't wait any longer," her grandmother said. "I was trying to get into this meditative state and be patient, to sit by the river and just let it flow by, but I can't wait another dang minute to hear about that murder at Marina City."

"I'm sorry. I should've called right away." *How inconsiderate of you. You know Gran ranks even higher on the inquisitive scale than you.*

"I'm not trying to make you feel guilty or anything," Gran said. "That's your mother's job. I just want to find out all about this guy who got whacked at Marina City."

"I'm headed toward Oak Park now. I could come straight to your house. The only thing is, I have a client at eight."

"Why don't you and Zach come for supper. I got some stew I could take out of the freezer."

Zach doesn't add a lot of cheer lately. Besides, if he's there you won't be able to talk about him.

"It'll be simpler if I come by myself."

Three cars succeeded in turning left as the light changed to red again.

Cassidy asked, "What river is it you're trying to sit by?"

"Any old river, I guess. A friend of mine insisted I had to read this book on Buddhism. She thinks I'm too hyper and need a little Zen in my life, but I've had about all I can take of trying to empty my mind and breathe slowly in and out. Relaxation may be all right for some people, but it's way too boring for me."

Chapter 11

Stepping into Gran's entryway, pushed from behind by a fierce wind, Cassidy shoved the door closed. She perused the short, sleek, black wig covering her grandmother's scalp. "Is that supposed to look Asian?"

"I thought it'd put me in the mood for Buddhism, but I can't say it did much good." The tiny, wrinkled octogenarian stroked her hair with the fingertips of both hands.

"Is your friend a practicing Buddhist?"

"A Buddhist, a Catholic, a Shaman, and a bunch of other things. I guess she picks her religion according to the whim of the moment, the way I do wigs." Hugging herself, Gran rocked up and down on the balls of her feet. "Boy, that outside air is cold. Let's go in the kitchen where it's warm and I can finish heating the stew."

Tossing her coat on the back of an easy chair, Cassidy followed her grandmother through the dining room. The bleached oak table held two red linen placemats, two blue and white soup bowls, a basket of bread wrapped in a red cloth, and a tall glass vase filled with yellow daisies.

Your table never looks inviting the way Mom and Gran's do. You're always running late and the best you ever manage is to fill the plates in the kitchen and plop them on the table. Seems like you missed out on the decorating gene.

Gran whisked through a set of Dutch doors and turned on the gas beneath a pot on the stove. "You want to pour yourself a glass of wine?"

"No wine for me. I have a client."

"Well, I don't, so you can pour some for me and then I want to hear all about the goings-on at Marina City."

As Cassidy talked, Gran filled their bowls and they sat down to eat. Between spoonfuls, Cassidy recounted every detail of the investigation. "So," she finished, scooping up the last of her broth, "we decided Andy wasn't gay and that left us with no justification for adding his name to the suspect list. Which means we only have three people. Four if you count Miles' son."

"I think you should count him. The kid could've been waiting in the hall, planning to call Miles and lure him out of his condo, but then he got lucky and Miles came out on his own."

"And the kid followed him to Henry's instead of grabbing him on the spot?"

"I can't come up with any reasons 'bout that. I already stretched my brain as far as it'll go with that first explanation." Gran finished the last of her French bread, washing it down with a big gulp of Merlot. "Joan is so lucky. I wish I could go with you on your interviews."

Cassidy patted Gran's age-spotted arm. "I do too."

"So who's your favorite suspect?"

Cassidy made a face. "Nobody's right. The kid had a great motive but I'm skeptical about the opportunity. Tessa had a motive but I can't imagine her committing such a cold-blooded crime. Sandra seems cold-blooded enough, but she's a little thin on motive and opportunity. Henry had the best opportunity but there's no sign of a motive."

"Well, you'll figure it out. You always do." Gran wiped her mouth with her napkin.

Pushing her bowl back, Cassidy plopped her elbows on the table and dropped her chin onto her hands. "I never had to try to solve any murders alone before. Well, not alone—I've got Joan. But she doesn't understand these things the way Zach does."

"He's still not doing so good?"

Cassidy hesitated. "There's one part of me that wants to say he's in terrible shape. But that probably isn't true. He's experienced a major loss and he's doing exactly what people do when they're depressed. I should leave him alone and let him find his own way out of it, but I keep wanting to fix it."

"'Course you do. You and me both always want to fix other people's problems."

"Instead of our own." She closed her eyes and pressed her fingertips against her eyelids. "You want to know the truth? I'm pissed at Zach for not being as patient, understanding and available as he was before. He's going through this horrible time and here I am feeling sorry for myself."

"Well, sure. Whenever we got something good, we don't want to lose it."

"I don't know when I turned into this needy, dependent little person. Most women don't have husbands who listen and talk the way Zach does— or the way he used to. I should be happy for what I've got and not expect so much from him."

"Now that's just plain silly. How could you possibly be happy about Zach not being himself?"

You know she's right. Of course you're feeling a loss. You said sometimes people need to whine. Must've been talking about yourself.

Gran tipped up her glass, letting the last few drops of wine trickle into her mouth. "Seems to me the important thing is, Zach has to get back to doing what he loves. I don't know why he doesn't tell that old editor to take his job and shove it."

"Because the only other major daily isn't hiring. Because it'd be a huge step down to go to a suburban paper. Because I don't want to leave you and Mom and all my clients and start over in New York or Washington, D.C."

"Well, then, Zach should investigate his editor. Dig up some dirt and hold it over his head. Then he'd have to let Zach do what he wants."

"But that'd be blackmail or extortion or something. And totally unethical."

"So what? Look what this guy's done to Zach. I read the *Post*. I know what a crackerjack reporter Zach is and that he hasn't written anything except these itsy bitsy stories since the new editor took over. Zach needs to do whatever it takes to get that jerk to stop walking all over him."

"If I don't get out of here soon, this totally unscrupulous idea of yours is going to take root my brain."

Starshine was in the wicker chair, right where she belonged, when Cassidy came into the waiting room. As she acceded to the calico's demand for food, she told herself she should lock the cat door so Starshine wouldn't disappear again that night. But by the time she'd covered the can with a plastic lid, her mind had moved on to the client who was due to appear at her door in ten minutes.

In the bedroom, she pushed playback on her answering machine. "Sorry to cancel at the last minute, but I have a migraine coming on. Can we reschedule for next week at the same time?"

Although Cassidy disliked eleventh-hour cancellations, she knew enough about migraines to be sympathetic. She left a message on the woman's machine confirming next week's appointment.

On the plus side, you can tell Zach now instead of later about this Gran-inspired idea you just had.

He was in the computer room next to the den. When she came up to stand beside him, he swiveled to face her.

She said, "I've got something I want to talk to you about."

He gave her a vague look. "What?"

"Let's go sit in the den."

"Soon as I finish what I'm doing here."

She went into the den and moved a footstool, placing it between their two chairs so they could share it, then parked herself in her chair and put her feet up. A short time later Zach joined her, resting his feet on the stool next to hers. She touched his black tennis shoe with the toe of her ankle-length boot.

"Gran says you have to find a way to get back to doing what you love."

"Yeah, well, that would be nice."

"She thought you should investigate McCready. Find something you could use against him and force him to give you decent assignments."

"Yeah, right."

"I know you can't blackmail him, but what if you found evidence he'd fabricated some of his stories? If you could prove he made up even one part of one story, it would ruin his career."

"I have no reason to think he ever did that."

"You said he turned in stories that weren't accurate when he worked for you."

"He was just sloppy."

"How do you know he wasn't making things up? In the last few years we've discovered there are a lot more dishonest reporters than anyone ever imagined. Nobody knows how widespread this thing is. It's probably been going on forever but editors didn't think to look for it before."

"You're grasping at straws."

"Turning in sloppy stories means he was lazy. He didn't want to work any harder than he had to. Isn't that the kind of person who'd make something up if he thought he could get away with it? And given the number of reporters who *have* been getting away with it, it seems like it's not that hard to do."

"Yeah, but it goes against all our training. Sure, there are a few bad apples, but it wouldn't even occur to most of us."

"Why are you so resistant?"

"Because you have nothing to base your theory on except wishful thinking. McCready and I were both in our early twenties when he worked for me. He hadn't learned his craft yet. He's been at the *Post* over four years now, and I haven't seen anything in his work to suggest that he's gone ethically awol."

"What about the fact that he's sidelined one of the paper's best and most highly paid reporters? Doesn't that imply a little ethical askewedness?"

"You haven't said one thing that makes me think it'd be worth the time and effort to fact-check McCready's stories. Even if I did discover inaccuracies, I couldn't tell anyone. Reporters never rat each other out. That's why the guy at the *Times* got away with lying for so long."

"It would energize you. Get you up and running again."

He lowered his brow. His mouth leveled into a thin line. "So this is just a back-handed attempt at doing therapy on me."

"No—I really believe McCready's the type to falsify stories. This is the sort of thing you'd have thrown yourself into before McCready came along. One reason depression is so hard to lick is that it leads to a vicious circle. The more depressed you are, the more hopeless you feel, so you refuse to do the kind of things that would lift you out of the depression."

"So if I don't do what you want, I'm refusing to help myself."

Thought you were going to let him deal with this on his own.

"Okay—I give. Go ahead and be depressed."

What a gracious apology.

Zach stood abruptly and started to leave the room.

"Please don't go. I know I'm out of line. It's just that—" *Don't say you miss him. It'll only make him feel worse.* "It's just that I have this really obnoxious part that always wants to fix things."

"Tell me about it." Zach sat down again. "So what else do you want?"

"For you not to go away mad."

"Okay, I'm not mad. At least not at you." He stared into space. "There was something I meant to tell you. Oh yeah. Bob—the reporter who's taken over my beat—he mentioned that the guy who went missing from Marina City hasn't turned up yet. Which means the cops haven't found any body parts, because if they had, the press would've gotten wind of it."

"I was surprised I didn't see anything about it in the *Post* this morning."

"Bob interviewed several residents and they all told him they'd heard that some guy disappeared the night before. With cops all over the place, Bob naturally suspects foul play, but he can't write it up unless he can get somebody to verify it, and the handful of people who know what really happened aren't talking. So all he's got is a missing-person story and that isn't news."

"Maybe the press won't get hold of it."

"That could happen. With the mess in the Middle East and all the other homicides in this town, there's a chance it won't get picked up."

Propping her elbows on the arms of her chair, she laced her fingers together. "What will the cops do if they don't have a body?"

"Can't say for sure. I've never seen a case like this before. But considering they've got evidence of a homicide, I'd guess they'll treat it like any other murder."

"I have one more question," she said as he started to get up again. "I hate to even think about this—it creates horrible pictures in my head—but how was the killer able to hoist the body over the drain?"

"Block and tackle. It's got pulleys to leverage the weight. Somebody your size could've hung the body without too much difficulty."

Chapter 12

It was eight-fifty at night when the phone rang. Cassidy was trying to clear up the mess on her desk.

"Please help me," a low voice said.

"Delia? Is that you? Where are you?" The caller ID was blank.

"I'm afraid I'm going to do something bad. The Dark Angels are after me. They never leave me alone."

Cassidy's hand tightened on the phone. Her stomach churned.

"If they catch me, I'll have to do what they want. I'm trying not to give in, but the voices just keep screaming. They're so loud I can't get any sleep. They keep telling me everybody hates me...I'm a bitch...the world would be better off without me and I should just do it."

"Do what?"

"I can't tell you."

"Do the voices want you to hurt yourself?"

Silence.

"The voices are wrong. Nobody hates you. I care about you and so does your therapist." *Not supposed to argue with her delusion.*

"This is a terrible place. I can't stay here but if I leave, the Dark Angels will get me."

"How can I help?"

"You could take me away. You've got white magic. If you come get me, the Dark Angels will leave me alone."

"Where are you?"

Another silence. "You have to promise not to tell the police. If the police come, I'll do what the Dark Angels want."

Oh shit! Cassidy swallowed. "All right, I won't bring the police."

"You can't tell Zach either."

"I won't tell anybody." *Unless I have to.*

"I'm in a boarded-up building. It's close to another one where people live. If you go between them, you'll see an open side door. That's how you get in."

"But I don't know where the building is. I need a street name, an address."

"It's down the block from Lowell School."

"I don't know where—"

"Please, Cass, you have to get me out of here!" The phone clicked off.

Oh my God! Sweat broke out on Cassidy's forehead.

You can't do this by yourself. You have to call the cops. It's insane to feel bound by a promise to a schizophrenic.

But what if she gets away from the cops? What if she kills herself? Even if she doesn't, she'll never trust you again.

Who cares? Unless you can get her into a hospital—which you can't seem to do—you can't help her anyway.

She's in a terrible place. She's frightened and alone and waiting for you to rescue her.

Cassidy went into the hall to gaze through the open doorway at Zach watching TV in the den. If she told him about Delia's call, he'd probably insist on accompanying her. That would be the sensible thing. For her to venture alone into a boarded-up building where homeless people lived was beyond stupid.

But if Delia sees Zach, she won't go with you.

Cassidy realized she was getting ahead of herself. The first step was to find out where Delia was. Cassidy sat at the computer and Googled Lowell School, locating an address on the thirty-seven hundred block of Hirsch Street in Chicago. *Smack dab in the heart of Austin.* Austin was a crime-ridden neighborhood on the west side of Chicago, an area many people hesitated to drive into. But because it lay directly east of Oak Park, it was familiar territory to Cassidy and not as frightening as it might have been to others.

In a residential section. And it's February. Even thugs don't hang out on street corners much when there's snow on the ground.

Still, we're talking a boarded-up building with scary people in it. And even if Delia comes with you, she probably won't let you take her to the hospital. Cassidy pictured Delia throwing herself out of the car as they approached West Suburban.

But she's waiting for you. You can't not go.

You also can't lie to Zach. She and Zach had a long-standing pact to be honest with each other, a pact she'd insisted on and he'd scrupulously observed.

She went back into the hall. Shifting her weight from one foot to the other, she stared at her husband. She tried to telegraph a mental command that he look up and ask why she was standing there. *If he asked, you'd have to tell him. Then you wouldn't need to do this thing behind his back.*

His eyes never wavered from the screen.

If only he'd ask, you'd have a reason to break your promise to Delia. But he's not going to, so you have to decide. You can tell him the truth—in which case he'll go with you—and risk that Delia sees him and runs away. You can disappear and leave him to worry when he discovers you're gone. Or you can lie now and seek forgiveness later.

She walked into the den and sat in the chair next to Zach's. "I got a call from the ER at Rush. The police brought Delia in and she's asking for me. I'm going to go spend some time with her."

"I'm glad they found her. You'll feel better knowing she's safe."

Cassidy descended the stairs, grabbed a flashlight as she went through the kitchen, and left.

When she reached the thirty-seven hundred block of Hirsch, she hunched over the steering wheel, slowed to a crawl, and started scrutinizing each dwelling. The housing stock in Austin was similar to Oak Park's, tall single-family homes with a few low-rise apartment buildings thrown in, the main difference being that the Chicago lots were smaller and the buildings set closer together. The only giveaway that this was a low-income area were the junk cars thickly lining the curbs.

So far in her drive through Austin she'd seen only a couple of boarded-up buildings, which made her wonder if the place Delia described might be part of her delusion. *If the building doesn't exist, you won't have to go in. Or feel guilty, either.*

Cassidy passed Lowell School, went halfway down the next block, and tapped the brake. Two side-by-side four-flats, their yellow-brick fronts abutting the sidewalk, stood on the south side of the street. The one to the right had lighted windows. The one to the left was dark, its windows and doors boarded. Scanning the string of cars at the curb, she spotted a small space near the southwest corner of the lighted building. *Parking. A minor miracle. Or maybe the work of the Dark Angels luring you into the building so they can get rid of both of you.* After considerable maneuvering, she was able to squeeze her Toyota into the tiny slot.

She sat frozen behind the wheel, staring at the narrow gangway about fifteen feet ahead.

You should have a gun. So what if they're illegal in Oak Park. Anybody demented enough to go into places like this should pack heat.

Unclenching her hands from the wheel, she stuffed her keys in her coat pocket, took out her flashlight, and hid her purse beneath the seat. Wintry air stung her cheeks and sent icy fingers down the neck of her coat. A large boat of a car roared past, its muffler dragging. She hurried to the gangway entrance.

The windows of the occupied building provided sufficient light for her to navigate around piles of trash and broken concrete. Sounds penetrated the glass. A baby screamed. A male voice bellowed. Foul odors assailed her.

She stopped in front of a rectangular opening where a side door used to be. The stink of urine and feces was stronger here. Shining her light into the opening, she could see the board that had covered the doorway leaning against the wall. She listened intently, but all she could hear were voices from the other building. Her light revealed a small entryway, with a short flight of stairs leading to the first-floor apartments.

When she stepped inside, her mouth was so dry she could barely speak. Working up some saliva, she called Delia's name, but the sound didn't seem to go anywhere. Several seconds passed, then she started up the stairs, walking around a pile of dog turds, broken bottles, a large boot. At the first-floor landing, two open doorways stood opposite each other. Both apartments were empty.

Cassidy climbed a long zigzag flight to the second floor, a murmur of voices becoming discernable as she neared the top. When she reached the landing, she saw candlelight flickering inside the apartment to her right. She turned off her flashlight, pressed her body against the wall, and peered around the doorframe. Half a dozen candles stood in cans on the floor. A mattress heaped with rags was shoved against one wall. As her eyes adjusted, she could see that the rags were people, maybe two or three. Across from the mattress two people of indeterminate sex sat on a sofa with stuffing protruding from holes in the upholstery. A young, hollow-eyed girl rocked back and forth on a straight-backed chair. A man stood in the corner gesturing and talking to himself.

Delia's one of those people on the mattress. Or she's in a back room. Or she isn't here. Cassidy would have to go inside and look for her. The thought of entering the room caused metal bands to clamp across her chest.

Creeping over to the mattress, Cassidy gazed down at three figures. None of them was Delia. She peeked around a corner into the kitchen. Two unfamiliar women sat on the floor, both talking at once. She crossed the living room and passed through a hall into a bedroom.

A thickset man with a wild white Afro, rheumy eyes, stubbly gray beard, and several layers of clothing, lumbered toward her. "Hep a man down on his luck?" His voice menacing.

Cassidy retreated into the hall. He lunged after her, grabbing her wrist and knocking the flashlight out of her hand.

"Gimme your money."

"I don't have any." She tried to jerk her arm away but couldn't break his hold.

He shoved her up against the wall, wrapping one hand around her throat and running the other over her coat, searching for pockets. When she struggled, he squeezed her throat tighter.

"Really," she choked out words, "I didn't bring any with me."

"Leave her alone!" Delia's voice shrieked from behind him.

"Fuck off!"

"Get your hands off her, asshole."

He dug out Cassidy's keys and threw them on the floor, then began ripping the buttons off her coat.

A board hammered down on the man's shoulder. As he swiveled around, Cassidy caught a glimpse of Delia holding the board, ready to hit him again.

The man raised his palms and shuffled back into the bedroom.

"Oh thank God! We have to get out of here. Soon as I find my keys." Cassidy squatted, running her hands over the uneven floorboards until her fingers touched her large round keyring. She grabbed it, located her flashlight, and rose to her feet. "Let's go."

Delia turned her head to the side and stared into space, then looked at Cassidy again. "You brought the police. They're downstairs waiting for me."

"No, I didn't. There aren't any police. It's just me."

"You're lying. I thought you were my friend but you're not."

Delia ran into the living room and Cassidy followed, watching as she went around the corner into the kitchen and out the back door.

Oh shit! She did it again.

Chapter 13

"So you lied about it," Zach said, his voice flat, his face remote.

Cassidy couldn't tell if he was mad or not, only that he was withdrawing from her. He sat at his desk in the bedroom and Cassidy watched him from her usual place on the bed.

"Isn't that what I just said?" *You're pissed 'cause you feel guilty. And 'cause he obviously doesn't want to hash it out.*

Zach looked at the clock on the bureau. Eleven-thirty. "It's getting late. Let's go to bed."

"And just forget about it?" Cassidy said, indignant.

"What's the point of talking? You're going to do what you're going to do."

More guilt oozed into her chest. "I don't think you realize how sorry I am. I don't ever want to do anything like that again."

His gaze rested on her face. "Oh, I know you're sorry. Sorry you thought you had to lie. But if you had to do it over, you'd do the same thing."

He nailed you. Maybe we should *go to bed.*

He scratched his jaw. "We could revise the rule and say we have to tell the truth except when it's expedient not to."

"We can't do that. We have to trust each other."

"I was just taking a cheap shot. Look, I do trust you. You lied once. So what? The real problem is, you want to turn this into a big argument and I want to go to bed."

You do want to pick a fight. You want him to be mad so you won't have to feel guilty. Plus you want him to pay attention to you.

"Sorry I made such a big deal out of it. It must seem pretty trivial compared to what you're going through at work."

"Work is what's trivial. I used to be able to put things out of my mind and not let them bother me, but it's harder when I have to go back and face the same shit every day."

Zach went to the walk-in closet on the other side of the room and began undressing. Cassidy hopped off the bed, slid past her husband, and went into the closet to get her fleecy lavender nightshirt. As she passed him on the way out, he wrapped his arms around her from behind and kissed her neck.

Warmth flowed through her, dissolving the tension. She crossed the room, sat in her chair, and leaned over to take off her boots. Then she sat up straight, suddenly aware of the calico's absence. "Starshine's gone again, just like last night. I was so worried about having to confess, I didn't even notice until now."

"Two nights in a row?"

"She must have found another family. She's started spending her nights at somebody else's house." *Curling up by that other person's head, purring them to sleep.*

"That's a pretty big leap, considering it's only been two nights." Zach pushed his arms into the sleeves of his cushy blue robe.

"I've heard about cats doing that. They make friends with someone other than their owner, the other person feeds them, then they start going back and forth between houses."

"Yeah, but Starshine doesn't walk up to strangers. You know how many times she's suddenly changed her behavior. She's probably just decided it's more interesting to be outside than stuck in the bedroom all night."

"It's too cold. I can't believe she'd stay out all night. I think she's got another family."

"I doubt it. Even if she does, as long as she shows up first thing in the morning, what's the harm?"

"She's *my* cat. I'm her primary love object, and I have no intention of sharing. Once I have her back in the house, she's going on lockdown."

Cassidy glanced at the clock. Eight forty-five, a client due at nine, and she was still in her lavender nightshirt. She'd been standing in front of her closet for nearly a minute. *Have to get dressed. Can't do therapy in your nightshirt. But how can you think about clothes when Starshine hasn't come home?*

Cassidy pulled out a mauve turtleneck with makeup smears on the collar. She tossed it into the laundry basket at the back of the closet. Next she reached for a fuchsia sweater that was badly wrinkled from being crammed onto an overstuffed rod. She put the sweater back and grabbed a powder blue top with a wine stain on the front.

Didn't you promise yourself you'd send this to the cleaners right away?

She decided the wrinkled sweater would have to do. *It's not like your clients expect you to be kempt or anything.*

Removing the sweater and a pair of black knit pants from the closet, she turned around and saw Starshine flopped out on the waterbed.

"How can you do this to me? Don't you know it makes me crazy? You're *our* cat. You have no business spending your nights at somebody else's house."

Just throw on some clothes. It's almost nine.

You need to lock the cat door now. You have four clients in a row and you're likely to forget if you wait till later.

She dashed down to the landing in the middle of the basement stairs. Above the landing was the window with the cat-flap in it. She set it so Starshine couldn't get out.

She was sprinting up the basement stairs when the back doorbell rang, indicating that her client had stepped into the waiting room. *Should've gotten dressed first!* She prided herself on being ready ahead of time, greeting her clients in a composed fashion, and giving them a full fifty-five-minute session.

What would be so bad if they discovered you're human?

Clients don't want their therapists to be human. They want them to be paragons and never screw up.

The phone rang while Cassidy was eating Campbell's soup at the dining room table. Swallowing quickly, she stood and lifted the handset from the wall phone in the kitchen.

"It's Tessa. I had the locksmith out this morning, so now I know what Miles was hiding from me." Her voice had the same high-pitched quality Cassidy had heard when she'd expressed her fear of being arrested.

"What did you find?"

"Financial records, mostly. Old income tax returns, copies of receipts he gave clients, broker statements. He was very secretive about money. He didn't want me to know how much he made or what his net worth was."

"You sound upset. Is it less than you thought?"

"Just the opposite. Miles used to talk as if we were barely getting by, but he had a lot more socked away than I ever would have guessed."

"So what's the problem?"

"A couple of things. One's a notebook showing he received payments of $25,000 at irregular intervals over a period of three years."

"What's wrong with that?"

"I've studied his tax returns and as far as I can tell it's unreported income. These payments started shortly after he went out on his own, and I don't know where the money came from."

"Is there anything else?"

"A divorce decree. I know he had a son but he never said a word about a previous marriage. I can't understand why he didn't tell me. Even though these past few years have been bad, we were in love when we first started out. I completely opened up to him, and he didn't even mention that he'd been married before. I'm starting to feel like I was living with a stranger."

"That's a lot to take in."

"There's one other thing. Except there's no reason this should bother me. I mean, he had affairs before and I really didn't care, so why should I care about this one?"

"What makes you think he was having an affair?"

"I found an eight-by-ten glossy of Sandra. In a slinky teddy. Signed 'With Love.' "

"It must feel like having the ground fall out from under you. Have you had a chance to talk to Joan about it?"

"She's leading a two-day seminar for retirees. I probably won't see her till after dinner. But I'm a big girl. I should be able to handle this by myself."

"I'm sure you can. But it never hurts to have someone to bounce things off of. I could come down to Marina City if you like."

You put up this front of being so kind and helpful, when what you really want is a chance to see everything for yourself.

Well, but you're not totally selfish. You'd probably make the same offer even if you didn't have an ulterior motive.

Tessa said, "It's so much trouble for you to come here three days in a row. I don't even know why I'm so...I don't know...agitated. I always thought of myself as a strong person."

"Well, and you are. But even strong people can hit a limit. You should have seen me after my divorce—a total basket case. I'd like to come. After all you've been through, you deserve a shoulder to lean on."

"Where's Amy?" Cassidy asked.

"Mom's been picking her up every morning and dropping her off at night. I've been so distracted, I haven't been able to give her the attention she needs."

The two women sat on the emerald sofa, the square coffee table in front of them. The plants that had previously occupied the table's surface were pushed to its far side to make room for the documents Tessa had lined up. Cassidy noted a stack of papers, a divorce decree, a medium-sized notebook, and an eight-by-ten photo laying face down.

You wouldn't want supercilious Sandra giving you her ice-queen stare either.

Cassidy laid a hand on Tessa's arm. "You probably aren't particularly eager to look at any of these, but I think we should go through them together. There may be something here that'll assist in my investigation, and even if there isn't, talking usually helps."

Tessa dropped her head onto the heel of her hand. She didn't move for about three beats, then straightened and aimed her large translucent eyes at Cassidy. "Okay, where shall we start?

"With the easiest one."

"I guess this would be it." Tessa handed the notebook to Cassidy.

The book contained nineteen entries, each a payment of $25,000 along with the date it was received. The earliest date went back nearly six years, the latest about three.

"You said he started his own business a short time before the first payment?" Cassidy asked.

Tessa nodded. "He had only a couple of thousand in savings when he did it, and we couldn't begin to live on my income. I thought he should wait till he'd built up more of a cushion, but he hated where he worked and he kept assuring me he could make a go of it. I don't think he had any clients for several months. I was getting scared we'd have to put our next mortgage payment on a credit card, but he just adopted this air of bravado, the way men do. It didn't fool me, though. I knew he was as nervous as I was."

Tessa nibbled her thumb. "Then he walked in one day and told me he'd gotten this great consulting job but I wasn't sure I believed him because he never seemed to be going to an office or working at home. But when the money started rolling in, I figured he must have a client."

"Did the consulting job coincide with the date of this first payment?"

"I can't remember but it seems like it must have."

"Since these payments don't show up on his income tax returns, we have to assume he was getting paid under the table. Is there any reason to think this wasn't just a little hanky panky he worked out with his client?"

"It seems pretty odd that the payments were all the same. With his other clients, he did big jobs, small jobs, the payments always varied. Besides, I can't recall any clients that started early on and stuck with him for almost three years. Of course, Miles didn't tell me everything and I was never good at remembering what he said about his business."

"You know, you're right. This does seem a little off." Scrunching her brow, Cassidy stared at the figures. "You think he might have been engaged in some illegal activity?"

"If an opportunity presented itself and he thought he could get away with it, his conscience certainly wouldn't have stopped him."

"Looks like we've gotten about all we can out of this one." Cassidy put the notebook back on the table. "Which is the next easiest?"

Tessa pointed to the divorce decree. "I got all riled up when I first saw this, but now it doesn't seem to matter. Considering he lied about all sorts of things, I guess it isn't surprising he didn't tell me he was married before."

Cassidy picked up a single piece of paper. "This is just the cover page. You have any idea where the rest of it is?"

Tessa shook her head. "Miles was famous for throwing things away. I suppose he didn't think he needed the other pages."

"Mind if I write down his ex's name?"

"Fine with me."

Cassidy recorded the information in her notepad, then looked at Tessa. "You said he lied about all sorts of things. Were you aware of his lying before now?"

"Not really. Either he was a world-class prevaricator or I was a real chump. When he bought a Mercedes last year, it dawned on me that he must be making more than he admitted, but except for that I thought he was pretty much on the up-and-up."

"Well," Cassidy said, "all we have left are the financial records, which wouldn't mean a thing to me, and Sandra's photo. Is it all right if I turn it over?"

"Go ahead."

Chapter 14

Sandra looked up at them out of imperious blue eyes, her full lips curving in a sensuous smile. Her dark hair fell in waves over her shoulders, and the nipples on her lush breasts tilted upward. She wore an amber teddy with a neckline that plunged almost to her navel and a skirt that barely covered her crotch.

"Wow!" Cassidy said.

"My reaction too."

"Does this still bother you? Or have you calmed down about it like with the divorce decree?"

Tessa turned the photo face down again.

"I guess it still gets to you."

"But it shouldn't! I was happy when he had those other two affairs. He ignored me, he was gone a lot, I got my hopes up that he'd leave me for the other woman. And the best part, he stopped pestering me for sex."

"Were you still having sex right up to the end?"

"Every now and then he'd wear me down and I'd give in. Would you believe, he hadn't gotten past that old-fashioned fifties idea that women owe it to their husbands. After he threatened to make Amy pay if I left him, I swore I wouldn't let him touch me. And most of the time I stuck to it. But there were a few occasions—I feel like such an idiot admitting this—when he'd get in a funk and I'd feel sorry for him and give him what he wanted."

So many of us women are afflicted by sympathy for men who don't deserve it. "Miles kept after you to have sex except when he was involved with other women?"

"When I said no, he just tried harder."

"Did he ever force you?"

"Never laid a hand on me. It was all verbal."

"So when he had those two previous affairs, he told you about them and his behavior changed. But none of those things happened with Sandra?"

"You think he *wasn't* sleeping with her?"

Looking at the photo again, Cassidy thought about it. "There are a couple of possibilities. Maybe Sandra was more important to him than the others and that made him want to keep it a secret. Or maybe Sandra was teasing him—reeling him in, then pushing him away—and they hadn't actually consummated it yet. That really fits with her personality. Or maybe she turned him down."

"If she did, he would've gone after revenge."

"Maybe he got his revenge and she killed him for it."

Tessa walked over to the glass wall and stared out. Turning around, she hugged herself tightly. "What bothers me the most is, I don't have a clue why that photo hit me so hard. When I first saw it, I assumed they were sleeping together, and that should've been a good thing. If he had gorgeous Sandra waiting in the wings, he probably would've divorced me. Why hang out with the ugly stepsister if Cinderella will let you in her bed?"

"Sounds like you thought you couldn't compete."

"But I didn't want him anyway."

"Most people aren't as sensitive to rejection as Miles, but nobody likes it. We generally can handle being the dumper, even if it makes us feel guilty. But we absolutely hate being the dumpee. I think that photo set off a mental scenario of Miles' leaving you. And even though you don't want him, the prospect of being left made you doubt yourself."

"You think that's it?" Tessa pushed one side of her thick golden hair behind her ear.

"What do you think?"

"It doesn't make sense but it feels right." Tessa let out a long breath. "People are so nuts. I don't know how you can stand to be a therapist."

"That's what makes it interesting." Cassidy stood. "Do you mind if I show this photo to Sandra? I'd like to hear what she has to say about why she gave it to Miles."

"She'll probably make it sound all innocent."

Holding up the photo, Cassidy grinned. "Innocent? This?"

Amidst a flurry of excited doggie yelps, Cassidy pushed Sandra's doorbell. She waited thirty seconds and pushed it again. *Probably at her health club trying to turn herself into a long-legged, gigantic-breasted Barbie, too top heavy to stand up. Or maybe at her plastic surgeon's choosing a new nose.*

A feeling of disgust welled up in Cassidy. She had no use for people whose sole purpose in life was to be admired. *You should feel sorry for her. Women hate her, men lust after her, but nobody loves her.*

Cassidy was just turning away when the door opened. The two small dogs greeted her joyfully, mouths slobbering, toenails digging into her jeans.

Sandra planted herself in the doorway.

"It's you again," she said. "Did I forget to tell you I wasn't interested in any more little talks?"

Cassidy displayed the photo. "Tessa found this in a locked drawer."

"Pretty good, isn't it? The best shot in my modeling portfolio."

"Why give it to Miles?"

"He was a connoisseur of feminine beauty and I wanted to show it off."

"You said your relationship was limited to weekly lunches. People usually don't give out sexy pictures of themselves unless there's more going on than that."

"Maybe *people* don't, but I do."

"Were you sleeping with him?"

Sandra shook her head. "You don't listen very well, do you?"

"Maybe it was only a flirtation. Miles pursuing, you playing the temptress."

"Now you're starting to bore me." Stepping back from the doorway, Sandra said to the dogs, "Come on, boys. Get back inside." As soon as the last wisp of tail passed over the threshold, she closed the door.

Cassidy returned the photo to Tessa and went home.

Leaving the usual layer of food at the bottom of her bowl, the calico sat on her haunches and scrubbed her triangular face. She purred contentedly and cast a moist gaze on her human.

"You love me now because your tummy's full. But when you run up against the locked cat door, you'll probably decide I'm the enemy."

Starshine ambled off to take a nap, and Cassidy began to think about dinner. Since it was only four o'clock, she had plenty of time to try out the casserole recipe she'd clipped from the paper. Before the new editor took over, Zach had frequently put in extra hours, but now he shaved his time, often appearing before six.

At six-thirty, Cassidy tried to call her husband, but both his office and cell numbers routed her to voice mail. *What did you expect? You know he hardly ever answers any more.* An uneasy feeling rippled through her. She tried to convince herself he was in the middle of an interview and couldn't leave. Dozens of times in the past Zach had gotten into situations where he could neither call nor tear himself away. *But not since McCready's reign started.* She took deep breaths and tried to calm herself, but the uneasiness turned to dread.

At seven-fifteen, the cold casserole sat on top of the stove. Cassidy, staring through her kitchen window into the kitchen next door, was finishing off a bag of peanut butter cups when she heard the back door open. As Zach came around the room divider, she noted the droop in his eyelids, the slackness in his face. Her stomach sank.

"Don't jump on me," he said in the stilted way drunks do when they're trying to sound sober. "A couple of guys insisted on taking me out for drinks to cheer me up. We got so involved, I lost track of how many rounds we had. But you'll be pleased to know I took a cab."

"How many rounds *did* you have?" She could smell the alcohol from several feet away.

"You back to counting drinks?" He put a hand on the kitchen counter to steady himself.

"You back to giving me a reason to?"

"Look, don't make this into more than it is. I went out after work and got a little sloshed. Happens all the time. I'm gonna go crash now and when we get up tomorrow morning, I expect you to put this behind you."

Put it behind me? Zach forget who he's married to?

"Why didn't you call and tell me you were going to be late?"

"I didn't fucking think of it."

"How could you not think of it when you knew you were going out for drinks?"

"I'm getting sick of having to be accountable all the time. If I want to have a few drinks, I will. Now—like I said before—I'm gonna go sleep it off, and I don't want you acting all pissy tomorrow morning."

Staggering slightly, he headed for the stairs.

Went out after work and got that drunk? Zach can hold his liquor better than anybody you know. Had to be gulping drinks. Or started earlier than he said.

And you're not supposed to be pissed?

Chapter 15

The bedroom light went on. Cassidy's eyes flew open. Adrenaline surged through her body.

Clad in his blue robe, Zach stood at the foot of the bed. "I know you hate being dragged out before dawn, but I have something I need to get off my chest, and I suspect you'd hate it even more if I dumped this shit on you at eight, then left for work."

Cassidy drew herself upright. The dread she'd felt earlier returned. The clock on the bureau said five-fifteen.

"Take as long as you want to get yourself awake. I've got mugs of coffee in the den. I'll wait for you there." He left the room.

Something he needs to get off his chest. Something you don't want to hear.

The windows were black and a sharp chill was in the air. She donned her burgundy robe and stuffed her feet into slippers. Tense and stiff, she sat in the den and wrapped both hands around the warm mug on the table beside her chair.

"It's cold."

"I turned up the heat. We should be okay in a couple minutes."

Zach stared at the blank TV screen and Cassidy sipped her coffee. Although in the past she had demanded that he tell her everything, a small voice said, *If he chickens out, you should go back to bed, pretend to be asleep, and never ask what it was he thought he had to tell you.*

Several seconds passed. Zach shifted in his chair. "You won't understand this unless I put it in context. Remember the cop who got killed about six months ago? And the rumor I picked up that the shooter was another cop?"

She nodded.

"All this time I've been developing a source. Somebody in the department who knows what went down. He called me shortly after the murder and said he could name names, but as soon as I asked a question, he hung up. He called again later and gave me the name of a rookie, but the rookie offered to rip me a new one. So all this time I've been getting calls from some amateur deep throat, and then a few days ago he agreed to a meeting. We were supposed to hook up in the lobby of the Hilton on Michigan at ten A.M. the day before yesterday."

"But something went wrong."

"I never got to the meeting. Which means there's a chance in hell I'll ever hear from him again."

"What happened?"

"When I went to work that day, McCready told me he wanted to go over my story list at nine-thirty. I didn't tell him about my source because I was sure he'd find a way to screw up the story, but I tried everything I could think of to get him to change the time. There was no reason it had to be nine-thirty. But the cretin had to have it his way, and then he called me in half an hour late. I almost walked out, but it would've given him an excuse to write me up. I couldn't even call my source because he'd refused to give me his number."

"You must've been so pissed!"

"So then yesterday morning McCready assigns me to go to O'Hare and interview this minor dignitary from Sweden. It was a bullshit story, never would've gotten in the paper. I started to drive to the airport, but I was so fucking sick of it all, I decided to stop and have a drink."

The room fell silent. Zach's eyes drifted back to the TV screen.

"What time did you stop?"

"It was almost eleven."

She could feel the blood drain from her face. "You were bingeing most of the day?"

"Somewhere around five I started to go the john and discovered my legs weren't working so well. That's when it hit me that I was in trouble. So I drank about a dozen cups of coffee before I came home."

"Coffee doesn't make you sober."

"It got me to the point where I could face you."

Closing her eyes, Cassidy took in a deep breath and let it out slowly. When she reached for her mug, her hand was shaking.

"Last night I thought I wouldn't tell you. You lied to me so I'd lie to you. But then I woke up around three and couldn't stop thinking about how we've always been honest with each other and what would happen to our marriage if we weren't."

"When you went in the bar, what exactly were you thinking?"

"What difference does it make?"

"Tell me."

"I figured I'd have a quick one, then go to the interview."

"A primary indicator for alcoholism is intending to have just one and not being able to stop."

"You're not going to get it in your head that I'm an alcoholic, are you?"

"You just went on a six-hour binge."

"I cut back to one or two drinks a day and I've maintained it all this time, so that means I'm not. After all the grief you've given me, I looked up the symptoms of alcoholism. Daily drinking isn't on the list. Getting drunk now and then isn't either. You live in a world of social workers who sip herbal tea. I live in a world of journalists and cops where drinking is the norm."

"Except for the ones in AA. Of which there are many."

"You have no reason to think I'm an alcoholic."

Cassidy rubbed her thumb over the large garnet in her wedding ring. "Alcohol has always been your way of coping, and you've got more to cope with now than ever before. When people are depressed, they often self-medicate. I know you weren't an alcoholic before, but what you did yesterday could be an indication that you've crossed the line."

"It was an isolated incident. You're blowing it out of proportion."

"Can you promise me you'll stay out of bars and limit yourself to two drinks a day?"

A long pause. "As much as I love you, I can't let you take over my life. There's nothing wrong with going into bars, and there are times when I need more than two drinks to get through the day."

Needs to drink to get through the day? If that doesn't sound alcoholic, I don't know what does.

"It's been killing me to see you so depressed. I can't bear the thought of watching you slide into alcoholism, too. It would destroy us."

"I've never sat around in bars during working hours before and I don't intend to do it again. You just need to give it some time and you'll see I'm not sliding into anything."

Except everything he says makes it sound like he is.

Zach tilted his mug to finish his coffee. "Okay, I made my big confession. Do you feel a need to keep raking me over the coals, or can I go read my email now?"

Cassidy's first impulse was to continue hammering at him in an effort to extract a promise. *But if he is an alcoholic, he won't keep it, and if he isn't, you don't need it.* "I guess there's nothing more to say."

It was only six A.M. and Cassidy was far too upset to start her day. The voices in her head made it impossible to think about anything other than Zach's drinking and what it might mean for their future. She needed Starshine, peanut butter cups, and more coffee. *Right. More caffeine because amping up your anxiety level is such a good idea.*

The Reese's and coffee were easy, but enticing Starshine into her lap might prove more difficult. The evening before, when the calico discovered that her door was locked, she sat next to it and howled for at least fifteen minutes. After that, she went into hiding in the basement. At bedtime Cassidy tried to lure the cat upstairs, but she refused to respond, and so far this morning she hadn't shown her face.

While Cassidy was refilling her mug, Starshine emerged from the basement and hopped onto the counter. She sat next to her bowl, which contained remnants of the breakfast Zach had provided earlier. As part of the cat's weight maintenance program, Cassidy had set a limit of three meals a day.

Starshine said her coaxing *mwat.*

"Are you open to bribery? If I feed you a second breakfast will you come sit in my lap?

The calico repeated her seductive sound.

You can't believe a word she says. But if you don't feed her, there's no chance she'll come on your lap, and if you do, there's a possibility she might.

After polishing off a second breakfast, Starshine followed Cassidy upstairs and into the bedroom.

Cassidy sat on the bed, pillows behind her back, her mug and the bag of Reese's on her nightstand. The calico curled up at Cassidy's feet, her eyes turning to slits, her head gradually dropping onto her paws.

"But I need you," Cassidy said.

Having a cuddle-in might make you feel better, said the part that wanted her to face reality, *but it's not going to change anything. You have to look at what's happening here. He started drinking before noon, wasn't able to stop, says he needs to drink to get through the day, and insists he isn't an alcoholic. What does that tell you?*

But it only happened once, said the part that wanted to look on the bright side. *You can't label him an alcoholic on the basis of a six-hour binge during a period of high stress.*

Maybe you can't label him yet, but a few months from now he could be full blown.

Cassidy's eyes felt gritty. Bile rose in her throat. Life without Zach would be a free fall into a black hole. Life with an alcoholic would be a bare-backed ride on bucking bronco.

Stop this right now! What do you tell clients? Not to dwell on worst-case scenarios. To distract themselves. To focus on something that'll take up their full attention.

Cassidy stood up, shook herself, and headed for the shower.

Cassidy saw two clients, then went upstairs, sat at her desk, and paged through her notebook. The last entry was her confrontation with Sandra over the slinky-teddy photo.

Would any woman give a picture like that to someone she wasn't involved with?

Except according to Tessa, Miles didn't act like he was having an affair, so maybe they weren't sleeping together.

But Andy Gearen, the dropout from the Lunch Bunch, said he got the impression that Sandra and Miles had a history together. And Henry said Sandra had a prior disappearance in her family.

Cassidy propped her elbow on the desk and pinched her chin. The more she thought about it, the more likely it seemed that some kind of relationship had existed between Sandra and Miles. Then something went wrong and Sandra made Miles disappear, just as someone in her family had disappeared previously.

Cassidy tried to picture Sandra hoisting Miles' body over the drain but the picture didn't work. Sandra didn't seem the type to commit such a messy, gory crime herself. She was too princessy, too used to getting others to do things for her.

Cassidy drew a cartoon face resting on balloon-sized breasts. The face displayed an evil grin.

Any possibility Sandra teamed up with Miles' son to do the deed?

Cassidy created a mental scenario of how that might have happened. Sandra would have witnessed or heard about Miles' son attacking him, then tracked the boy down and asked him to help her get rid of Miles. The son would have hated his father enough to agree to it. The night of the murder, Miles would have called Sandra to tell her he was going to drop by after he left Henry's, and Sandra would have alerted the son. When the boy arrived at Marina City, Sandra would have buzzed him in, and he would have gone straight to the sixtieth floor to set up his equipment. Then, when Miles showed up at Sandra's, she would have drugged him to make him easier to handle. The boy would have waited with Sandra until the deepest part of the night, then taken his father up to the rooftop room and killed him.

Cassidy tried to evaluate her theory objectively. It wasn't entirely plausible, but neither were many of the crimes she read about in the paper. And if she had to pick the person most likely to kill, Sandra would definitely top the list.

There were two people Cassidy wanted to talk to. The first was Danno, the second Henry.   She called Joan to ask for their numbers but Joan didn't answer, so she got them from Tessa.

"Remember me?" Cassidy said to Danno. "I was with Joan when you told her about Miles' son waling on him in the lobby."

"Could I forget a gorgeous broad like you?"

That's not me so he must not remember.

"So, what's up, babe?"

"I was just wondering who else was in the lobby when Miles' son jumped him."

"Didn't pay no attention."

"What about Sandra Brown? Any chance she was there?"

"Coulda been."

Cassidy thanked him and disconnected. *Least he didn't rule her out. So it's possible she saw the fight, followed the security guards, and introduced herself to the son after the guards dumped him outside.*

Cassidy started to call Henry, then put the receiver down. Getting people to talk was so much easier face-to-face than over the phone, where they could say they were busy and tell you they'd call back. *Of course they can always slam doors, but Henry seems too polite for that.* The other advantage of paying a visit was that she could watch his expression and body language and try to get a fix on whether he was telling the truth. *And the best reason of all, a trip to Marina City will distract you from worrying about Zach.*

She glanced out the window. The sky was overcast, the light subdued. Dirty puddles stood in the street.

She thought about calling ahead to see if Henry was home but concluded it would be better to take him by surprise, even though it meant risking a wasted trip. *What's one more parking fee on top of all the others?* She then took a moment to consider how Joan would react to Cassidy's flying solo on an investigation they had undertaken together.

Joan likes to be in charge even more than you do. When she finds out what you've been up to, you're going to get the full brunt of her disapproving stare.

Okay, so you'll have to put up with being treated like a bad child. But there's no way you're going to wait around for Joan to make herself available.

Chapter 16

Henry, his brow deeply furrowed, clad in a navy blue jacket and gray slacks with a knife-like crease, stood in his doorway. "I know I've met you but I can't think of your name."

Something about his performance seemed a little off. Cassidy's gut told her he was merely pretending not to recognize her.

"I'm Cass McCabe. Joan and I interviewed you about Miles' death."

"Oh yes, now I remember. Is there something else you need from me?"

"A few questions came to mind after we talked last time."

"I thought Joan was responsible for the report and you were just helping out."

"Well, yes, that's true...." *How do you explain away the fact that you're horning in on someone else's territory?*

"So where's Joan?"

"She had a seminar to teach. These questions kept nagging at me and I couldn't get hold of Joan so I decided to come here on my own and see if you'd be kind enough to answer them."

"I'm a very private person. I don't want to appear rude, but I'd prefer not to be interrogated."

"Please don't say no. Here I've taken the time to drive to Marina City and the car parkers are funding their retirements off my ancient Toyota and these questions aren't even about you. Oh please, let me come inside and tell you what the questions are and if you don't want to answer them, I'll be out the door in no time."

He smiled. "You don't give up easily, do you, Ms. McCabe. All right, I'll accept those terms." He stood back from the doorway and allowed her to enter.

Cassidy sank into the same oversized chair she'd occupied before. *Practically eats you alive. Must've bought it at The Little Shop of Horrors.*

She said, "You mentioned that Miles told you one of Sandra's relatives had disappeared."

"I said that? I wonder why I even brought it up."

"You don't remember?"

"At my age, I'm lucky if I can recall what I had for breakfast this morning."

Doubt this guy forgets much of anything.

"How long ago do you think Miles told you about the missing relative?"

Tenting his fingers, Henry rested his chin on one of the points. "I have no idea. It could've been two months or two years. Ever since I retired, the days just run together."

"Why do you think he told you?"

"Men usually don't admit to gossiping, but the truth is we do indulge in it now and then. I expect it was an interesting little tidbit he picked up and thought he could trust me to keep to myself. Which turned out not to be the case since I passed it on to you."

"Did you tell the police?"

He shook his head. "I was more cautious with them."

"Were you aware that Miles and Sandra had some sort of relationship beyond the weekly lunches?"

"Can't help you there. I'm the last person to notice things like that."

"Do you know anything about Sandra's family?"

He squinted in thought. "She referred to a sister a couple of times. I don't believe she ever told us the sister's name. I have the impression they weren't on good terms." He paused. "I don't remember her mentioning anyone else."

He looked at Cassidy, his eyes displaying the same gleam of amusement she'd seen before. This time she felt he was playing with her.

"Why ask me about Sandra's family?" he wanted to know. "Isn't she the one you should be talking to?"

"Well," Cassidy said, "I've taken up enough of your time."

"I answered your questions but you didn't answer mine. Why not ask Sandra?"

"I seem to have offended her. I came to you because I didn't think she'd talk to me."

He gave Cassidy an understanding nod. "Well, if you're finished with your questions...." He stood and she did also.

As she waited for the elevator, she tried to make sense out of Henry's behavior. *Playing dumb, pretending not to be as smart as he is. Why try to get you to underestimate him? Because he wants you to think he's too old and doddering to commit a complicated crime?*

In the below-ground lobby, Cassidy headed toward the escalators. Behind the escalators stood two banks of mail boxes. She noticed Tessa and Andy Gearen talking to each other between the two banks. Cassidy stopped to watch them, remembering that Andy had mentioned networking with Tessa. She studied their body language. *Totally innocuous. Nothing to suggest they're anything but acquaintances.*

Why are you looking at them as if they were suspects? Well, Tessa is, but there's no reason to think of Andy that way.

You should get out of the investigation business. It makes you almost as paranoid as Delia.

* * *

At five-twenty Zach phoned. "I'm just leaving so I should be home before six."

"Uh...okay."

"See you soon."

Cassidy hung up, then stared at the white phone sitting in the corner of her polished wood desk. She could not remember any other time when Zach had called to tell her he was leaving his office. A suspicious thought floated to the surface of her mind but she quickly squelched it. She had worked all day to convince herself that yesterday's binge was just a fluke and she was not about to let a new qualm worm itself into her brain.

She was frying hamburger for spaghetti sauce when Zach came into the kitchen.

"I've got something I want to talk to you about," he said. "It could wait till you're done but I'd rather do it now."

Her stomach churned. She searched his face for clues, but his expression was shuttered, giving nothing away.

"Now is fine." She put the pan in the oven so Starshine couldn't treat the half-cooked meat as a self-serve buffet.

"How 'bout I pour you a glass of wine?" Zach asked.

"That bad?"

"It's just that you look so tense. It's easier to talk when you're more relaxed."

He filled a glass, handed it to her, then led the way into the living room. After they'd taken their seats, he said, "This isn't going to be easy so don't beat up on me, okay?"

She moistened her upper lip. "The reason you called tonight. It was to set it up so you couldn't stop for a drink, wasn't it?"

He gazed at the opposite wall. "Sometimes I wish you didn't know me so well."

Cassidy took shallow breaths and waited.

After what seemed like a long time but probably wasn't, he turned to look at her. "When you accused me of being an alcoholic, my defenses shot straight up and all I could think of were arguments to prove that I wasn't. But you're right about tonight. I almost had myself convinced there was no reason not to stop for a drink and that you didn't need to know about it. Then I realized I was thinking like an alcoholic."

"Are you saying—" She gripped the bubble part of her glass with both hands.

"Don't talk yet. Let me get this all out before you say anything. So after I recognized that my thinking was off base, I had to acknowledge the other little things I'd been pushing out of my mind. Sometimes I wake up at three A.M. and feel like I have to have a drink or two to get back to sleep. Except for that, I haven't been sneaking drinks, but I've had to fight off the urge more times than I care to admit."

Cassidy took a large swallow. "I can almost understand. I can't tell you how glad I was to have you pour me this glass of wine tonight."

"But it's not the same for you. You might think you need a drink, but if you don't get it, you forget about it. I haven't been able to stop obsessing about booze since McCready took over."

"Does that mean you think you *are* an alcoholic?"

"I'm not ready to say that. Before my job turned to shit, I was perfectly content with a drink before bed. It's only since I started to feel so helpless that the drinking's turned into a problem. If I can get more control over my life, I think I'll go back to being the way I was."

"That could be true." *You desperately want it to be true.* "If the alcohol is just self-medication, once the depression lifts you may not need it anymore."

"Two days ago you tried to convince me to fact-check McCready's stories. I wasn't interested because I had no reason to think he'd made anything up. But now that I'm being honest with myself, I can see I've got to do something. If I investigate McCready, it'll give me a sense of purpose, a reason to get up in the morning. Even if I come up empty, it'll get the juices flowing again. I've got two weeks' vacation coming. I'm going to take that time and find out everything I can about the asshole. I don't know what I'll do with it if I uncover anything, but I'll certainly enjoy the process."

A sense of relief washed over Cassidy. *Hey, don't jump the gun. This doesn't mean everything's fixed.*

"I think that's a great start. But what if you don't find anything and after the two weeks is over, the depression returns?"

"Then I'll have to consider medication."

"I don't get it. Why so resistant?"

"I thought I told you."

"I mean the real reason."

"I feel like I should be able to do this on my own. Like taking meds is a weakness."

"But drinking isn't?"

"Tough guys always drink. My frontal lobes know there's nothing wrong with taking meds or seeing a therapist, but my lizard brain is convinced that medication is for sissies."

"I thought you were a twenty-first century man."

"Nah, I'm really a Troglodyte."

"What if the excessive drinking continues?"

"I'm sure you won't let that happen."

* * *

When it was close to bedtime, Cassidy went hunting for Starshine. She found the calico asleep on the sofa in the living room. Cassidy grabbed her up and wrapped both arms around her, the cat digging her hind claws into her human's arm, squirming and wriggling to get free. Cassidy carried her up to the bedroom, shut the door, and deposited her on the bed.

Starshine's ears twisted back, her whiskers retracted, the tip of her tail twitched.

Zach looked up from the magazine he was reading at his desk. "She doesn't look too happy to be here."

"When we turn off the light, she'll curl up between our heads. It's programmed in. She won't be able to stop herself."

"We'll see."

Starshine leapt onto Cassidy's desk, knocked over the mug that served as a pen holder, and pushed several pens to the floor. She chewed on the corner of a stack of papers. She walked across the phone, turning on the speaker light.

Cassidy scrambled to pick up the pens and turn off the speaker phone, worrying that Starshine would lay waste to the objects on her desk. *But if you yell at her, she definitely won't sleep with you.*

"Why don't we go to bed now and see if she settles down?"

"I'm willing to give it a shot." Zach headed for the bathroom.

After the lights were out, Cassidy heard a jingly little bell roll across the floor, one of the numerous cat toys Starshine had squirreled around the house. Gritting her teeth, Cassidy waited, still hoping that the cat's curling-up-between-their-heads programming would kick in.

A few minutes later, Zach's bedside lamp went on. "Do you really want to lie awake all night listening to that?"

Cassidy turned on her own light. "I guess she's not going to sleep with us."

"You never learn, do you?"

"Learn what?"

"That you can't win when you get into a battle of wills with Starshine. You may be able to get around all the people in your life, but Starshine's even more intractable than you."

"You think I should put her in the basement?"

"I think you should stop trying to control her. Open the cat door and let her come and go as she pleases. The more you try to force her to stay inside, the more determined she is to get out. Maybe if you let her do what she wants, she'll get tired of this new family of hers and start spending the nights with us again."

Cassidy's stomach sank. *Or maybe she'll pick the other family over us.*

"I hate having to compete for her affection with somebody I don't even know."

"You can't make her love you."

Why do I keep forgetting that?

Cassidy followed Starshine down to the basement, unlocked the cat flap, and watched her disappear into the night.

Chapter 17

After Zach left for his last day of work before taking vacation time, Cassidy was eating an English muffin at the dining room table when she heard the cat flap bang. Relief pulsed through her. *You're really afraid she'll move out permanently, aren't you?*

A moment later the cat, who never moved in a straight line if she could zigzag, jumped on the credenza, hopped to a chair, and climbed onto the table. She sat in front of Cassidy, revved up her motor, and sniffed the half-eaten muffin on her human's plate. Cassidy picked it up quickly before Starshine could lick the butter. Reaching across the plate, the calico touched her nose to Cassidy's mouth. It was the first display of affection she'd received in days.

"I *can* make you love me. All I have to do is give in to your every whim."

The phone rang while Cassidy was rinsing up.

Joan said, "I hear you've been busy while I was away teaching for two days."

Cassidy bit back the defensive words that wanted to leap out of her mouth. She took a moment to get her therapist part in control. "I guess you're not too happy about my going off on my own."

"I thought we were supposed to be working together. Which I took to mean that neither of us would talk to a suspect without consulting the other."

Forcing herself to see the situation from Joan's point of view, Cassidy realized the former principal had every right to be angry. "I can see why you'd be upset with me for not waiting until the seminar was over." Cassidy knew an apology was in order, but she didn't feel sorry and she didn't want to placate Joan with words she didn't mean.

"So," Joan said, not sounding particularly mollified, "are we clear that in the future we'll discuss things before either one of us goes off half-cocked?"

You should say yes. After all, you wouldn't even know who the victim was if Joan hadn't called.

But you've never let anyone tell you what you can and can't do. Besides, you don't entirely like her way of bullying people.

Cassidy said, "I'd like to renegotiate."

"Are you trying to take over the investigation?"

Well, yes, but I'm not about to say so. "I've always acted independently. It just isn't in me to discuss everything I do before I do it."

"Then perhaps the best choice would be for you to step aside and let me conduct the investigation on my own."

"I'm sorry, Joan. I understand that it must seem like I'm encroaching on your territory, but I think I can do some good here, and I'm not willing to just let it go. I'll be happy to stay in touch and include you whenever I can, but I can't guarantee I'll check everything out with you before I do it."

"So you're going to ignore my wishes and just do what you want?"

"I like you, Joan. I think it's terrific the way you've created a sense of community in the West Tower. I really hope we can get past this and be friends."

"I'll have to think about that."

By the time she got off the phone, Cassidy's skin was feeling prickly. She didn't like confrontations any more than anyone else. *You want everyone to like you, and you also want everything your own way. And there are a lot of times when you can't have both.*

Cassidy saw her morning clients, then sat at her desk and dialed Zach's work number. "How did it go?"

"I probably should've mentioned that company policy requires a two-week notice prior to taking vacation time."

"What happened? Did he fire you?"

"Almost, but then he lost his nerve. I said I was going to be out of the office for two weeks starting tomorrow, and he reminded me of the vacation policy and told me I couldn't do it. Then I said half the stories I've written since he became editor haven't made it into the paper, and the other half could've been handled by a cub. He blustered around for a while, told me it was a fireable offense, then backed down."

"Considering how much he doesn't like you, why wouldn't he fire you? And why didn't you tell me it could happen?" She jiggled a pen between her fingers.

"I was pretty sure he wouldn't do it and I didn't want to worry you. McCready's a brand new editor and I've been covering the crime beat for fifteen years. Plus a lot of the higher-ups consider me something of a star. If McCready canned me, the publisher would do an exit interview, and that'd give me a chance to fill him in on the type of assignments I've been getting. Since I was the paper's first choice and McCready only got the job because I turned it down, I doubt that he wants the publisher looking too closely at how he's been treating me."

"But I thought you didn't want him to write you up."

"Yeah, well, I've got my confidence back. You've been pounding it into my head that I haven't been myself of late, and in fact I've been so far down I let that little prick intimidate me. But he's not going to get away with it any longer. It felt damn good to stand up to him this morning, and even if he *had* canned me, it'd be better than sliding back into that sense of helplessness."

"Well, I'm glad you won that round. I'd much rather see his head roll than yours. But that's not the only reason I called. I'd like you to use Lexus/Nexus to track somebody down. Sandra Brown. She's a woman Miles may have been involved with, and she told him that a member of her family disappeared. If that's true, it means Sandra's known two people who simply vanished, and I don't believe in coincidence any more than you do. Sandra denies the disappearance story, so I need to talk to some other member of her family, and the only one she's ever mentioned is a sister. So, can you do that magic techie thing you do and locate the sister of Sandra Brown?"

"What've you got on Sandra? A social? Birthdate? What's her condo number? How old is she?"

Cassidy recited the condo number. "Since her highest priority is to never look a day over twenty-five, it's hard to tell about her age, but I'd guess she's in her middle thirties."

"Hang on a minute." After a brief pause, Zach said, "The sister's name is Ann without an 'e' Brown."

"How'd you do that?"

"Followed Sandra's previous addresses back as far as they went—a place in Berwyn. Since she was living there twenty-two years ago, I figure this is her family home." He gave Cassidy the address. "Then I checked other occupants and came up with George, Elizabeth, and Ann Brown. George and Elizabeth both had previous addresses but Ann didn't so she must be the sister."

"Can you get Ann's current address?"

"The name's too common. Lexus/Nexus would generate dozens, maybe even hundreds, of women with that name, and without some kind of identifier there'd be no way to zero in on the sister. If you hadn't given me Sandra's address, I wouldn't have been able to track her either."

Cassidy sighed. "Guess that means I have to drive to the Berwyn place and knock on doors."

"You don't *have* to do anything. In case you haven't noticed, you aren't a police detective or a P.I. You throw yourself into investigations for some of the same reasons I do, except I get paid for it, and all you ever get is threatened or beaten up. You do it for the excitement, the adrenaline rush—only you usually get more than you bargained for."

"No I don't, I..." Her brain could not generate a single defense. Even though she knew he was right, she hated to let him win.

Zach laughed. "Good luck with the door knocking."

Cassidy stood in front of the bedroom window watching large wet snowflakes fall to the ground. *There's no reason you have to do it today. You'd probably find more people home on the weekend. And if you wait, it'll give you time to think up a good pretext for asking about Ann.*

But she was too impatient, too eager to find out whether the disappearance story was true, and if it was, how Sandra was involved.

Chicagoans are tough. You can't let a little snow stop you.

Bundling up in a coat, boots, gloves, and neck scarf, she was heading out the door when another thought struck her. If she went charging off alone only hours after Joan had rebuked her for not being a team player, the former principal might never forgive her. *Joan could cut you off from her friends at Marina City. You can't afford to have her as an enemy.*

She removed her gloves and called her erstwhile partner. When Joan came on the line, Cassidy explained what she planned to do and invited Joan to come with her.

"You don't mean right this minute, do you? I need some advance warning." Joan's voice sounded less chilly than in their previous conversation.

"Actually, I do. When I get a brainstorm like this, I'm fairly obsessed to see it through."

"But I have other plans. There's no reason it can't wait till tomorrow."

"No reason except my irrational sense of urgency. I'd like to have you with me, but I feel a real need to do it now."

"All right, go ahead. As long as you keep me apprised."

Cassidy hung up, then rolled her head to relieve the tension in her neck. *Boy, did you luck out. You managed to appease Joan without having to take her with you.*

Chapter 18

Cassidy drove toward Berwyn, a suburb that bordered Oak Park on the south, the windshield wipers leaving white smears on the glass. She always thought of Berwyn as Oak Park's less-expensive, more conservative stepsister. The citizenry was composed of a burgeoning population of Hispanics, a dwindling population of Eastern Europeans, and a small population of people who were Oak Parkers at heart but couldn't afford the village's high taxes and pricey real estate.

She parked in front of the address Zach had given her, a red brick bungalow with leaded glass windows and weathered aluminum awnings. *Should've asked Zach if the Browns still live here.* She stayed in the Toyota a while working on her story. Once she'd devised a convincing ruse, she climbed out and trudged through the mound of snow at the curb, feeling an icy chill as some of the white stuff spilled inside her boots. She followed the shoveled path to the front door. A brawny brown-skinned man reeking of tobacco opened it.

I'd say this isn't Sandra's father.

Cassidy asked, "Do you know anything about the Browns? The people who used to live here?"

"I have no English."

To the left stood a two-story limestone Georgian, a house considerably more upscale than the surrounding bungalows. Cassidy rang the doorbell twice but nobody answered.

To the right stood a modest bungalow with a bowed multipaned window in front. As Cassidy approached it, she saw a framed glass square hanging on the front door. The square displayed a picture of a dove, the word *Peace* written beneath it.

She banged the brass knocker and a few seconds
later a woman's face appeared in the door's round
window. A strong face, with blunt cut iron-gray hair
and age lines undisguised by makeup.

Speaking through the glass, the woman asked,
"Who are you?"

"Cassidy McCabe. I'm trying to locate Ann
Brown."

Narrowing her eyes, the woman stared at
Cassidy for about three beats, then opened the
door. She wore a paint-smeared smock, jeans, and
leather sandals over thick white socks. "Everybody
says you should never open your door to strangers,
but I just hate having to be so distrustful all the
time. My husband may come home someday to find
the house ransacked and my mangled body lying in
a pool of blood, but I'm not sure that'd be any
worse than going through life being suspicious of
everyone. Well, as long as I've gone this far, you
might as well come in out of the weather."

"My boots are wet."

"Just leave them on the mat."

Cassidy removed her boots, stuffed her gloves in
her pockets, and rubbed snowflakes out of her
eyelashes.

"Now why on earth are you out in this storm
looking for Ann?" the woman asked. "Don't you
know most people aren't home during the day? And
even if they were, a lot of them wouldn't open their
doors."

"I realize this was a stupid thing to do, but
when I heard Ann Brown might have the Brown
family bible, I was so excited I couldn't wait."

"Let's sit down." The woman waved Cassidy into
the living room. "This is likely to be a long story."

"It's not that long."

"It may take longer than you think. I'm not about to tell you anything unless you convince me you're legit, and at the moment I'm having some doubts."

Pressure built in Cassidy's chest. Although no one had ever challenged her lies, she always felt guilty and expected to be caught. Taking off her coat, she sat in an angular purple chair. Her hostess chose the matching couch.

"Okay, have at it," the woman said.

"There's hardly anything to tell. I'm a genealogy nut. Traced Dad's ancestors back to Lithuania in the sixteen hundreds. Now I'm working on Mom's side. When her family came over from Europe four generations ago, the immigration agent changed their name to Miller, and nobody knows what it was before that. My grandmother is certain somebody had a family bible that went back ten generations, but she doesn't know what happened to it. So I put the question up on a message board, and this morning I got an email from a man who thinks Ann Brown has the bible."

The woman's finger traced a paint spot on the front of her smock. "So how did you know Ann's family used to live next door?"

"The man who emailed me gave me that address."

"The Browns didn't seem like the kind to have a family bible. They weren't churchgoers, had no interest in genealogy, never talked about their extended family."

Cassidy shrugged. "This guy who emailed me could be wrong, but I won't be satisfied until I talk to Ann and find out for myself."

"What do you know about Ann?"

"Nothing."

"I used to babysit for her. She was the sweetest kid."

"You know how to reach her?"

"We keep in touch."

"So will you tell me how I can locate her?"

"Simplest thing would be for me to call and ask if she has the bible. If she doesn't, it'll save you a trip."

Oh shit! Ann will say no and then you'll have to tromp through the snow and try to find someone else to con.

"Be back in a minute." The woman set off down a hall at the end of the living room.

She returned ten minutes later, a slight frown on her face. "Tried three times but the line was always busy, so I guess I'll go ahead and give you the address." She handed Cassidy a slip of paper.

God bless busy signals!

"Thanks so much. I was afraid I might have a hard time finding her." Cassidy rose and put on her coat.

"Before you go," the woman said, "I'd like your opinion on something." She led Cassidy across the entryway and into the kitchen, stopping in front of a
Formica table. On the table were pots of paint, brushes, and three pale blue tee shirts, each sporting a different design: a peace symbol; footprints surrounding the words *No War*; and a box enclosing the words *Peace Now.*

"We're preparing for an anti-war march in the spring. I've been playing around with different designs and can't decide which I like best."

"Who's the 'we?'" Cassidy asked, buying herself time because she couldn't decide either.

"The UU social justice committee. That's Unitarian Universalist."

"At Unity Temple?" Cassidy was referring to the famous Frank Lloyd Wright building in the center of Oak Park.

"That's the one. Now which would you choose?"

"Um...the footprints."

Cupping her elbow in her hand, the woman squeezed her chin between her thumb and index finger. "No, I think *Peace Now* is better."

So why ask me?

Keeping her expression neutral, Cassidy replied, "Yes, I believe you're right."

She drove to Riverside, a charming suburb with a wide variety of architectural styles, curving twisty streets, and old-fashioned gas street lights.

After getting lost twice, she drew up in front of Ann's small Tudor. Since early that morning she'd been trying to come up with a rationale for inquiring about the family disappearance, but her creative powers had deserted her. She could not think of a single credible reason for asking the questions she wanted to ask. Her only option was to fall back on the truth and hope for the best.

A woman in her early thirties, soft and cushiony, with undistinguished features and short sandy hair, opened the door. She had nothing in common with her sister except the blue of her eyes, which were warm and welcoming, not icy. A yellow lab stood beside her.

"You must be the genealogist," she said. "I hate to disappoint you, but I've never heard of a family bible. This guy who emailed you must've gotten his wires crossed."

"That's not the only reason I wanted to talk to you. This snow is coming down hard. I realize you don't know anything about me, but I'd appreciate it if you'd let me come inside and explain myself."

The dog wriggled past its owner to sniff Cassidy's coat.

"I see both you and your sister are dog lovers," Cassidy said, hoping the reference to Sandra would buy her a ticket into the house.

Ann's plain face hardened. "What does my sister have to do with this?"

"Sandra and I both own condos at Marina City. One of the residents disappeared recently, and I heard a rumor that a member of Sandra's family had disappeared as well. This strikes me as a little too coincidental, which made me curious about the earlier disappearance. I'm afraid I didn't get off to a very good start with your sister, and now she's refusing to talk to me."

The younger woman's pale complexion went a shade lighter. "You better come in."

Cassidy took off her boots and hung her coat on a tree just inside the door. They went into a large living room. A sofa with a fuzzy pink afghan draped across one corner faced a terra cotta fireplace, flames dancing above the ceramic logs. Chairs stood at either end of the sofa, both laden with books, jackets, backpacks and other kid-related debris. Ann lowered herself on the sofa next to a skein of blue yarn connected to a half-knitted scarf. Cassidy sat on the other side of the yarn.

"Who are you?" Ann asked. "What's your connection to the man who disappeared? Why so interested in our family disappearance?"

Cassidy winced. These were questions she never had good answers to. "My name is Cassidy McCabe. I'm a friend of Joan Frasier and she's on the association board. Head of security, that's her title. Since she manages building security, she wanted to see what she could find out about this guy's disappearance. I'm married to an investigative reporter and I've had some experience with this sort of thing so I offered to help."

"But why are you here instead of a cop?"

"Because I didn't report the rumor to the police. I probably should have, but I didn't." Cassidy stared into the fire. "I have such an urge to solve things myself I have trouble letting go." She turned her head to look at Ann. "Will you talk to me?"

Ann bit her lower lip. The lab laid his head in her lap. She scratched behind his ears, then instructed him to settle at her feet. Picking up her knitting, she said, "All right, I'll tell you. Then I'll call the police and tell them." A long silence. "My mother disappeared eleven years ago. She was only forty-six." Blinking rapidly, Ann covered her mouth and looked away.

"What a terrible thing," Cassidy said in a soft voice.

"Yes, it was terrible. At least to me. It certainly wasn't to Sandra. She never liked Mom. The only person she cared about was Dad, who always gave her what she wanted. Sometimes I thought she was just using him and didn't really like him either."

"How did it happen?"

"It started with my mother's decision to give me her jewelry. She had some gorgeous pieces— diamonds and rubies, really valuable stuff—handed down from her grandmother. Next to the house, it was the most valuable asset we owned."

"It must've been pretty important to all of you."

"You can say that again. Let's see—I was twenty-three, Sandra was twenty-seven. I was married and had my own place but she still lived at home because she spent every cent she made and was always broke. She was Dad's favorite and I was Mom's. I had two little girls and Mom just adored my husband and children. At the same time,

Sandra was modeling for a *Victoria's Secret* catalogue and Mom was pretty horrified about it. She thought modeling in skimpy lingerie was almost as bad as being a porn star. So one day when Mom and I were at lunch she told me she'd decided to give all the jewelry to me."

"You mean, leave it to you in her will?"

"No, she wanted me to have it then. Ron—that's my husband—he worked for a foundation so we attended a few black tie events. Mom thought it would be great if I actually had a chance to wear some of the pieces instead of leaving them locked away in a safe-deposit box all the time."

"And the reason she was giving you the jewelry was that she disapproved of Sandra?"

"Mainly she wanted to make sure it stayed in the family. She knew she could trust me to pass it on to my daughters but she doubted that Sandra would ever have children. She was also afraid Sandra would sell it since she was always so broke."

"Makes sense to me."

"I felt a little guilty about Sandra not getting her share, but I was pretty sure Mom was right about her selling it. When Mom announced she was giving it to me, I said she shouldn't breathe a word of it to Sandra, but Mom insisted it wasn't fair not to tell her."

"Why didn't you want Sandra to know?"

Ann shuddered. "Because I knew she'd be furious. When Sandra was mad, the whole house shook. She used to terrorize me when we were kids."

"But your mother told her anyway."

"Yeah, and Sandra threw the biggest fit I've ever seen. Then she calmed down and stopped talking about it, which struck me as strange." Ann took in a breath. "Three weeks later Dad had to go out of town on a business trip."

Cassidy thought she knew what was coming next. The muscles in her neck tightened.

"I used to call Mom every day and most of the time she was home. Then, right after Dad left, I called early in the morning and she didn't answer. I kept calling but I couldn't reach her, so after dinner I left the girls with Ron and drove to my parents' house. When I saw her car in the driveway, I panicked. I thought maybe she'd fallen and was unconscious or something. So I let myself in and she wasn't there. Everything seemed normal—her purse where she always left it, her clothes in the closet—but no sign of her."

"What did you do?"

"I called Dad. He said he'd catch the first flight out. Then I called the police but they told me she hadn't been gone long enough for them to do anything. They did come out the next day, not that they were any use. They told us there was no sign of forced entry and that she might have had some reason to take off on her own. It was obvious they thought my father was abusing her and she'd used some kind of underground railroad to disappear. I felt sorry for him. I knew he'd never been abusive to Mom or anyone else." Ann frowned deeply. "It was just plain stupid. I told the cops about her fight with Sandra and pointed out that no woman would walk away and leave her purse with her money and keys inside. But they kept telling me they couldn't do much without a body."

"Did they investigate at all?"

"They talked to a lot of people but nobody knew anything. Of course Sandra made sure she had an alibi. She pretended to be all broken up about it but I don't think she fooled anybody. She never was a very good actor."

Cassidy cleared her throat. "I hate to even ask this, but are you assuming your mother's dead?"

Ann put her knitting down and glared at Cassidy. "I *know* she's dead. She never would've left Dad or me. She's dead and Sandra did it. Not with her own hands, but she got somebody to do it for her."

"You must feel so helpless—knowing your mother was killed and not being able to do anything about it."

"Right after it happened, I confronted Sandra and she just gave me this smug look. Then I tried to convince Dad, but he'd never believe his little princess could do anything wrong."

"That must have made you crazy."

"And you know what else? Dad gave Sandra the jewelry."

"What!"

"She said she needed it more than I did because I had a husband and family and she had nothing. I was so mad I stopped talking to my father for a while. But it was more than I could take, being cut off from my entire family, so I let him back into my life. But not Sandra. I haven't spoken to her since the day I accused her of killing my mother."

"Who would?"

Ann's eyes shone with emotion. "I feel so cheated. I thought I'd have my mother for years to come. That she'd be my best friend, a grandmother to my girls, that we'd go shopping and have lunch. This is the kind of thing you never get over."

I've got a mother who's alive and well and would love to go to lunch and I try to avoid her.

"It's important for the cops to hear your story. You need to call District Nineteen and ask for Detective Roloff."

"You think it's possible Sandra could be arrested for this new disappearance?"

"One thing you can count on, they'll take a good hard look at her after they find out about your mother."

Chapter 19

With snow still drifting down, Cassidy hunched her shoulders and hurried from the garage toward her back gate. Starshine ran out to meet her, uttering a series of welcoming *mwats.* If it had been summer, the cat would have rolled on the sidewalk, but since the concrete was frozen, she dashed ahead of her human to the door.

"Why are you out in this cold?" Cassidy scolded, sticking her key in the lock. "You used to stay inside in bad weather."

As Starshine trotted around the room divider into the kitchen, Cassidy hung her coat in the closet. Following the calico, Cassidy expected to find her sitting next to her dish, but instead she was perched on the other side of the sink washing her face.

Cassidy felt jealousy snaking through her. "Does this mean you've started lunching with your new family as well as spending the night?"

It was only four o'clock, which meant she had a little time to spare before tackling dinner. "Here, kitty, kitty," she said, walking toward the stairs at the front of the house. To her surprise, Starshine jumped down and came along with her.

A tall cabinet stood at the head of the stairs. Cassidy kept the calico's favorite toy, a stick with feathers attached to the end of a cord, on top of the cabinet. It was the only place high enough that the cat couldn't take the birdlike toy out for herself. Starshine reached up and planted her paws on the side of the cabinet, signaling that she wanted to play with the bird.

Cassidy settled on the bed and began whipping the well-chewed feathers around. Starshine hid behind a pillow, pounced on the toy, jumped a couple of feet into the air, captured the bird, and started to walk away with it clamped between her teeth. Cassidy tried to yank it free but the worn cord broke and the calico remained in possession of her prize.

She carried it to her water bowl, which sat on top of the radiator cover, and dropped it in. After it was thoroughly soaked, she tried to fish it out, splashing water everywhere. Cassidy hopped off the bed and grabbed the bowl before Starshine could knock it to the floor. After mopping up, Cassidy tossed the bedraggled stub of feathers to the cat, who pranced around the room with the bird in her mouth.

"I don't know why I try so hard to keep you home. If I had any sense, I'd encourage you to spend *more* time at the other house."

At five-thirty Zach walked into the bedroom. Before he arrived, Cassidy had started chicken breasts simmering on the stove, washed the green beans, and set out a package of rice, then returned upstairs to do paperwork at her desk.

Standing in the middle of the room, Zach said, "Come here."

As he pulled her to him, she pressed her body against his, looping her arms around his neck. He leaned down and gave her a big wet open-mouthed kiss. She began to feel hot and tingly and moist.

Panting slightly, she stepped back and said, "Maybe I should turn off the stove."

"Why don't you do that?"

They made love for a long time. Sitting in bed afterward, Cassidy leaned her back against Zach's bent knees. He said, "Standing up to McCready was better than any pill I could ever take. I have no interest in drinking. All I can think about is digging in and investigating that little prick."

"It's so good to have you back."

"I should have listened when you first suggested it."

"Sometimes things have to get worse before they get better."

"Do all therapists talk in clichés?"

She made a face. "I try not to but sometimes they just pop out."

He massaged her neck.

"What if you don't find anything?"

"I'll quit and go deliver pizzas or something. No matter how this turns out, I'll never put myself in a position where McCready can grind me under his heel again."

Cassidy stabbed a bite of chicken and two green beans with her fork. "She's gone again. She had lunch with her other family and now she's returned for dinner. Maybe she likes them better because they feed her whenever she wants. They obviously don't care about keeping her weight down the way I do."

"You don't know that she's visiting some other family," Zach said. "You don't even know for sure that she has another family. She could just as easily be out sniffing bushes or hiding in the basement."

Cassidy chewed and swallowed. "One thing I can be sure of, and that's that somebody else is feeding her. Breakfast was always her favorite meal and now, whenever she's been out all night, she has no appetite the next morning."

"You seem to have this fixed idea that somebody is deliberately trying to steal Starshine's affections." Zach reached for another serving of chicken and rice. "It could be entirely innocent. Maybe one of our neighbors thinks she's a stray and is feeding her out of the kindness of her heart."

Frowning, Cassidy drew herself up. "Nobody could mistake Starshine for a stray. She has a collar with a magnet on it and her grooming is impeccable. Strays always look unkempt."

"Maybe the neighbor thinks she's lost. Or a cat who got left behind when her owners moved."

"If she was lost, she'd stay with whoever's feeding her instead of going back and forth between houses. No, I'm sure this is an alienator of affection we're dealing with here. And just to prove it, I'll go buy a tag with my name and number on it right after dinner—while you're cleaning up the dishes. Then we'll see whether Starshine's other family gives me a call."

When Cassidy returned from purchasing the tag, Starshine had reappeared. Cassidy attached the tag to the cat's collar with no expectation of hearing from the person who'd been keeping the calico overnight.

Upstairs, the printer was whirring noisily. "What are you doing?" Cassidy asked her husband, who was staring intently at the monitor.

"Printing up all the stories McCready wrote while he was at the *Post.*"

"I'll get out of your way."

She went into the bedroom and sat at her desk to ponder Miles' demise. Having heard what Ann had to say, Cassidy was convinced that Sandra was behind the Marina City murder.

She made her mother disappear because she wanted the jewelry. Then she made Miles disappear because something went wrong in their relationship.

Sandra had an alibi for the night her mother disappeared, which meant she solicited someone else to do the dirty work. That someone was either a hit man or a boyfriend willing to kill for her. Cassidy knew amateurs usually weren't slick enough to get away with such complicated crimes, but professionals were expensive and Sandra was always broke. *Bet she got her boyfriend to do it and he was either lucky enough or smart enough to carry it off.*

So who did it this time? Miles' son?

Would an eighteen-year-old be capable of killing someone, draining his blood, and disposing of the body? He might, if Sandra masterminded the crime.

Thinking there was a good chance Miles' ex was the mother of his son, Cassidy searched her notes for the name she'd copied from the divorce decree. Marla Nisbitt. *Good she kept her maiden name. Ups the odds you'll be able to find her. Now here's hoping she doesn't have an unlisted number.*

Cassidy borrowed Zach's laptop, clicked on Switchboard.com, and came up with three Marla Nisbitts in Illinois. The first was in Springfield, the second in Western Springs, the third in Chicago's South Loop.

She lifted the receiver, then put it down again. *You completely forgot about Joan. You should have told her about the disappearance of Sandra's mother.* Cassidy tried to remember if she'd made any promises. She didn't think she had. She also wondered if she was obligated to inform Joan that she wanted to meet Miles' ex.

The real deal is, you don't want her accompanying you on interviews. It was a matter of getting people to talk. Although Joan was very effective on her own turf, Cassidy was afraid her pushiness wouldn't go over so well with strangers.

She had more confidence in her own style of gaining rapport, and she didn't want Joan undermining her. Cassidy decided she would continue to go it alone, and Joan might never need to know about her extra-curricular activities.

Looking at the three addresses, Cassidy decided to call the South Loop number first.

"My name is Cassidy McCabe and I'm calling in regard to your ex-husband Miles."

"I have absolutely no interest in discussing Miles with you or anybody else." The phone clicked down.

Bingo! The right Marla. But you should have started off by telling her Miles is dead. Who could resist hearing about the murder of their ex?

Cassidy's next two calls were routed onto voice mail. She dialed again and Marla picked up.

"If you don't stop harassing me, I'll call the police."

"Are you aware that your ex was killed last Saturday night?"

"What?"

"Did you know he'd remarried and was living at Marina City?"

"I haven't spoken to him since the divorce."

"My husband and I own a condo at the twin towers, and someone there got a glimpse of the murder in progress."

"How did it happen? Who killed him?"

She's taking the bait.

"I'd rather tell you in person." Cassidy picked up a couple of pens from her desk and dropped them in the mug where they belonged.

"This is a scam, isn't it?"

"I know this sounds like an offer of riches from Nigeria, but I really am on the up and up. My husband Zach Moran is a reporter for the *Post*, and

I've learned a lot about investigating from him. Since the head of Marina City security is a friend of mine, I offered to help her follow up on as many leads as possible."

"I still don't get it. If your husband's the reporter, why isn't he calling? Or the police?"

"Because the body disappeared. The police can't rule it an official homicide until the DNA results come back."

"You mean they don't know if he was murdered or not?"

"They know all right, they just can't act on it. Look, I'd really appreciate it if you'd give me half an hour of your time. I'll tell you everything I know, then maybe you can answer a few questions for me."

"I'm leaving town on a business trip in the morning."

"How about tonight? It's only eight-thirty."

"I don't feel comfortable letting strangers into my house."

"Is there a bar or restaurant where we could meet?"

"Lalos. It's right across the street from my apartment. You have my address?"

Cassidy said she did.

"How soon can you get there?"

"I can be there by nine."

"I'll be waiting just inside the door."

"You know, it's odd," Marla Nisbitt said. "When you first told me Miles'd been murdered, I was shocked, of course. But now I don't seem to feel anything. Just detached. The kind of non-reaction I have when I hear about the assassination of a third world despot. It's almost like there's something wrong with me. Here we were married for seven years, and you tell me Miles was killed in this really gruesome way, and I don't have any feelings at all."

"I think that's pretty normal," Cassidy replied. "After all these years with no contact, Miles must seem like a stranger."

Marla flicked back one of the long dark curtains of hair that lay along the sides of her face. She was several inches taller than Cassidy, slender, dressed all in black, and managed to be both brisk and amiable at the same time.

The two women sat across from each other at a blond wood table. The restaurant, bright, colorful, piñatas and woven hangings on the wall, was packed with bodies. High-decibel clatter filled the room. Marla touched her tongue to the salt on the rim of her huge glass.

Cassidy asked, "Did you and Miles have any children?"

"No, thank God."

Damn! You were hoping she'd be your ticket to finding the son. But maybe there are other things she can tell you.

"We were only a few months into the marriage when I began to have my doubts," his ex-wife continued. "It took me long enough to get out, but at least I didn't do anything irrevocable like having a baby."

"Why the doubts?"

"Before we were married, he put on his Prince Charming routine. Then afterward, his real self started to shine through, which, it turned out, was cold and indifferent. He was basically so self-centered he couldn't be bothered with anybody else. He just wanted a wife to hang on his arm and make him look good."

"But you stayed for seven years." *If anybody can understand staying too long, it should be you.*

Cassidy had remained with her womanizing ex until he dumped her.

A wizened old man, guitar strapped over his shoulder, small round toupee perched on top of his head, asked if they would like a song. Cassidy politely declined.

Marla looked directly at her. "You're asking why I didn't leave earlier."

"I'm sorry. That was rude of me."

"That's okay. I don't mind." Marla tasted the salt on her glass again. "At first, whenever I'd broach the topic of divorce, he'd sweet-talk me out of it. And for a while, he'd be Prince Charming again. Then, after we'd been together a few years, he turned nasty." She stared down at her drink.

"Nasty how?"

"I'd revealed something in confidence and he threatened to tell my parents." A three-beat silence. "Oh hell, what difference does it make now? I had a lesbian relationship when I was in college and my parents were very conservative. I was young and stupid and I allowed Miles to intimidate me. What I should've done was pack my bags and let him say whatever he wanted."

"How did you finally get out?"

"Miles dropped the bomb. He told me and everybody else that he was the father of Renee's five-year-old son. We lived in this neighborhood where people threw block parties and backyard barbecues and everybody got along. My two best friends were Jen and Renee. And then I find out my husband's been banging Renee for years." Marla's face darkened.

"How awful!"

"Awful and humiliating. I immediately moved back in with my parents. Whenever Miles called, I told him he had to go through my attorney and I'd hang up. The only person I talked to was Jen, and when I found out she was still friends with Renee, I quit talking to her."

"You lost everything at once. Your home, your friends, your marriage."

"I didn't completely lose my friends. When I came to my senses, I realized Jen had done the right thing in refusing to take sides. So I worked myself up to call her, and she was very understanding. I got a new job, moved into the city, and now I'm glad the whole thing happened. If Miles hadn't made such a mess of everything, who knows how long it would've taken me to leave."

A waitress stopped by their table and said something in a mixture of Spanish and English Cassidy couldn't understand. Assuming she was asking if they wanted a refill, Cassidy said to Marla, "Another Margarita?"

"I have to go." She tipped back her drink and finished it. "I still have to pack."

"Please bring the check," Cassidy said to the waitress. As the woman trundled on, Cassidy had no idea whether the check would be forthcoming or not.

She looked at Marla. "I have one more question. Do you know anything about Renee or her son?"

"Jen's the only person I stayed in contact with, and I told her I didn't want to hear Renee's name."

"Aren't you curious?"

"I suppose. But talking about her always puts me in a funk."

"All these questions I asked tonight. They'll probably put you in an even bigger funk."

"Probably. But the tradeoff is, I got to hear about Miles' getting killed."

"Do you think Jen could put me in touch with Renee?"

"I expect she could." Marla tilted her head. "Why so interested in Renee?"

"Because she's the mother of Miles' son." Cassidy went on to tell Marla about the fight between the boy and his father.

Marla said, "Give me your card and I'll pass your number on to Jen. She can decide whether or not she thinks it's a good idea for you to talk to Renee."

Chapter 20

"I'm going to jump," Delia shouted at Cassidy, who stood on the opposite side of the West Tower roof.

"No, don't!" Cassidy cried out. She wanted to run across the rooftop and grab Delia but her feet were rooted to the concrete floor. "Don't jump! I can help you!"

"I'm a worthless piece of shit. I don't deserve to live." Delia climbed over the railing and launched herself into the air.

Cassidy screamed, her voice shrill and insistent like the ringing of a phone.

Zach gently shook her shoulder. "Somebody named Jen is asking for you. You want me to take a message?"

"No, I'll talk to her." Cassidy brushed her tangled hair back from her face and struggled to sit up, dragging the sheet over her bare breasts. *This is insane. You know you're totally incoherent before coffee.*

Zach handed her the cordless and Cassidy said a mumbly hello.

"This is Marla's friend, Jen. She told me about your conversation last night."

Jen? Who's Jen? And who for that matter is Marla?

Zach set a mug on her nightstand. Cassidy dropped the sheet and gulped half her coffee, her brain cells immediately perking up.

"Yes, of course," Cassidy said, her voice growing crisper. "Marla told me you have Renee's number."

"Well, I do, but the story you told Marla sounds so bizarre I'm not certain I believe it. Did somebody really cut Miles up into little pieces and throw him in the trash?"

"All I know for sure is that Miles was killed at Marina City and it seems likely his body parts were carried out and disposed of."

"I guess I just needed to hear it directly from you. Getting it second-hand made it seem a little unreal. Miles stepped on so many people it's no great stretch to imagine someone hating him enough to do that."

"Did he step on you?"

"I never had anything to do with him. Even though he worked so hard to be Mr. Wonderful, I could tell from the get-go he was slime. Since I always disliked him, I don't even have to pretend to feel sorry he's dead."

The cold air raising goosebumps on her arms, Cassidy tucked the burgundy comforter over her bare skin. "Have you talked to Renee? Is she willing to see me?"

"She said it's fine with her if you want to come to her place." Jen paused. "I guess you wouldn't know about her circumstances."

"All Marla could tell me was her name."

"Her situation is pretty grim. She's got MS, been confined to a wheelchair for quite a while, plus she has a third-floor walk-up apartment. She gets Medicaid, SSDI, and food stamps, but even when Kenny was working—that's her son—they never had enough to move to a wheelchair-accessible place. Far as I know, she hasn't left her apartment in over a year. So for her, the prospect of anybody paying a visit is appealing."

"That really is grim."

"And that's not the worst of it. As long as Kenny was working, she could pay the rent, but he's been unemployed for months now and it looks like she's going to lose her apartment."

So that was the trigger for the kid's going off on Miles.

Cassidy asked, "What will happen to her?"

"I hate to even think about it." Another pause. "I brought her some groceries a while back, but it makes her feel terrible to accept charity. And it makes me feel terrible to sit back and watch what she's going through."

"Well, thanks for cluing me in. Can you give me her phone number and address?"

Jen complied. After a short silence, she added, "Marla said you think Kenny might have killed his father."

"It's a possibility."

"Renee would never tell you, but I think you ought to know that Kenny's been arrested twice for assault."

"Was he convicted?"

"I don't think so. Both times, Renee called and sobbed over the phone, but afterward she refused to talk about it. Acted like it never happened."

Cassidy donned her heaviest nightshirt and padded into the computer room to talk to Zach. Dressed in a black tee inscribed with the words, *Beer: Helping Ugly People Have Sex,* he swiveled to face her. "So, who's this Jen person that calls at such an uncivilized hour?"

Cassidy told him about her attempt to track down Miles' son, then asked, "How long've you been up?"

"Couple hours. Two weeks is not a lot of time. I'll probably have to pull some all-nighters." Several stacks of computer printouts, some with highlighted sections, sat on the long table he'd built to accommodate his techie equipment. He'd also been making notes on a spiral pad.

"How's it coming?"

"Barely scratched the surface."

"Jen said something about Miles being cut up and thrown into the trash. Got me to wondering whether the police have found any body parts yet. I know your reporter friend said they hadn't on Monday, but that was several days ago. I also wondered if the cops could get search warrants based on body parts without waiting for the parts to go through a DNA test."

"It's possible the dicks could find some judge who'd issue a warrant based on the parts alone. If you really want to know where things stand, call Emily."

Emily was both a friend and a Chicago Police Detective working out of Area Three. Although Cassidy, Zach and Emily now enjoyed an easygoing relationship, getting to that point had not been easy. When Cassidy and Zach first met, he had recently broken up with Emily, and she was still attempting to get him back. Even after he moved in with Cassidy, the two women viewed each other as rivals. But as time went by, Cassidy overcame her jealousy and Emily was able to settle into a friendship with her ex and his wife.

Cassidy showered, dressed, poured more coffee, and made the call.

"Hey, Emily, how you doing?" A mug in one hand, the phone in the other, Cassidy sat in her chair in the den.

"I was wondering when you'd call," the detective said good-naturedly.

"You were expecting to hear from me?"

"Don't play dumb. Every time you want a police leak you call me."

"How'd you know I'd need insider information?"

"You were the one who notified the police in the Marina City murder, weren't you? When have you ever gotten that close to a homicide that your crime-solving compulsion didn't kick in? So, what do you want this time?"

"Did the police find any body parts?" Cassidy hooked her toes beneath the footstool and pulled it into place.

"Nary a one. They searched every dumpster on the block and even went digging through the landfill but didn't find a thing. We're thinking this guy's so good, he must be a professional. Which means there isn't much chance he'll be caught."

"Not what I wanted to hear." Sipping her coffee, Cassidy rummaged around in her head to see if she'd missed anything. "Any idea when the DNA results'll get back?"

"Should be soon. The boss put a rush on it, and he's leaning on the lab."

"Well, Emily, thanks for helping me out one more time."

"This was an easy one. Since my colleagues haven't gotten very far, I didn't have to betray anybody. Now, I've got a question for you. None of us can figure out why Zach didn't have a story in the *Post* the day after it happened."

Oh shit. What can you say? "Um...Zach's been reassigned. He has a new editor who doesn't appreciate him as much as the old one did."

"You saying he's having trouble at work?"

"Please don't tell anyone."

"Sorry to hear it, but if I know Zach, he won't let this new editor keep him down very long."

Clicking off the cordless, Cassidy propped her elbow on the armrest, laid her cheek against her palm, and thought about what Emily had told her.

If the killer's a hit man, it can't be Miles' son. So maybe Sandra isn't broke anymore. Maybe she did hire a professional. Or maybe the hit man was willing to take his fee out in trade.

Cassidy felt a letdown. If the Angel of Death was a contract killer, she might as well give up now. But giving up just wasn't in her. At least, not until every stone had been turned and every lead followed.

There's still more you can do. And the cops aren't always right. Just because the killer's so savvy doesn't mean he has to be a professional. Could've been a very smart amateur.

She called Renee and set up a meeting for that afternoon.

Chapter 21

Cassidy parked on a street in Uptown, a neighborhood in the early stages of gentrification that still contained plenty of low-rent housing. She walked to Renee's building, read the hand-lettered sign that told her the buzzer wasn't working, and hiked up three flights of stairs, panting as she reached the top.

Renee opened the door and looked up at her from an ancient wheelchair. "How nice of you to come all the way from Oak Park to tell me about Miles," she said, smiling shyly.

A black lump of guilt settled in Cassidy's chest. "I can't take that much credit. I think you deserve to hear the story of Miles' death, but I have to admit, I have my own agenda as well."

"I don't see anything wrong with that. At least you sort of went out of your way to come here and tell me what happened." Turning her wheels manually, Renee backed away from the door so Cassidy could enter the smoke-filled apartment. The woman's face was lined with worry and pain, but Cassidy could see vestiges of its former beauty in the fine bone structure and lively brown eyes. Flanking Renee's hollow cheeks hung limp strands of gray-brown hair that fell to her shoulders. She wore a small gold cross around her neck.

Renee positioned her wheelchair next to a rickety dinette table blemished with cigarette burns. It held a pack of Marlboros, an ashtray, a phone, and a stack of romance novels.

She said, "Make yourself comfortable in that chair over there and then you can tell me about this agenda of yours."

Cassidy sat on a cracked vinyl recliner facing a new-looking wide-screened TV. A sagging sofa piled with a pillow, sheet, and quilt stood to her left. She swiveled the recliner halfway around so she could look directly at Renee.

Cassidy asked, "Did Jen tell you Miles was murdered?"

Renee's eyebrows shot up in surprise. "She just said he died. I figured it was natural circumstances."

"There was nothing natural about it." Cassidy went on to tell the whole story.

"He wasn't very nice, but nobody should have to die like that." Renee lit a cigarette, then looked up from under her brow. "You still haven't said how I can help you."

Cassidy's throat constricted. *What you're here for is to get something you can use against this poor woman's son.* "I'm a friend of the person who's head of Marina City security and we're investigating the murder together."

"What does that have to do with me?"

"Probably nothing. To tell you the truth, we've talked to everyone Miles knew in the present and run into a complete dead end. So I decided to dig around in his past, which probably won't shed any light. But there's nothing else for us to do. His ex told me you and Miles were involved in a neighborhood scandal, and I was hoping you'd be willing to explain it from your point of view."

Renee took a deep drag from her cigarette, then set it in the ashtray. She gazed at the wall behind Cassidy's head. "I've tried so hard to forget."

"Look, if this is too difficult—"

"It's so nice to have company. Jen comes by when she can, but she's kind of busy. And I do have some friends I talk to on the phone, but it's not the same. Since you came all this way to see me, I'll try to answer your questions."

"I understand you and Miles lived on the same block."

"We were two houses apart. We belonged to the same social circle. In fact, Marla was one of my closest friends. Of course there was some flirting going on, but that didn't bother me. I developed sort of early and had pretty big boobs, so I was used to male attention. Mom said it was a curse, but I loved having boys chase after me. I didn't realize how right she was until my life fell apart."

"Did you get involved with other men besides Miles?"

"Un-uh." She coiled a spiral of hair around her finger. "I never slept around. I was fairly good looking in those days so I got the sense that a lot of guys considered me sort of a trophy, and that didn't appeal to me. Besides, having plenty of options made it easy to say no."

"So what was different about Miles?"

"It was almost more about my husband than Miles. I married Jim when we were both in college, then I dropped out so I could work to support him. He was the sweetest guy back then. Not in any hurry to jump my bones. Long conversations late into the night. Always sensitive to my feelings. But after he graduated and went to work for a corporation, everything changed."

Remembering her own first marriage, Cassidy said, "I guess that's pretty common. Especially when people marry young." She rubbed the large garnet on her wedding ring.

"Once Jim had his foot on the bottom rung of the ladder, all he could think about was moving up. He put in long hours. Scarcely noticed I was around. But I guess I can't blame him. I was working part-time at the Jewel, so I didn't have anything very interesting to say. I was like, "Did you know the price of potatoes went up five cents today?"

"I can't believe you were ever like that."

"The worst part was, he kind of expected me to handle everything at home, including the repairs, but he was too cheap to pay for any help. He'd get all mad at me because the garage door didn't work, but I couldn't fix it myself and he wouldn't let me hire anyone."

"Doesn't sound like much of a marriage."

"I just sort of thought husbands were like that. Mom kept telling me I needed to be more assertive, so I figured it was partly my fault. Anyway, one night when I was drinking wine with Marla and Miles, I complained about Jim, and Miles said he'd be happy to fix some of the things around my house. Marla even encouraged me to take him up on it."

"Is that how the affair got started?"

Renee chewed on her bottom lip and nodded.

"Marla never suspected?"

"Usually we'd do it when she was away on a business trip. The funny thing is, I never felt guilty. I thought we'd just keep it to ourselves and nobody'd get hurt. The only time I felt bad was when I was with Marla. She was always so nice to me." Renee stabbed out her cigarette and lit another.

"Did you know Miles was the father when you got pregnant?"

She ducked her head. "I was pretty sure. Jim was so tired all the time we didn't have sex very much, and I got pregnant during a month when we didn't do it at all."

"How did you feel about the pregnancy?"

"I was terrified. I thought Jim would figure it out because we were hardly ever intimate. Or that the baby would look like Miles. But Jim was so tuned out I don't think it ever crossed his mind that I might be screwing somebody else. And then there was a part of me that was glad 'cause I really wanted a baby."

"What about Miles? How did he feel?"

"Well, first he was pissed 'cause I wouldn't get an abortion. And I have to say, I can't blame him, since it was my fault for forgetting to take the pill. Then I thought we should end the affair but he talked me out of it. So after Kenny was born, we slipped back into our old routine. The surprising thing was, Jim turned out to be a pretty good dad and Kenny just adored him."

"So what went wrong?"

"When Kenny turned five, I felt like I ought to take him to church. It started off that I was doing it for his sake, but then I realized I was the one who needed to make my peace with God." She looked down at her hands. "One day, after we'd been going to church for several months, it came to me what a sinner I was. It just hit me that Miles and I had been committing adultery all those years and it had to stop. That night I told him it was over."

"How did he take it?"

"Oh, it was horrible!" Renee turned her head sharply away. "I couldn't believe how mad he was. Well, I could sort of understand. Mom always told me that all guys want to get into your pants and it's the girl's job to stop them."

What century is this woman from?

Renee added, "So here I'd been jumping into bed with him all those years and then suddenly— for no reason he could understand—I cut him off."

"He got mad? Was that all he did?"

Renee lowered her face, letting her hair fall forward. "He kind of threatened me. Said he'd tell Jim he was Kenny's father. That he'd insist on a paternity test."

"What did you do?"

"I didn't believe him. It didn't make sense that he'd let Marla know he'd been cheating on her just to hurt me. And once I realized how sinful I'd been, I couldn't go back. So I told him I was sorry he felt that way and asked him to leave." She raised her cigarette to her mouth with a shaky hand.

"What I did that night changed everybody's life. I've gone 'round and 'round in my head, trying to figure out how I could've done it differently, but I never come up with anything that would've stopped Miles from doing what he did."

"What was that?"

"Miles told Jim and a couple weeks later Jim was gone. But walking off and leaving us with almost no money wasn't enough. He had to take his anger out on this poor little boy who was crazy about him. He told Kenny he wasn't his father and didn't want anything more to do with him. It just broke my son's heart."

"And yours as well."

"It didn't matter about me. I sort of deserved what I got. But Kenny was an innocent victim. First his father disappeared, then we had to move in with my mom, then I went back to work. It was like his whole life got turned upside down."

"It must've been really hard on him. Most kids'd be pretty angry after something like that."

"Well, he did sort of act out in kindergarten, but his teacher was understanding and he got over it after a while."

Got over it? With two arrests for assault? I don't think so.

Cassidy asked, "So how did Kenny do in school?"

"He was real bright. Almost a genius, they said. But if he didn't like a subject, he wouldn't study, so his grades weren't that hot. I kept hoping he'd use those brains he had to get ahead. Then my MS got so bad I couldn't work and he had to drop out of school. He's a real wizard with computers, so he was able to get a pretty good job. Up until a few months ago, he was earning enough to pay all our bills."

"What happened a few months ago?"

"Lost his job. It was the boss's fault. No matter how hard Kenny tried, the bastard was never satisfied."

Could be true. Or could be Kenny took a swing at him.

Cassidy asked, "Does Kenny have a problem with his temper?"

The furrows between Renee's eyes deepened. "Oh no. He's just the sweetest kid. You wouldn't believe how hard he works at taking care of me. You see that big TV? He bought it for my birthday. And he does all the cooking and laundry."

"What about Miles? Did he have to pay child support?"

"Told me if I took him to court he'd get visitation and make me sorry I let Kenny go anywhere near him." She sighed. "After what he'd done already, I wasn't about to take a chance on that, so I signed a paper saying I'd never go after him for child support. I felt real bad losing out on the support 'cause the extra money would've made Kenny's life easier. Bad things just kept happening and it was all on account of my sins."

"You think it's all your fault?" Cassidy asked. "Don't Miles and Jim deserve some of the blame?"

Renee waved her hand, brushing off what Cassidy had said. "That's just what men do. Women have to be smart enough not to let 'em get away with it."

Cassidy felt like gagging. *Men should get a free pass because they're jerks?*

She tried to come up with more questions. She'd covered all the territory she initially intended to, but she wanted to extend her stay in hopes that Kenny would make an appearance. For some reason she didn't quite understand, she wanted to see what he looked like.

This is ridiculous. It's not as if he'll have "killer" stamped on his forehead. And it's also not true that piercings, tattoos, or gang colors would reveal a propensity for homicide.

But Renee likes having you here, so there's no reason not to drag this on as long as possible.

Cassidy asked, "So how have you been getting along since Kenny's been unemployed?"

Before Renee could answer, the phone rang and she picked up. She talked for a minute, then put her hand over the mouthpiece and said to Cassidy, "Do you mind? It's a friend I haven't heard from in ages."

"Go right ahead. Okay if I use the bathroom?"

Sure." Pointing to a hall at the rear of the room, Renee resumed her conversation.

Chapter 22

Cassidy went into the dim corridor, which lay outside Renee's line of vision. *A chance to scope out the rest of the apartment. But you better be quick so you don't get caught. Nah, Renee's not the short-winded type.*

To Cassidy's left stood an open door leading to the bathroom, to her right a closed door. Since she felt certain Renee slept on the sofa, she assumed the closed door led to Kenny's bedroom.

She reached for the doorknob, then withdrew her hand. *What if he's in there? He could've been surfing the Net or listening to his iPod the whole time you've been here.*

Holding her breath, she leaned her ear up close to the door. No sound came from within.

She looked at her watch. She'd been in the apartment for nearly an hour. *Teenagers can spend way longer than that holed up in their rooms.*

Okay, so there's some chance you'll run into him, but how bad could that be? He's not likely to hack you up in his own bedroom with his mother just a few feet away.

Not quite believing her own rationalization, she opened the door a crack and peered in. When there was no response from the other side, she pushed it wider and slipped inside. Scanning the room to make sure Kenny wasn't in it, she blew out a long, whooshing breath of relief.

Her eyes were instantly riveted to the far wall. Tacked to it were a drawing and several photos. She gasped when she realized what she was looking at. On one side was a sketched ground plan of Marina City with the entrances and exits highlighted. In the middle were half a dozen enlargements of a man who had to be Miles going into and coming out of the building. On the other side were five black and white shots of Miles that had been edited to show red blood spurting from various wounds on his body: his face blown off, his stomach sliced open, his heart cut out, his hands missing, his body decapitated.

Cassidy took several deep breaths to calm herself. She wished she'd allowed Zach to talk her into buying a camera cell phone. But even if she had, it would be in her purse on the living room floor.

She tore her gaze away from the display on the wall and looked around the room. It was crammed with computers, printers, televisions, and other gadgets she didn't recognize. An unmade bed stood against the inner wall. Clothes and empty vodka bottles were strewn across the darkened hardwood floor.

Her eyes returned to the photos on the wall. *Certainly looks like he wanted to kill his father. And maybe succeeded.*

Footsteps sounded in the hall. Panic swept through her. Her knees went weak and her heart began to pound.

The door opened and a tall, muscular teenager came through the door. His shoulders and arms bulged, he had clean shiny hair that brushed the neckline of his shirt, and he carried her purse in his hand. He closed the door and stood in front of it.

"What are you doing in my room?" he demanded, his eyes glinting with anger.

She clenched her hands together and held them against her throat, not able to think of a single excuse.

He waited.

"Well, I guess I was...What I mean is...I suppose I was looking around." She took in a breath. "I know I shouldn't be here."

"You came because you thought I might've killed the jaggoff. Now that you've seen my artwork, you're sure of it."

Cassidy opened her mouth to deny it, then realized she'd never be able to change his mind. Drawing herself up, she asked, "Well, did you?"

He threw back his head and laughed. Then, in a serious voice, "You came here, asked a lot of prying questions, then snuck into my room. You think I eradicated Miles but wouldn't hurt you?" Reaching toward a nearby table, he picked up a pair of large, pointed scissors and turned them in his hand.

Cassidy felt light-headed. Her vision began to blur at the periphery.

Stepping closer, his sour breath warm on her face, he said in a low tone, "I scare you, don't I? You want to scream? Go ahead. There's nobody in this dump that'd pay any attention."

She backed away from him.

"If I wanted to, I could dispose of you and nobody'd be able to prove I did it. Fortunately, I'm not as violent as you think. I'd rather resolve things peacefully. You should know that as soon as you're out of here, the artwork's coming off the wall, so if any cops show up later, it's your word against mine. Now that the jaggoff's dead, I don't have any further use for it anyway."

"Can I have my purse back?"

He handed it to her. "Give me your driver's license."

"What?" She tucked her shoulder bag under her arm and held on tight.

"So I can find you if I need to."

"But I'm listed in the directory. And on Switchboard."

"Consider it a toll for having trespassed." He stretched his lips into a menacing smile. "You keep talking, the toll will get higher. I might decide I want your underpants as well."

She gave him her license and went into the living room. She thanked Renee, who was still on the phone, and left.

Cassidy climbed into the Toyota and began searching for her keys. She was so flooded with anxiety she could barely think straight, and the trembling in her hands made it difficult to hold onto things. She felt around in three different compartments, then thrust her hand to the bottom of her bag. *Why don't you have one of those small purses that's so trendy now? What makes you think you have to carry everything you own around with you? This damn bag swallows things up like Jonah's whale.*

When she managed to get the key in the ignition, she let the engine warm up and tried to decide what to do next. One part of her was outraged that Kenny had taken her license and wanted to call 9-1-1. Another part was scared and wanted to get away as fast as possible.

The problem is, you don't know whether the cops would force their way in on your say-so, or if they'd take you to the station and make you wait while they got a search warrant.

Since the thought of having to go to the station again made her want to scream, she opted for finding a safe place where she could think things through before doing anything about her stolen license.

She would go home and Zach would hold her and comfort her. Or he would go barging into Kenny's apartment and try to make the hulking teen give back her license. Or get mad at her for putting herself at risk in the first place. She didn't know what he would do, but she did know that as soon as she presented him with the mess she'd created, he would put aside his own investigation and focus on her.

You can't expect Zach to rescue you. You have to take care of the situation yourself, then go home and tell him how you handled it. Besides, Zach isn't your only source of comfort. You always have Gran as backup.

"You don't look so good," Gran said, standing in her open doorway. "You better come in and tell me all about it."

Cassidy grimaced. "And here I thought I was so good at maintaining a neutral expression."

"Well, you are." Gran pulled her inside and closed the door. "Most people wouldn't notice anything's wrong. It's just that I know you so well." Gran straightened the shaggy, strawberry-blond wig that framed her wrinkly face.

Bending over, Cassidy removed her boots.

"You don't need to bother with that. A little water won't hurt anything."

"You might not mind if I track muddy water all over your house, but I do."

Cassidy hung her coat in the entryway closet and went into the living room. Gran's carpet and walls were gold, with red and blue pieces of pottery on display in a wall unit. The furniture was upholstered in an assortment of different fabrics, all royal blue with small patterns in yellow or red. On one side of the room, a sofa and loveseat faced each other. On the other, five small, mismatched easy chairs stood in a wide semi-circle in front of the brick fireplace.

Cassidy plopped into the middle chair. Her socks were wet, her feet chunks of ice. She stretched them toward the low gas flames.

Gran said, "How 'bout some wine or brandy? That oughtta put the color back in your cheeks."

"Make that hot tea. To warm up my insides. And put it in a mug so I can wrap my hands around it."

"You got it." Gran trotted off toward the kitchen. A couple of minutes later, she handed Cassidy a mug wafting the sweet scent of ripe peaches. She sat in the chair next to Cassidy's, turning it so she could see her granddaughter's face. "Now you just let it all out, and if there's anything you don't wanna talk about, that's okay too."

"I don't know what I'd do without you. You have to live forever, or at least as long as I'm still around."

Gran sat up straight, patted her wig, and preened. "I'll be happy to keep on breathing as long as you want me to."

"Okay, here goes." Cassidy told Gran about Kenny and what he'd done to her.

Gran's face scrunched in anger. "Why that blinkety-blank punk. Zach and me oughtta get us some assault guns and scare the bejeesus out of him."

"Blinkety-blank?"

"I think it'd be an awful lot of fun to cuss, but I can't bring myself to do it. Maybe Zach can teach me sometime."

Cassidy grinned. "If only assault guns would do the trick. But we need a more subtle approach."

"Like what?"

"That's the problem. I can't decide. If I tell the police what I saw on Kenny's wall, they'll either search the apartment or bring him in for questioning. But by the time they get to his place, all the incriminating stuff will be gone, and he'll deny he took my license. Now the police are likely to believe me, since I have no reason to lie and Kenny was seen beating on Miles, but it may be impossible to build a case against him." Cassidy pictured Kenny turning the scissors. "And once the cops show up at his door, there's a good chance he'll come after me."

"Boy, after what you said about those pictures, I'd sure be afraid of him."

Envisioning the black and white photos splattered with red ink, Cassidy shuddered. "I've run into some scary types before and Kenny's right up there with the worst of them. It's that obsessive streak of his. He's obviously been brooding about killing his father for a long time. People like that don't just give up and go away. He strikes me as the kind of guy who might have a bright future as a serial killer."

"You're pretty sure he whacked Miles?"

Cassidy drew her brows together and reflected on the murder. "I keep going back and forth. For a while, I had myself convinced he did it, but there are some holes in my theory. I'm not sure an eighteen-year-old—even a genius eighteen-year-old—could have executed such a complex crime. The killer had to get Miles up to the sixtieth floor without being seen, drain his blood, cut him up, take him out of the building, and make all the body parts disappear. I don't know if anybody other than an experienced professional could have done it. On top of that, if it *was* Kenny, he had to be planning it well in advance. And if a plan was already in the works, why do something as clunky as beat up his father in front of witnesses?"

"So maybe he was just thinking about it, and somebody else beat him to the punch."

"There's no way to tell."

"Well, that's not the important thing," Gran said. "The important thing is keeping you safe."

"Are you telling me I shouldn't call the police?"

"Didn't you say he's gonna come after you if you do?"

"The police need to know about those pictures. I have to do what's right."

"How can you say it's right to put yourself in danger? If he did kill his father, what's to stop him from killing you? And then think what it'd do to Zach and your mother and me. I'd just want to wither up and die. Besides, didn't you say he might not get arrested even if you do tell the cops?"

Propping her elbows on her knees, Cassidy dropped her forehead onto the heels of her hands. "There's a good chance he wouldn't, since as far as I know there isn't any evidence against him. And if he did get arrested, Renee wouldn't have anybody at all. God, that would be so awful! Almost worse than Kenny getting away with killing his father."

"Does that mean you're not going to tell the cops?"

"I don't know. I don't know. I'm so torn."

It'd be pigheaded and selfish to tell the police. Making yourself feel righteous and possibly getting killed for it. Hurting Renee and all the people who love you.

But if you don't call, you'll be letting that punk scare you out of doing what you know you should do.

Cassidy reached over and took Gran's bony, age-spotted hand. "I'm sorry. I hate making you worry. But I have to tell the detective what I saw."

Gran's face crumpled and tears brimmed in her faded eyes. She wiped them with her hands, then pulled a tissue out of her pocket and blew her nose. After several seconds of rapid breathing, she put on a brave face and said, "I know you gotta make your own decisions."

You are such a jerk! Gran's always been there for you and this is how you repay her.

"You know," Cassidy resumed, "this isn't half as bad as I said at first. I was really jumpy when I got here, so I built Kenny up into some kind of monster. But the fact is, he's nothing more than an overgrown kid who had it in for his father. Even though he made some vague threats, I'm not an important person to him, so he's not likely to obsess over me the way he did over Miles. I realize he may try to retaliate after the police pay him a visit, but there's no reason to assume he'd succeed. After all, I've had thugs try to hurt me before, but none of them ever managed to inflict much damage."

Gran pasted a wobbly smile on her face. "I know you always come out ahead in the end."

She doesn't believe a word you said. And neither do you.

"So how's it going with Joan?" Gran asked. "I bet she's impressed with all the information you dug up."

Guilt swelled in Cassidy's chest. "I haven't exactly kept her up to date."

"Oh, well, I'm sure you know what you're doing."

"Actually, I've been acting like a spoiled brat. Joan wants us to work together, which is a perfectly reasonable expectation considering she told me about Miles in the first place. But instead of cooperating, I've been running my own show behind her back."

"You must have your reasons."

"Yeah—I don't want to share. I want to make my own decisions without having to take anybody else's opinion into account." *Like you did just now when you ignored Gran's feelings about telling the cops.*

"There's nothing wrong with wanting to do things own your way."

"Gran, you are *sooo* not objective. Now that you've got me thinking about Joan, I can see I haven't treated her very well. I need to 'fess up, throw myself on her mercy, and see if she'll take me back."

"Look at all the stuff you found out about Kenny. She should consider herself lucky to have you."

Somehow I don't think lucky is what she'll feel when I tell her.

"I should get going," Cassidy said. "I may have to drive to District Nineteen before I go home tonight."

"You don't have your license. You should let me drive."

Gran doesn't want me to go, but she's willing to take me. How loveable is that?

Cassidy stood, turning around so the fire could warm her backside before she went out into the cold. "In all the years I've been driving, I've only had to show my license twice. I'm sure I can make it there and back without being stopped."

"I'll let you off this time," Gran said sternly, "but you gotta promise you'll let me take you to the

Secretary of State's Office first thing tomorrow morning."

"As long as it's not before ten."

Chapter 23

It was four-thirty when Cassidy climbed into the Toyota. There were three people she had to explain herself to and none of the encounters would be easy. Roloff would be pissed at her for interfering with a police investigation. Joan would be pissed for her failure to communicate. And Zach would be torn between feeling pissed and protective.

She called District Nineteen and asked for Detective Roloff. When he picked up, she realized she'd been hoping to get his machine.

"I've come across some information that may be relevant to the Marina City murder."

"What would that be?"

"Are you aware Miles had a son?"

"Yeah, we know that."

"Well, I found the son and while I was at his apartment I saw some pretty disturbing things on his wall."

"You *found* the son? Does that mean you were looking for him?"

This was the part where she had to admit she'd been playing detective and then he'd yell at her.

"I said, were you looking for him?"

"Yes."

"You're going to have to come down to the station and give me a statement."

"Yeah, I was pretty sure I'd have to do that."

"How soon can I expect you?"

"About forty-five minutes."

Cassidy sat across a table from Roloff in a room that looked much like the room he'd questioned her in before. The detective had taken her through her story a couple of times, and she hoped he was nearly done with her.

"I asked around about you." He thrust his clean cut face slightly closer to hers. "This isn't the first time you've messed around in a police investigation, is it?"

She shook her head.

"So you probably already know what police think of civilian interference."

"They hate it."

"You know why?" He brushed his straight brown hair back from his forehead.

She didn't like to think about why. "I'm sure you're going to tell me."

"They can influence witnesses, contaminate evidence, and generally screw things up. They also run the risk of getting hurt. Take for instance the fact that this weirdo kid caught you in his bedroom and knows where you live. You get yourself capped, we've got another murder on our hands."

"If I get killed, I'll do my best to make sure it doesn't happen in Area Three."

Pinching his lip, he stared at her for several seconds. "What's the matter with you, anyway? C'mon, you're a shrink. You should be able to explain this problem of yours. Because the fact that you've meddled in several investigations is definitely a problem."

She wanted to say, *Not only have I meddled, I've actually solved them.* But she was fairly certain that wouldn't help her case.

"I enjoy trying to figure things out," she replied. "Like people who do crosswords." *Except crosswords are way too tame for you.*

"Doing crosswords is fine. Interfering in a homicide investigation is an obstruction of justice."

Cassidy felt her backbone go rigid. "Did Ann Brown tell you about the circumstances of her mother's disappearance?"

Glaring, Roloff nodded.

"And I presume she mentioned how she happened to get in touch with you?"

He didn't respond.

"Today I drove down here to tell you about the photos on Kenny's wall. Is that what you call obstruction?"

Roloff's boyish face hardened. "I'm telling you to stay the hell out of this investigation. You want to solve murders, apply to the Police Academy."

She stood. "Are we done?"

He stood also. "Go on. Get the hell out of here."

When Cassidy returned to the house, Zach was reading a document on the computer screen and listening to NPR. A terrible multi-tasker herself, she envied his ability to do two things at once. *Whenever you try it, you screw up at least one of them—sometimes both.*

She leaned against the doorframe. "Did you even take time to eat?"

"I grabbed a bite when I went out to run down some of the sources McCready quoted in his stories. I was sniffing around to see if any of them had a problem with what he'd written. Only one of them did, and that was because the source blabbed more than he intended to."

"How do you approach these people? You can't come out and say you're looking for inaccuracies, can you?"

"No, of course not. I have to go at this very delicately. If McCready even suspected what I was up to, I'd be canned on the spot and blackballed across the country. I've been saying the *Post* is having a slow news week and I'm on a fishing expedition looking for some follow-up on the story McCready did earlier."

Cassidy traced a finger beneath her lower lip. "I'm definitely interested in your investigation, but I have to admit that what I'm really doing here is stalling."

He studied her face. "Stalling about what?"

"About what I have to tell you." She drew in a breath. "Let's go sit in the den."

Cassidy adjusted the footstool so they could both rest their feet on it. "Remember I told you I was going to visit the mother of Miles' son?" She went on to describe what she'd seen in Kenny's bedroom, how he'd threatened her, and the lecture she'd received from Roloff.

Zach's jaw clenched. "You have no idea how tempted I am to go on a rant and tell you what an idiot you were to go inside that thug's bedroom. But if I'm honest with myself, I have to admit I would've gone in there too. However, the fact that I take stupid risks is no excuse for you to do it."

"If I hadn't gone in that room, no one would know he's an obsessive stalker."

"Did you hear what you just said? He's an obsessive stalker and now he's likely to start stalking you."

Turning her head away, Cassidy gazed out the window.

"You deserve to be locked in your room till he gets thrown in the joint for some other crime."

"I know," she said in a small voice.

"Look, I realize I have no business giving you such a hard time since I've been guilty of doing similar things, but it kills me to think of anything happening to you."

If the situation were reversed, you'd feel the same.

He asked, "Would you like me to get you a gun?"

A gun would make you feel safer. But your aim is terrible and Kenny'd probably take it away and use it against you.

"I think I'm better off without one."

"When it comes right down to it, there isn't a single thing either one of us can do to protect you. I don't know how many times you've gotten yourself in situations like this. What would you say to a client who keeps putting herself at risk?"

Another version of Roloff's question.

"That she wanted to die. Or she felt she deserved to be punished. Or she was trying to prove something."

"Well, it's not the first two, so what are you trying to prove?"

She bit the inner lining of her lip. Although she was usually completely open with Zach, this was something she didn't want to tell anybody. *You're trying to prove you're tough and strong and not afraid of anything...because you feel so small and needy inside.*

After Gran schlepped her to the Secretary of State's Office, Cassidy sat at her desk staring at the phone. As much as she hated acknowledging she'd been wrong, her talk with Gran the day before had forced her to realize she'd treated Joan unfairly. *All she asked was that you keep her informed, and you couldn't even do that.*

Cassidy briefly considered trying to make amends over the phone, but she knew her chances of appeasing Joan would be greater if she did it face to face. *You owe it to her to let her wale on you as much as she wants before she takes you back.*

She lifted the receiver and punched in Joan's number.

"This is Cass. I'm calling to apologize. I got so involved in chasing down leads I forgot to tell you what I found out."

"I wondered when I'd hear from you."

"It should've been two days ago."

"So why wasn't it?" Joan snapped.

"Because I get so single-minded I lose track of everything else. I know I've been remiss, but I'd like to sit down with both you and Tessa and fill you in on everything I've uncovered in the past couple of days."

"You can tell me now and I'll relay it to Tessa."

"I'd much rather do it in person. I'll come down whenever you want and the three of us can strategize about where to go from here." *If there's anything you haven't done already.*

"Initially I liked the idea of us working together, but you've made it painfully obvious you prefer a lone gun approach. After the way you've excluded me, I don't see any reason to trust you again."

Cassidy's cheeks grew warm with shame. "I know I've treated you badly. There's no excuse for my going off on my own the way I did. You have every right to be angry and not want anything more to do with me, but I really wish you'd give me one more chance. Just let me come to Marina City and bring you and Tessa up to date, then you can decide whether you want to continue working with me."

Joan sighed. "Well, I do want to hear what you've uncovered. I guess there's no harm in letting you come here and tell us." She paused. "I suppose you learned how to manipulate people in your therapist training."

This cookie is way sharper than you ever gave her credit for.

Cassidy asked, "What would be a good time?"

"Can you be here at three?"

"Absolutely."

She disconnected, then checked her calendar to make sure she had nothing on it for the afternoon. *Thank goodness, no clients. If there were any, you'd have to reschedule them. Because right now your top priority is to prove to Joan you can do things her way.*

Chapter 24

Cassidy and Joan followed the corridor to Tessa's condo and pressed the bell. The door was flung open by a small girl with blond curls and dark brown eyes that definitely had not come from her mother.

"Hi Joan," the girl said.

"Hi back atcha, Amy."

The child wore red and yellow striped pants and a neon orange top covered with Pooh Bears in various poses. Coming up behind her, Tessa said, "She's at that stage where she insists on picking out her own clothes."

Joan squatted on her heels in front of Amy. "And don't you look grand!"

Giggling, Amy tugged at her mother's hand. "What'd she say?"

"She gave you a compliment. Now remember, you promised to watch Blues Clues while I talk to my friends."

The child put up a protest, but Tessa used a combination of incentives and threats to convince Amy to stay in her room.

The women sat around the square coffee table with its assortment of plants in red pots while Cassidy told them everything she'd done since her last visit to Marina City.

"I can't believe it!" Tessa said. "When you first wanted us to investigate, I thought you were crazy. But here it is, a week later, and you've practically solved the case. In fact, if you're right about Sandra getting Kenny to do the deed for her, you really have solved it."

"That's just a theory. One possible scenario." Cassidy propped her elbow on the sofa's rolled armrest. "The cops wouldn't take it seriously unless we could prove there was a connection between Sandra and Kenny. And right now, I don't see any way of doing that."

Cassidy looked at Joan, who hadn't said a word since Cassidy started speaking. The woman's mahogany face was unreadable.

Has to be impressed with how much you found out. But the fact that you were able to do so much without her might make her even madder than she was before.

Cassidy asked, "What do you think, Joan?"

"You managed to pull together a lot of information," she said grudgingly. Then, a more cordial note creeping in, "I guess I ought to be pleased with all you've done."

Sounds like a truce.

"Now you need to hear what I discovered." Joan slid a pot half an inch forward to make the arrangement more symmetrical. "On the morning after Miles' disappeared, somebody turned the security camera off at 4:02 at the parking level exit. You know the one I mean?"

"The one where you can go out but the door locks behind you and you can't get back in?" Since Cassidy had never lived in the building, she'd used the exit only a few times. "As I recall, that area's usually deserted. It'd probably be the best way to leave the building without being seen."

Joan said, "The murderer must have turned the camera off and taken the body out through that exit. So then I questioned all the car parkers who were on duty at that time and one of them said he saw someone leaving with a very large suitcase in tow. He couldn't say for sure, but he thought might've been Henry."

Cassidy fished out her notepad and jotted down what Joan had said. "Have you asked Henry about it?"

"He told me he didn't wake up until a little before six and then the first thing he did was call Tessa. Besides, if you're so sure Sandra's behind the murder, it couldn't have been Henry."

"Not unless they were working together," Tessa said. "And if Sandra wanted someone to kill Miles for her, she wouldn't pick an old man."

"Well, but we don't know for sure she did it," Cassidy countered. "It's not like we have a confession or anything. I suppose it's possible Henry killed Miles and the two disappearances are just a coincidence. Or that Sandra and Henry worked together."

Joan looked at Cassidy as if she were nuts. "The car parker said it *might've* been Henry. That's about as unsubstantial as you can get. The only credible suspect is Sandra."

"You're right," Cassidy said. "We shouldn't let ourselves get distracted by some vague possibility." She rubbed her left hand back and forth against her thigh. Speaking to Joan, she continued. "I'm sure you've done a thorough job of interviewing the people involved with the security camera breakdown, but if you wouldn't mind, I'd like to hear what they have to say for myself."

Joan gave her a cold look. "I suppose you think you can get more out of the security manager than I did."

There you go, stepping on Joan's toes again.

"No, really." Cassidy shook her head vigorously. "It's not because I think you missed anything. I just like to hear what people have to say for myself."

"So do I," Joan said pointedly.

Still digging at you because of the way you went around her. Well, I guess you have it coming.

"Oh, all right," Joan said. "We can chase down the security manager after we finish here."

"I'd appreciate that."

Joan smoothed her soft beige A-line skirt over her knees. "If we're agreed that Sandra had Miles killed, I guess our work is done. All we can do now is hope the police find enough evidence to convict her."

Tessa clenched her hands into fists and banged them together. "Ever since I found that photo of Sandra in her teddy, I just hate her. The cops've got to nail her for this!"

"Don't count on it," Joan replied. "I can't see how the police could ever get enough evidence to arrest her."

"This feels so unfinished." Cassidy drummed her fingers on the armrest. "We can't even be sure Sandra did it. There must be other people we could talk to."

"Not that I can think of," Tessa said.

Joan asked, "What about Miles' mother?"

"She doesn't know anything. Miles was even more secretive with her than me."

"You never can tell," Cassidy said. "I've gotten useful leads from people I thought were completely out of the loop." *You just want to prolong the investigation because it makes life zingier and keeps you out of Zach's hair.*

Joan nudged another pot, moving it a hair's breadth sideways. "You think Miles' mother would talk to us?"

"There's nothing Bernice likes better than an excuse to air her gripes. But it might be a little overwhelming if all three of us descend on her at once. Since I'm the one who didn't want to get involved in the first place, why don't I set up the meeting and let the two of you go by yourselves?"

Cassidy said, "She might talk more freely if you're there."

A silence ensued.

You grabbed up all those other interviews. You should give this one to Joan.

But I don't want to miss anything.

It's time you learned to share.

"Since I've done so many of the others, I don't mind sitting this one out," Cassidy said, not entirely truthfully.

Another brief silence, then Joan said to Cassidy, "I'd like to be there, but it's obvious you have a knack for getting people to open up. Well, of course, that's your job. So I think you should go."

Tessa looked at Cassidy. "When would be a good time?"

"Let's see...tomorrow's Saturday." *Hard to believe it's only been a week.* "I have three clients in the morning but I'm free after that."

"I'll call Bernice and see if tomorrow afternoon's okay with her." Tessa spent five minutes explaining to her mother-in-law why she wanted her to talk to Cassidy, a woman she'd never met before.

Hanging up, Tessa said, "She'll be happy to have us. It'll give her an excuse to bake these special applesauce cookies all the neighbors used to rave about forty years ago. She just had a hard time grasping why I wanted to bring you with me."

As Tessa's door closed behind them, Joan said, "The security manager's office is in the basement beneath the East Tower."

She and Cassidy rode the elevator to the lobby, walked the nearly block-long distance between the two towers, then took the stairs to the basement.

The office consisted of two small concrete rooms, windowless, with pipes running overhead. The lighting was cold and bright, the temperature uncomfortably warm.

In the outer room, a man sat hunched over a bank of monitors. His head was shaven, his arms tattooed. Clad in a tee shirt bearing the face of Charles Manson, he was so emaciated he appeared either anorexic or strung out on drugs. He neither looked up nor spoke when Cassidy and Joan entered the room. Across from the monitors stood a large metal desk with two molded plastic chairs in front of it. A doorway in the far wall provided a glimpse of the lunchroom.

Joan said to the man, "Tell Dora that Joan Frasier wants to talk to her."

Without taking his eyes off the screens in front of him, the man radioed the message to Dora.

Cassidy gazed at the back of the man's skull-like head, long neck, and bony shoulders. *Security guards are supposed to make people feel safe. Maybe he's an underground troll and never leaves the office.*

A short, stocky black woman with a pouty bottom lip came strolling in a few minutes later. *That annoyed expression. Bet it's not just for us. Bet it's the face she shows the entire world.*

"This about that camera breakdown?" Dora asked. "I already told you everything I know."

Joan pointed her chin toward Cassidy. "She's working with me and she'd like to hear it for herself."

"You want me to go over the whole story again? If this is gonna be long and dragged out, we might as well sit down. I been on my feet enough today." Dora plunked into the chair behind her desk and the other two women settled in front of it.

Cassidy asked, "What caused the camera to stop?"

"Somebody cut the wire."

"How'd they do that without being caught on tape?"

"Easy. The camera's focused on the door to keep people from breaking in. The wire-cutter just walked up behind it."

"Would it take any special expertise to find the right wire?"

"Yeah. The guy'd have to not be blind. The camera wires are right out in plain sight."

"I suppose the building's well lit at night?"

Dora made no response, which Cassidy took to be an assent.

Leaning forward, she clasped her hands in her lap. "It sounds so risky, hauling a big suitcase out into a lighted area with car parkers and maybe even a resident or two around."

"Not really," Joan said. "Even on Saturday nights the traffic's pretty thin at four A.M. If a resident dropped his car off, he probably wouldn't stand out in the weather looking around. The car parker I talked to said there were only two guys on duty that night, and when they're not working, they sit inside that glass house and watch TV. It was pure accident he happened to look out the window and see the killer leaving. And even at that, the guy was so bundled up nobody could've made a positive I.D."

"Then what made the parker think it was Henry?"

"He said it was the slow careful way he walked. The way he carried himself."

Nobody spoke for about three beats.

"You done now?" Dora frowned and extended her lip even farther. "I got things to do."

Cassidy squinted in thought. "There's something else—something I can't quite get hold of."

"I don't have time—"

"Wait, I've got it. The killer left the building at four but then he'd have to come back in Sunday or Monday. So the West Tower security tape ought to show somebody coming in who never went out." *Unless it was Kenny. He wouldn't have to go back in.*

Joan said, "We need the tapes for Saturday, Sunday, and Monday."

"Too late. The police picked them up Monday."

"Dang!" Joan said. "We've put so much work into this. I hate to have the police beat us out."

Quelling her own disappointment, Cassidy said, "It's probably better that the police do it. I'm not sure I could stand watching that many hours of tape. Even if I could, I wouldn't be able to keep track of everybody."

Dora said, "If the killer knew what he was doing, he could've walked in with a bunch of people and kept his face hidden. There are always a few that get by."

Chapter 25

At nine-thirty that night, Cassidy sat on the waterbed, a book in her hand. A few inches away Starshine slept on her back, her snowy stomach spread wide, a paw draped over her eyes to keep out the light.

Cassidy tried to focus on her book, but her mind kept veering to the cat. *Usually disappears before nine. Does this mean she's going to grace us with her presence tonight? Or just that she can't tell time and she's running late. Maybe you should close the door so she can't get out.*

When you locked her inside before, it just made her hate you.

If she does stay home tonight, does it mean she's over her living-in-two-houses phase? Or maybe her other family isn't home. Or they did something to offend her and now she's in a snit at them.

Starshine rolled onto her side and stretched all four legs, turning her short, stubby self into a long cat. Climbing aboard Cassidy's lap, she gave her human a moist green gaze and purred ardently.

Zach came into the bedroom, sat in his chair, and swiveled to face her. Cassidy was surprised to see him, since he spent almost all his waking hours either sitting at the computer or talking to people McCready had written about.

He said, "Since I still haven't found any creative writing in the asshole's stories, I'm going to try something new. I've got sources all over town, and I plan to start asking them if they've run across anybody with a hard-on for McCready."

"You mean, you're actually going to let people know you're investigating him?"

"I realize this isn't the safest thing to do. If any of my sources have a score to settle with me, this would certainly give them the opportunity to do it. But since I won't go back to the *Post* if McCready's there anyway, I don't have that much to lose."

"You haven't finished fact-checking all his stories, have you?"

"Not by a long shot. But I figure I can do the checking during the day, and meet with these guys at night. In fact, one of the reasons I wanted to discuss this with you is that I generally meet these people in bars, and I don't want you to worry about my drinking."

Cassidy's chest tightened. "This doesn't sound like a discussion. It sounds like you telling me what you're going to do."

"The reason I'm telling you ahead of time is so I can make sure you're okay with it."

"I can see why you need to do it, but that doesn't mean I won't feel a little anxious when you walk out the door."

"You haven't heard my plan yet." Zach put his hands on his knees and sat forward. "I'll drink beer instead of bourbon, and I won't order more than one beer per person. That means no more than three or four beers over the course of an evening."

"Oh," she said, feeling the tension ease. "I could probably even go to sleep if I knew you wouldn't be drinking any more than that."

"Let me tell you, I'll be highly motivated to keep my wits about me."

"It helps that you spelled it out ahead of time." She smiled. "You've been putting in such long hours. How are you holding up?"

"I'm okay, thanks to caffeine and adrenaline. The only thing is, I kind of miss hanging out with

you. Here we are, both working in the same house,
I feel like I never see you."

"You don't. You're so preoccupied, you walk
right past me without a word."

"I'm going to take a break and watch the ten
o'clock news. I know it's not your favorite thing, but
maybe you could watch it with me so we could
spend some time together."

"Sitting in front of a TV isn't spending time
together."

"Sure it is. Women always have to talk, but guys
are happy just being in the same room together. It's
sort of like parallel play."

"Okay, I'll watch the news with you. Even
though it's all sound bytes and arsenic-in-the-
water, radon-in-the-basement scares of the day."

"It's so good to see you," Bernice said to Tessa,
ushering Cassidy and her daughter-in-law into the
living room of her tony East Roger's Park condo.
"And your friend too."

Bernice was tall and lean, attired in an off-white
shirt and pants, her thicket of hair a close match to
the color of her outfit. She had a narrow face, with
coarse features and wire-rimmed glasses perched
low on her long beaked nose.

Bernice looked at Cassidy suspiciously. "I have
to admit, I still don't understand why you want to
talk to me."

"My name is Cass McCabe." She moved a half
step closer to the older woman. "Tessa and I have
been working together to make sense out of your
son's disappearance."

"Tessa must have told you I hardly know
anything about Miles. And most of what I know I
learned from her."

"She did say that. But I thought there might be something from his past—from the time before Tessa knew him—that could have a bearing on his death."

"Not likely. But as long as you're here, we might as well have a nice visit." Bernice gestured toward a glass coffee table holding a platter of cookies, small plates, napkins, a coffee carafe, dainty cups and saucers, a sugar and creamer. Behind the table stood an off-white sofa jammed with off-white pillows standing upright like soldiers at attention.

Cassidy hesitated, wondering if she was supposed to sit on the pillows or put them someplace else, although she didn't know what that someplace else would be. Tessa piled them on the floor, then sat down, so Cassidy did the same.

The walls, area rug, and easy chairs, as well as the sofa and pillows, were all slightly different shades of off-white. *Mushroom, eggshell, cream, ecru, champagne,* Cassidy recited to herself, trying to think of all the different names she'd heard for colors in that family. *Here's a woman who wants to play it as safe as you can get when it comes to decorating. Or maybe wants to disappear into the background.*

Without asking, Bernice poured three cups of coffee, then piled cookies on three plates. Selecting a cup and plate, she settled in a chair across from her guests.

Let's see...I'd guess that one's champagne.

Cassidy added cream and sugar to her coffee, then tried one of the cookies. It was soft and chewy and tasted of apples and cinnamon. *No wonder the neighbors raved. I don't even mind that it's not chocolate.*

"I don't know what will become of me," Bernice said, her gaze fixed on Tessa. "I never imagined

Miles would go first. He was all the family I had. Except for you and Amy, of course."

Tessa tensed, her lustrous gray eyes losing some of their softness. She said, "I understand what a terrible loss this is."

After a brief silence, Bernice resumed. "I realize Miles and I were never close, but I always thought he'd be there to help me when I needed him. My neighbor across the hall fell and broke her hip, and her son watched over her every step of the way. Visited her in the hospital, handled the bills, you name it. 'Course I know Miles didn't care about me the way that boy cared about his mother, but I always thought he'd do what needed to be done." She looked at Tessa again.

"It's fortunate you have the inheritance," Tessa said. "At least you'll be able to pay for the help you need."

The cords on Bernice's neck stood out. She compressed her lips, then said in a fierce voice. "What will happen when I have to move into a retirement home? Will I have to pay strangers to sort through my things? To pack my boxes? Times like that, you're supposed to have family to turn to."

Tessa said, "Now Bernice, you know Miles wouldn't have been any help anyway."

The older woman twisted her hands together. "I just don't know what went wrong. Sometimes it seemed like he didn't love anybody."

Cassidy set down her cup, the saucer rattling slightly against the glass table. "You must've thought about it a lot, why Miles wasn't as caring as most adult children."

Bernice turned toward Cassidy, her brown eyes flat. "Tessa told me you're a therapist, so I suppose you think Miles' being so cold was my fault. That's what everybody thinks. The mother always gets blamed."

"I don't think it's ever just one person's fault. Sometimes nobody's to blame. It can be brain chemistry or genetics." Cassidy brushed at the crumbs on her grape-colored sweater. "What do you think made Miles so uncaring?"

"George. It was George leaving me for that other woman. And then bad- mouthing me to Miles after he left."

Why does that name ring a bell?

Cassidy said, "I know this is none of my business, but would you mind telling me what led to your divorce?"

Bernice peered at Cassidy over the tops of her glasses. "George and me grew up in Houston. When we got married, I just naturally assumed we'd stay close to our families, and we did for a few years. Those were good times. Miles was born thirteen months after the wedding. We had this darling little house and got to spend a lot of time with our folks. I wanted things to stay like that, but was George satisfied? Not him. He wanted a better job. He wanted to get away from our families. He said they were always interfering."

"And that's what brought you to Chicago?"

"Well, first it brought him. He got a job here at Sears' headquarters and then he wanted me to move up after him, but I didn't want to live in some crummy little apartment. I waited six months until he found us a house to rent, and then I came to Chicago to be with him." She shook her head. "Worst mistake I ever made."

"You said there was another woman. Was he already seeing her?"

"Seeing. Now that's a nice way to put it." Bernice's coarse face darkened in anger. "When I first arrived, I could tell something was wrong. I should've turned around and gone back to Texas, but stupid me, I wanted to save my marriage. I tried to get George to go to counseling, but he wouldn't. He moved out less than a year after I got here."

"To live with the other woman?"

"To live with the *slut*. She got herself knocked up so he'd feel responsible and go live with her. I always thought he would've stayed with me if she hadn't gotten herself pregnant. But since she had a bun in the oven, he felt obligated to marry her."

Why feel more responsible for the woman he got pregnant than the woman he already had a son with?

"How old was Miles when his father left?"

"Nine. Him and his father were real close and he took it pretty hard. What really got me was that Miles blamed me for the divorce. He said it was because I didn't go to Chicago right away, or because I didn't treat his father right, or because I wasn't as pretty as the new wife. It really tore me up to hear him say stuff like that."

Cassidy rubbed her thumb over the large garnet in her wedding ring. "It must've seemed so unfair."

"And that wasn't all," Bernice said, her outrage palpable. "Miles wanted to spend every minute he could at the other house."

Odd he didn't want to stay home with his mother, considering how much fun she must've been.

"I'm surprised you didn't take Miles and move back to Texas."

"I was going to, but Miles wouldn't have it. He said if I left Chicago, he'd run away and go live with his father."

Making threats already.

"The thing that really bothered me," Bernice said, "was the way he doted on Elizabeth's baby."

Elizabeth and George. Omigod! Ann's parents.

Bernice curled and uncurled her knobby fingers. "Miles always complained about being an only child, so when he had a little sister, even though she was ten years younger, he just loved taking care of her. That baby ruined my life and here was my son sneaking over to George's so he could be with his father and that bastard child. I just hated her. The only person I hated more was the slut."

Cassidy sat very still. "What was the baby's name?"

"Sandra."

"What?" Tessa's jaw went slack.

Cassidy said, "Sandra Brown?"

"How'd you know that?" Bernice asked.

Tessa pressed both hands to the sides of her face. "Sandra Brown lives in Marina City. She and Miles were friends—maybe more than friends—but Miles acted like they'd just met."

Bernice frowned, one hand clenching into a fist. "That lying little shit. He promised me he wouldn't have anything more to do with her."

"When was that?" Cassidy asked.

"Years ago. He hadn't spoken to me for a long time, but then he needed money so he started being nice. It always made me mad that he was such good friends with that selfish little bitch Sandra. So before I gave him the money, I made him promise not to have anything more to do with her."

And she believed him?

Tessa said, "You told me you were broke before you got your inheritance."

"I was. I had to beg my uncle for the money even though I knew he was going to leave it to me eventually."

"So that's why Miles didn't tell me Sandra was his sister. He was afraid I'd pass it on to you and you'd write him out of your will." Tessa hugged her arms tightly against her ribs. "I just can't get over it. Here I was thinking..." She paused, her eyes widening. "Oh God!" She paused again. "Bernice, do you think there's any chance they were...um...you know."

"Oh no. Miles wouldn't do that. I know he was mean sometimes and he lied a lot, but he wouldn't do that."

Or so his mother says.

"The thing that threw everybody off," Cassidy said, "was the different last name. Why was Miles a Gerlinski instead of a Brown?"

For one instant Bernice's lips pulled back to show her teeth like a dog baring its fangs. Then her face relaxed, settling into bitter lines. "Because I wouldn't let him be a Brown. I went back to Gerlinski—that's my maiden name—and I got it put in the decree that Miles would have my last name instead of George's. He was in a big hurry to marry his little tart, but I wasn't going to agree to anything until after the baby was born. She was conceived in sin and I wanted to make sure she was born out of wedlock."

Venom's so thick in the air I don't know how much longer I can go on breathing.

Cassidy said, "So you made George back down on a bunch of things and one of them was Miles' name."

"I wanted my son to have my name since his father didn't care enough about him to keep the family together."

Cassidy looked at her watch. "The time's gotten away from me. I have to get going."

Disappointment washed over Bernice's face. "Oh not so soon. I'm here alone so much of the time. I was hoping for a nice long visit."

"I'm sorry," Cassidy said, "but I have to get home to see a client." *Who will arrive at your door three hours from now.* Giving Bernice an insincere smile, she added, "It was very good of you to answer all these questions. And the cookies were out of this world."

Tessa said, "I'll come back next week and bring Amy."

The two visitors stood. Cassidy walked around the coffee table and took Bernice's hand. "I'm sorry for your loss. Having a child murdered is about the worst thing that can happen to anyone." Cassidy was surprised to realize that her statement was more genuine than her smile. *No matter how self-pitying and vitriolic Bernice is, nobody deserves to lose a son the way she did.*

Chapter 26

Cassidy slid behind the wheel of her Toyota and Tessa climbed in beside her. The young widow slammed the door, buckled her seat belt, then turned to face Cassidy. "So what do you think? Was Miles screwing his sister?"

"That's the question buzzing around in my head too. But I'm not sure there's any way to find out."

"What about that photo she gave Miles. Isn't that at least a clue?"

"It's possible she was just showing off for her big brother."

"Can't you tell if somebody was sexually abused by their behavior? Wouldn't incest explain Sandra's preoccupation with her body and the way she kind of oozes sexuality?"

"Therapists used to think so, but there really isn't any way to tell. She's clearly narcissistic, and that could explain her grandiosity and her need to be admired."

Tessa pushed one side of her golden hair behind her ear. "Isn't there some way of getting a fix on this?"

"I doubt that we'll ever have an ironclad answer, but we could see what her sister Ann has to say. Younger sibs usually watch their older sibs pretty closely."

Cassidy parked next to a fireplug near the Dearborn Street entrance to Marina City. "I could call Ann now. That way you wouldn't have to wait to hear what she has to say."

"Yes, please do. I don't know why, but the idea of his having sex with his half sister really disturbs me."

"I think it'd be pretty strange if it didn't." Cassidy took out her cell phone.

"Hi Cass," Ann said. "Have you got anything new?"

"I just found out that the murder victim—Miles Gerlinski—was your half brother."

"Miles! Oh my God! Here I told my story to that detective and the whole time he talked about the victim—he never used a name—so I had no idea it was Miles."

"Were you close to Miles when you were kids?"

"Heavens no. He was way older. He spent a lot of time at our house and I just hated it, because he and Sandra thought it was so much fun to make me cry."

"Miles' wife and I just finished talking to Mrs. Gerlinski. She said Miles took to Sandra right from the start."

"That's what my mom said too. She told me he loved the idea of having a little sister. He watched over her when she was little and then, when she got older, everybody could see they were like two peas in a pod. They both had a wild streak, they both thought they were better than everybody else, and they'd both go to any lengths to get what they wanted."

Cassidy gazed out the windshield at a woman struggling to push a double-seated stroller uphill against the wind. "We've been wondering if they were sexually intimate."

"I don't think anything happened when Sandra was young. Miles was always getting in trouble and Mom never let him out of her sight. But once Sandra was old enough to get around by herself, she was out all the time. At that point, who knows what they might have done. But I never sensed any sexual vibes between them."

"I had myself convinced Sandra got someone to kill Miles for her," Cassidy said. "But now that I hear how close they were, I'm not so sure. What do you think?"

"I don't know what to tell you. Fifteen years ago, Sandra adored him. But I've seen her get mad at people and cut them off completely. A person who'd kill her own mother"—Ann's voice cracked—"is capable of anything."

It was close to eleven A.M. on Sunday when the phone rang. Cassidy, folding laundry in the basement, ran upstairs to grab the receiver before the fourth ring, all the while telling herself she should let the call go to the answering machine. She lifted the handset off the kitchen wall just before the machine clicked in.

"It's me, Joan." Her words were nearly drowned out by the sound of a screaming child. "The police just finished searching Tessa's condo and I'm afraid she's losing it."

"No I'm not." Tessa's voice, high and thin, in the background.

That means the DNA results came back and the gunk in the drain belongs to Miles. Which doesn't come as a revelation to anybody.

Cassidy asked, "Can you put Tessa on the phone?"

She heard Tessa and Joan arguing. Then Tessa came on the line. "It was awful...they pawed through Miles' drawers...tore the bed apart." She was gasping out the words.

"I'd like to have you do some deep breathing. Would that be all right?"

"I guess so."

"Take a long slow breath. Pull the air all the way into your abdomen while I count to five." As

Cassidy counted, she could hear Tessa inhaling. "Now hold your breath to the count of five." Next she instructed Tessa to exhale to the count of five.

Cassidy continued for several minutes, then asked, "How are you feeling now?"

"Better."

"Can I speak to Joan again?"

"She looks a lot calmer," Joan said. "I never knew it would be so handy to have a therapist just a phone call away."

"What's the situation over there?"

"Amy freaked when these two cops came barging in. Tessa called me to come get Amy, but she had to stay and watch them tear her place apart. Now Amy wants to go stay with her grandma, which I heartily endorse, but I'm not about to let Tessa drive and I don't think she should be left alone here either. Maybe I'll take both of them to Grandma's house."

"Not me!" came from the background. "I have to stay and clean up."

To Tessa, Joan said, "You're in no condition to go back into that condo. Even though you've stopped hyperventilating, I can still hear the anxiety in your voice."

"I can't leave it the way it is," Tessa replied, her pitch higher than it should be. "I have to straighten it up now."

"Joan," Cassidy said into the mouthpiece. "Joan, are you there?"

After a brief pause, Joan returned. "We seem to be at an impasse. You have any suggestions?"

"How far away is grandma's house?"

"Evanston. It'll take at least an hour to get there and back."

"I'll come to Marina City. Then you can drive Amy and I can help Tessa."

"You sure you don't mind?"

"Actually, I'd rather deal with Tessa's mess than finish the laundry or clean my own place."

Cassidy disconnected and took a good look at the floor beneath her feet: dirt streaks, spilled food, clumps of cat fur. She felt a twinge of guilt, aware that she was always looking for excuses to avoid housework. Then she mentally slapped herself. *How could you even begin to think that a clean floor is more important than helping Tessa get through this crisis?*

She headed back down the basement stairs. *At least you can finish folding the clothes instead of leaving them in the basket where they'll soon start to resemble a pile of Shar-Pei skins.*

As she neared the laundry table, she noticed muddy paw prints criss-crossing the clothes she'd already folded. Starshine, happily ensconced in the basket of unfolded clothes, greeted her with a *mwat*.

Well, so much for preventing wrinkles. No point moving her now, since you're going to have to rewash the whole load anyway.

After scratching the calico behind her ears, Cassidy went upstairs to tell Zach where she was going.

She went out into a grimy world. Although the temperature had risen into the fifties, the sky was overcast, the light murky. Most of the snow had melted, leaving a dirty ridge along the wooden fence to the south and a large crusted hump at the curb to the north. The yard was matted with dull brown grass, and a pint liquor bottle had been tossed over their chain link fence. Cassidy focused on the job ahead and walked toward the garage.

Chapter 27

"Boy, am I glad to see you." Joan led Cassidy into her living room. "I practically had to barricade the door with my body to keep Tessa from going back to her condo."

Cassidy glanced at her hostess, whose diminutive frame would not present much of an obstacle to leaving. *But that intimidating stare would stop almost anyone in their tracks.*

Tessa sat with Amy in her lap, both faces wearing a sullen expression. "Just because I had that one panic attack is no reason to think I can't function like a normal human being."

Cassidy said to Joan, "Seems to me her attack was fairly minor. I don't see any problem with Tessa and me cleaning up her condo while you take Amy to her grandmother's."

The child wrapped her arms around her mother's neck. "I want Mommy to take me."

Tessa leaned her head close to Amy's. "I know it was scary but the police are gone now, and Mommy needs you to go with Joan so she can put things back together."

Joan and Amy donned their coats and headed toward the elevators, while Cassidy and Tessa walked the short distance to Tessa's condo. She paused in front of the door, drew in a breath, and inserted the key with a trembling hand.

"It must be hard to go back inside."

Nodding, Tessa pushed the door inward. In the galley kitchen to their left, a few pots and pans were scattered across the counter and some cupboard doors hung open. A small trash can with garbage spilling out stood in the middle of the floor.

To their right, the sliding doors of the coat closet were open. Some of the coats were still on hangers but others lay heaped on the floor. In the dressing room beyond the coat closet, a few pill bottles had fallen out of the medicine cabinet into the sink below. Three open cardboard boxes sat on the floor.

The women moved on into the living room. All the abstract paintings hung askew and the two emerald easy chairs were out of place. The seat cushions on both the sofa and the chairs had been disturbed. The previously locked bottom drawer of the desk was pulled out and empty. One of the red pots from the coffee table lay in pieces on the floor, its plant looking sickly and forlorn.

"Oh my poor miniature rose!" Tessa ripped a cardboard flap off one of the boxes and slid it beneath the plant and its dirt. She carried it into the kitchen and repotted it in a bowl. "Just for now. So it doesn't die."

"What's your bedroom like?" Cassidy asked.

"Come on, I'll show you."

Since Tessa owned a two-bedroom unit, the master bedroom was somewhat larger than the one in Zach's condo, but even Tessa's bedroom was slightly cramped. It contained a king-sized bed, a huge closet, two dressers, a television, and a small desk. The bedding was piled on the mattress, a number of drawers were open, and a few articles of clothing lay crumpled on the floor.

Cassidy asked, "That your desk?"

"Uh-huh."

"Did the police go through your desk or just Miles'?"

"The search warrant said they could take the answering machine, Miles' computer, and his papers. They wanted to look through my desk but I said absolutely not and they backed off. They opened my dresser drawers but as soon as they saw they were mine, they closed them back up."

"What about Miles' clothes? Are you ready to get rid of them? Or would you like to keep them a while longer?"

"I want them out of here! If I hadn't been feeling so overwhelmed, they'd be long gone."

"This might be a good time to pack them in garbage bags."

"You'd be willing to help?"

"Sure."

"Oh Cass," Tessa placed her hand on Cassidy's arm. "You have no idea how much I've been dreading this. Sometimes I dream I've disposed of all his things, and then he comes back and is furious. Getting his clothes out of here will be such a relief!"

"Since this'll be the biggest job, let's do everything else first, then hit the bedroom.

After straightening the other parts of the condo, Tessa and Cassidy moved the bedding into the living room so Tessa could wash it later. They picked up slacks, shirts, and suits from the closet floor, rolled them into tight bundles, and stuffed them in plastic bags. Then Cassidy tackled the clothes still hanging on the rod and Tessa scooped underwear and tee shirts out of Miles' drawers.

They'd been working on the bedroom for about half an hour when Tessa said, "There's only one more bag in the box. I'll have to go downstairs and buy more."

Cassidy took a pair of pants off its hanger, then turned to face Tessa. "We're nearly finished."

"You want to stop now?" Tessa asked, a pinprick of anxiety in her large gray eyes.

Cassidy started to say she could stay as long as Tessa needed her, then realized she would probably regret that statement later. "I don't have to leave any time soon."

"Thank goodness! Having someone to do this with makes it so much easier. I'll just run down to the store and get another box of bags." Tessa dusted off her hands, combed her golden hair, and left the bedroom.

Cassidy rolled up the last shirt, stuffed it in a bag, tied the top, threw it over her shoulder, and started toward the living room. As she passed Tessa's desk, she heard a thunk. Dropping the bag on the bed, she turned around to discover she'd knocked a pile of papers to the floor. She glanced at each one as she picked them up. They included newsletters, printouts from various websites, a couple of theater reviews, and an invitation to a Red Cross benefit.

Cassidy stroked her jaw. *Red Cross. Somebody mentioned that recently.* She could almost hear the person's voice in her head but couldn't tell who it belonged to.

Remember how you wanted to search the condo right away but Tessa refused? And you thought she was hiding something?

But Tessa's your friend and you've already picked Sandra as the killer.

Tessa's one of the two prime suspects and you don't have a single piece of evidence against Sandra. Just because you like Tessa doesn't mean she didn't kill her husband.

Cassidy opened the pencil drawer, poked around a little, ran her hand beneath the bottom of the drawer, and closed it. She repeated the process with the next two drawers. As she was pulling out the bottom drawer, she heard the condo door open.

"Hi, I'm back," Tessa called from the other room.

"I'm just finishing the shirts," Cassidy said. Her fingers encountered an item attached to the underside of the drawer. She tore at it with her nails, pulling it free. A card, with lace-covered roses on the front. She stuffed it beneath the mattress just before Tessa came into the room. As Cassidy got to her feet, she was not surprised to see Tessa staring at her with a puzzled expression on her face.

"The bag I was carrying knocked the papers off your desk," Cassidy explained. "I think I got all of them, but if anything's missing you'll find it on the floor."

"Don't worry about it. Most of the stuff on my desk ends up in the garbage anyway."

Later, while Tessa was taking a bathroom break, Cassidy pulled out the card and opened it. The printed message was romantic and sugary, the sort of pap she was happy not to get from Zach.

At the bottom of the card, the sender had written: *Our time is coming soon.* He'd signed it with a distinctive capital A, the letter tall, angular and steeply pitched. An image of Tessa and Andy talking near the mailboxes flashed through Cassidy's mind. She pushed the card to the bottom of her purse, this time not regretting that she carried a bag the size of a ten-pound potato sack.

Tessa and Andy. Well, what do you know?

You can't be certain it's Andy. He isn't the only male whose name starts with A.

A short time later, a heap of plastic bags sat in the living room awaiting a trip to the Salvation Army. Tessa gave Cassidy a big hug. "I can't thank you enough for all your help and support."

Wait till she notices that some of the things in her drawers have been rearranged. Or reaches for the card.

She headed toward Joan's condo with the intention of showing her the card, then stopped to weigh the consequences. She thought Joan could probably get her hands on a sample of Andy's signature, which should enable them to determine whether he was the sender. But Tessa and Joan were friends, and Joan might want nothing to do with an outsider who snooped through Tessa's drawers and found a card that could be used against her. Not for the first time, Cassidy realized what a mistake it would be to alienate Joan.

While Cassidy was trying to decide, Joan came out of her condo, unaware of Cassidy's presence, and walked toward the elevators.

"Hey Joan," Cassidy called after her. "Wait up."

Joan turned around. "I'm glad to see you. I've got a situation that could be serious and I'd like to have you with me." Joan started walking again and Cassidy fell in beside her.

"What is it?"

"Sandra's neighbor called. Apparently Sandra didn't come home last night."

"What did she say?"

"I'd rather not give you a second-hand version. You can hear it for yourself in just a minute."

They rode the elevator three floors up. As they headed toward Sandra's unit, they could hear her dogs howling. The neighbor came out into the hall to talk to them. In her fifties, she was a large woman who carried herself well. A sense of competence emanated from her.

She planted her hands on her hips. "I'm so worried. Dammit, Sandra should've given me a key.

There were a couple other times she was late—not like this, of course—and I told her it was hard on the dogs to keep them cooped up so long. But would she give me a key? Not paranoid Sandra."

"I'll go get a key," Joan said, "but could you fill me in a little first?"

The neighbor said, "I take care of Han and Luke whenever Sandra's away. Those dogs are such sweethearts, I almost wish they were mine. I've been looking after them since they were puppies, and I hate that she leaves them alone so much. Up until now, whenever she was going to be gone overnight, she'd lend me a key, but this time I guess she forgot about poor little Han and Luke."

Hope that's all there is to it. After what happened to Miles, impossible not to think the worst.

"But it's hard to imagine how she *could* forget," the neighbor continued, "considering they poop and pee all over the place when they don't get walked." She sniffed the air. "I can smell it from here. Well, Sandra's going to get what she deserves when she comes back.

"But those poor doggies don't deserve to be left alone like that. I expect their anxiety levels have gone through the roof. Joan, you should get that key right away so they don't have to suffer a minute longer than necessary."

"This shouldn't take long." Joan started for the elevator.

The neighbor turned toward Cassidy. "You a friend of Joan's?"

Cassidy nodded. "Cass McCabe."

"Celia."

"Sandra's lucky to have somebody as responsible as you watching over her animals."

"I first heard them howling around nine last night. They do that when Sandra doesn't get home

on time. Since I have to get to work early, I put in
earplugs and went to sleep. But then when they
were still howling this morning, I started to get
concerned. It occurred to me that something might
have happened to Sandra. Although knowing her, it
seemed more likely she'd gone off with some
boyfriend and hadn't made it home."

"Considering the circumstances, wasn't there
somebody you could get to open the door?"

"I could've gone to the management office, but
then I'd have to explain why I needed to get into
Sandra's condo. There's a rule against dogs, but
management usually looks the other way unless
somebody complains. I was afraid if I said anything,
they'd make Sandra get rid of the dogs, and I didn't
want to see that happen."

"Must've been hard to leave them and go off to
work."

"I would've taken the day off except they're so
damn short-handed at the hospital."

"You a nurse?"

Celia nodded. "Since Joan is head of security, I
figured she could get a key without having to
explain herself. So I left a detailed message on her
machine and assumed she'd take care of it."

"But she just found out about it, didn't she?"

"I guess she was in the shower when I called
this morning, and she went all day without
checking her machine. I called again a few minutes
ago."

A moment later Joan returned with the key. As
she approached the door, the howls turned to woofs
of excitement.

"Wait a minute," Cassidy said. "The dogs are
going to be all over us. Maybe Celia should go first
since they know her."

Opening the door, Celia sat on her heels to greet the small canines. They jumped on her and yipped furiously. The stench of urine and feces drifted into the hall.

"The smell is so bad I'm going to grab their leashes and food and take them to my place." Darting inside, Celia returned with the leashes, snapped them on, and led the dogs into her unit. Then she made a second trip for a bag of Science Diet dog food.

Chapter 28

Joan and Cassidy stared at each other.

"I suppose it's possible Sandra forgot," Joan said.

"But not likely." Cassidy moistened her bottom lip. "I have to go in there. To make sure she's not unconscious or...." Her words trailed off.

Joan clutched her arms across her chest. "You'll just run in, see if she's there, and come back?"

"If there's no sign of her, I'll have to look around." Cassidy thought of what Ann had said about no woman leaving her purse behind. "I want to see if it looks like she packed up and left, or if her purse and clothes are still there."

Cassidy went into the entryway and Joan followed. Turning around, Cassidy looked the former principal in the eye. "You don't have to do this. Everybody knows how competent and strong you are. It'd be okay to let yourself off this time."

Joan's erect posture slumped a little. "I'm getting old. Nobody else notices, but I do. Every day I have to prove to myself I can still cut it. Now don't mess with me about coming in here."

Cassidy checked each room. When she was sure Sandra's body wasn't in the condo, she took out a tissue and used it to open the closet doors. Each closet was crammed with clothes. The hanging bag of shoes was full. The medicine chest held bottles of Clonapin and Xanax. *If she went to stay somewhere else, probably would've packed her meds.* Five purses sat on a shelf above the coats but all of them were empty. Cassidy searched for a purse containing keys, credit cards, makeup—the things Sandra would never leave behind—but she was unable to find it.

She said to Joan, "I can't think of anywhere else to look."

"I'd say we're finished here." They returned to the hall. "Guess it's time to call the cops."

Cassidy heaved a large sigh. "I can't tell you how much I hate the thought of cooling my heels in one of those interview rooms. Or making another statement. Or getting lectured by Roloff again."

"I don't see any reason your name has to come up. You just happened to be in the wrong place at the wrong time. Let me go explain to Celia that you weren't really here."

After returning from Celia's condo, Joan said, "She's fine with it."

Cassidy shifted her weight. "I guess I might as well get going then."

"And I have to call the police."

Neither woman made a move to leave. A few seconds passed, then Joan said, "I don't suppose it would hurt anything if we went to my place and spent a few minutes trying to figure this out before I make that call."

Cassidy sat on Joan's navy blue sofa gazing at the view while Joan busied herself in the kitchen making coffee. Five-thirty, and the sun had already dipped below the horizon. The sky, reflecting the glow from the city, was an eerie shade of mauve. Cassidy could see the headlamps of vehicles moving slowly through traffic and street lights blinking on in all directions. They marked out a near-perfect grid, with occasional diagonal lines cutting through it.

When the coffee was poured, they sat across from one another in the living room. Joan said, "Remember when we talked to Sandra, how she seemed afraid of the murderer? Maybe she knew who did it and decided to make herself disappear before the killer could do it for her. After all, her purse was gone so she must've taken it with her."

"Yes, but everything else was there. My guess is the killer snatched her off the street. She was so meticulous. She'd never have allowed the dogs to make such a mess."

The room fell silent.

Joan said, "If Sandra's dead, that's two out of three Lunch Bunchers. Which seems to point to Henry as the killer."

"Or maybe somebody's out to get all three, in which case Henry'd be next. In fact, it might be a good idea to check on him."

"Why would anybody want to kill three people who have lunch together?"

"Because they rejected him. Because he's a psychopath. People commit murder for all kinds of reasons that don't make sense to those of us who are sane."

Joan pressed her fingertips to her cheekbone. "You don't think I'm at risk, do you? I mean, I've been asking a lot of questions."

"I don't see you as fitting the pattern. So far, the disappearances seem connected to either the Lunch Bunch"—*Don't say it. It'll only get you in trouble*—"or Tessa. But you still should take precautions."

Joan's back went rigid. "What do you mean, 'Tessa'? There's no connection between Tessa and Sandra."

"Do you remember Tessa saying how much she hated Sandra?"

Joan made a dismissive gesture. "People say things like that all the time. It doesn't mean anything."

You have to tell her about the card.

"I found something that raises questions about Tessa. I'd like to show it to you but I don't want to get you mad at me again."

Joan's eyes narrowed. "Sounds like you've been up to no good and you're hoping I'll give you a free pass on it."

"Uh...I suppose you could say that. Tessa and I were packing up Miles' clothes and she went down to the store to get more bags. While she was gone, I looked through her desk and found this"—Cassidy handed the card to Joan—"taped to the underside of her bottom drawer."

Tight lines formed around Joan's mouth. She glanced at the card but didn't open it. "You went through Tessa's desk behind her back? I suppose if I left you here alone, you'd do the same to me."

Forcing herself not to sound defensive, Cassidy said, "Tessa's a suspect. You're not."

Silence.

Finally Cassidy said, "I really think you ought to look at it."

Joan skimmed the message, then closed it. "Somebody sent her a love note. So what?"

"'Our time is coming soon.' What do you think that means? That they're planning to kill Miles?"

"More likely that they won't have to keep their relationship hidden once the murder's solved."

"I'm guessing the card came from Andy and the two of them are having an affair."

"This certainly doesn't prove they were sleeping together. But considering the way Miles treated her, I don't see how anyone could blame her if they were."

"An affair would ramp up Tessa's motivation. I had trouble imagining her committing such a gruesome crime on her own, but if Andy did the dirty work, then I could see it."

"Tessa said she had nothing to do with it and I believe her." Joan held the card in her lap, flipping it back and forth like a fan. "Why show this to me if you knew I'd disapprove?"

"Look at how unusual that 'A' is. I was hoping you could get hold of something with Andy's signature on it so we could compare."

"I could, but I won't. As far as I'm concerned, Tessa's not a suspect. I know her. She'd never hurt anybody. Not even a snake like Miles."

Gotta admire Joan. She's not going to let anyone undermine her faith in her friend.

Either that, or she's in denial. You never can tell which.

"Can I have the card back?" Cassidy asked.

"It doesn't belong to you."

"What are you going to do with it?"

"I *should* give it to Tessa."

Hasn't decided yet. If you don't push her, maybe she won't tell Tessa what you did.

"I better leave now so you can call the police. I really appreciate your keeping my name out of it."

Joan retrieved Cassidy's coat from the closet.

As Cassidy put it on, she asked, "Okay if I stop at Henry's and see if he's all right?"

"Yes, I think you should do that."

"Don't tell me your name," Henry said, standing in his doorway. "It's on the tip of my tongue." He held his chin between his thumb and forefinger. "I believe you're Ms. McCabe, the inquisitive young lady who keeps popping up with more questions. Last time I let you get around me, but today I intend to stand firm." A small twinkle in his faded eyes took the harshness out of his words.

"I don't need to come in. I just want to tell you something I think you ought to know." As the full horror of Sandra's disappearance came over her, a shivery feeling ran down her arms. She described what she and Joan had discovered at Sandra's condo.

Henry's face registered shock. "Are you telling me she's disappeared too?"

"That's what it looks like."

"I simply don't believe it. There's not nearly enough evidence to support such a theory. She could be in a drug-induced state of confusion, or with her boyfriend, or in a hospital somewhere."

"I hope you're right."

"I can't think of a single reason why anyone would make both Miles and Sandra disappear."

"Two out of three Lunch Bunchers."

Henry frowned deeply. "Are you implying I might be next?"

"The thought crossed my mind."

"That's absurd. Why would anybody want to get rid of three unrelated people who just happen to have lunch together?"

"I was hoping you could answer that question. Do you know of anyone who showed particular interest in the Lunch Bunchers? Or who might have felt rejected because they weren't invited to join?"

Henry stared into space for several beats, then shook his head. "It doesn't make sense. Even if I grant you that Sandra may have disappeared, it's far more likely something was going on between Sandra and Miles and that's what got them killed."

"But you can't deny the possibility that someone might have it in for all three of you. Perhaps you could stay away from Marina City for a while. Go on vacation or check into a hotel."

A stern look came over his face. "It's presumptuous of you to give advice to your elders.

Your assumption that someone is trying to kill all three of us is frankly ridiculous. Now, if you'll excuse me...." He stepped back from the threshold and closed the door.

As the Toyota approached Cassidy's house, which stood on the southeast corner of Briar and Hazel, she saw a yellow Miata parked near her back gate. *Bryce,* she thought, her spirits lifting. Her stepson, a sophomore at Northwestern University, kept himself so busy she didn't get to see nearly as much of him as she would have liked.

She entered her waiting room and heard two male voices that weren't arguing. *Of course not. You just haven't adjusted to the new them yet.* She felt a sense of satisfaction over the role she'd played in getting father and son to work out their differences.

At the age of seventeen, Bryce had reluctantly appeared at their door. He arrived bristling with hatred toward Zach because his mother had deliberately poisoned his mind against his father. Then his mother discovered that her life was in danger and sent her son to stay with Zach, the one person who could keep him safe.

Zach didn't know he'd sired a son, but when confronted with the boy's attitude, he responded in kind. Over the years their relationship improved to some degree, but a prickliness remained just beneath the surface. Then a crisis in their relationship had occurred the previous fall, leading Cassidy to step in as mediator. She convinced them to face the basic issues keeping them apart, and since then a genuine closeness had developed between father and son.

"Hi Cass," Bryce said as she came into the dining room. "Glad you got home before I had to leave."

Zach and Bryce sat across the table from each other, a large flat open box between them. Only a few pieces remained of what had once been a giant-sized pizza.

"Why didn't you wait for me?" Cassidy demanded. "I'm starved!"

Zach said, "We had no idea when you'd get here."

"You could have called."

"Maybe he just wanted some guy time with me," Bryce said.

Isn't that what you always hoped for? That they'd form a bond with each other and stop using you as the switchboard?

Yes, but you hate being left out of anything.

Cassidy took a seat at the head of the table, pulled the box close, and started gobbling lukewarm pizza. Holding a slice in the air, she chewed and swallowed, then asked Bryce, "What brings you all the way out to Oak Park?"

"I was in the area and thought I'd stop by. Wanted to see how you all were doing."

"Wanted to see how *I* was doing," Zach said.

Cassidy knew she wasn't the only one who'd been worried about Zach.

"You're my tough guy role model," Bryce said. "You have to make that jagoff pay for what he did to you. If you can't find anything to use against him, maybe you should just beat him to a pulp."

"I hate to tell you, but he's in much better shape than I am. In case you haven't noticed, I'm beginning to develop a paunch."

"Nah, it doesn't show. And don't let Cass put you on any diets, either."

"You're ganging up on me," she protested. "Getting you guys to talk was obviously a mistake."

Bryce said to Cassidy, "Zach showed me some cool stuff about fact-checking. Nothing I like better than filling my brain with useless information. Guess that's why I don't mind studying."

Zach shook his head. "You and I can't possibly be from the same gene pool. I hardly ever studied. Mostly I just faked it."

Bryce shoved his chair back. "Look, you don't have time to sit and chat with me. You've got a reputation to destroy."

Chapter 29

As they stood in the entryway watching Bryce leave, Cassidy said to Zach, "A lot happened today at Marina City and I'd like to bounce it off you. You think you could wait a little longer before getting back to work?"

"Sure." He headed toward the kitchen. "I'm going to get a Pepsi. You want anything?"

"Bring me one too."

Cassidy took the small blue chair in the living room. Zach handed her a glass and lowered himself onto the blue paisley sofa to the right of her chair. He plunked his soda on the glass coffee table, ignoring the coasters that sat within easy reach. Cassidy moved to sit beside him so she could put a coaster under his Pepsi can.

She told him everything that had happened that afternoon. When she finished, she noted that Zach's face had grown tense.

"So now you've got a second disappearance. Shit, I don't like this at all."

"Well, of course, no one likes the idea of people disappearing. Not even insufferable people like Sandra."

"What I don't like is the implication. You told me Sandra seemed scared after Miles was murdered. Obviously she had a reason to be. As to your theory about someone knocking off the Lunch Bunchers, I'm with Henry. That sort of thing only happens in those mysteries you read. What makes the most sense is that Sandra was killed because of something she knew."

"But how would she know anything?"

"Considering Miles and Sandra were tight since they were kids, he may well have opened up to her more than to his wife. So Miles knows somebody's out to get him, and he tells Sandra, which means she has a good idea who the doer is. Somehow the killer finds out—or maybe just guesses—that she knows, so he has to get rid of her too. But not in Marina City, because his previous crime scene was discovered. So this time he has to grab her someplace else."

"If Sandra knew who the killer was, why wouldn't she tell the police? Or go into hiding?"

"She doesn't tell the police because she's afraid that if she does, she'll be next. And she doesn't go into hiding because she doesn't think the killer's on to her. The thing that concerns me is, if Sandra was killed for knowing too much, you and Joan could be in danger too."

"We don't know who killed Miles."

"You've collected a lot of information. Maybe you've got the key and just don't know it yet." A three beat pause, then Zach started up again. "And Miles' killer isn't the only one you have to watch out for. There's a nutcase teenager who's pissed at you for reporting him to the police."

"If Kenny was going to do anything, I think he would've done it by now."

"Why in God's name would you say that? This is a kid who stalked his father over a long period of time. For all you know, he's creating a new photo exhibit with you as the star. Dammit, Cass, how can you be so smart when it comes to investigating and so stupid when it comes to protecting yourself?"

She looked down at her lap. "I probably shouldn't have told you about Sandra. You've got enough on your mind without worrying about me."

Stretching his arm behind her back, he squeezed her shoulder. "Don't you even think about not telling me. If you stopped talking, I'd really be worried."

Shortly before ten, Zach came into the bedroom where Cassidy was feeling sorry for herself because she didn't have a cat to pet.

"I'm going to have a drink while we watch the news. I'm so foggy from lack of sleep, I decided to bag it and go to bed as soon as the news is over. You want a glass of wine?"

"Sure."

Ever since Zach first convinced her to watch the news with him, it had become a nightly routine. *Much as you hate to admit it, there is a certain comfort in parallel play.*

They settled in the den, their sock-clad feet sharing the footstool. Zach clicked the remote. Four attractive people sat behind the anchor desk: a Latina, a black man, and two white men. One of the Caucasians said, "Stay tuned. Coming up next—mouse droppings and rotten food found in a popular Chicago restaurant." A commercial started and Zach switched channels.

Cassidy remarked, "I bet every anchor team in the country consists of three men and one woman, and out of that group two are minorities and two are white—usually two white men."

Zach switched back to the original channel. The Latina anchor said, "Coming up next. The Virgin Mary appears in a stain on the wall of a far north Jewel."

Been hearing about these Virgin Marys for years. Wonder what they look like.

Cassidy put her hand on Zach's arm. "I want to see this one."

"This is an old chestnut of a story. Stain on a wall, cracks in cement, face in a pizza. I could probably tell you almost verbatim what the reporter's going to say."

"Don't change channels!"

"The gullibility of the public knows no bounds."

"Obviously. But I want to see what these gullible people do."

Cassidy sipped wine, drummed her fingers, and fidgeted in her chair during the commercials, which seemed to go on forever.

The anchors reappeared and the Latina talked some more. "The devout flock to a stain where they see the Mother of God. Linda Dorne is reporting live from the scene."

Dorne said, "We're here in the parking lot of the Jewel at fifty-two hundred north Ashland where the faithful have been gathering all day to pray in front of this image, leaving lighted candles and tokens of their devotion to the Virgin Mary."

Behind the reporter, Cassidy saw a few individuals waving at the camera, and farther back, a crowd standing in front of a wall where a shrine of candles, flowers, and teddy bears had been erected. The worshippers blocked Cassidy's view of the shrine.

A hand clutched the reporter's arm. As the camera focused on the person, Cassidy could see it was a woman wearing a pair of man's pants, a dress over the pants, a hooded sweatshirt, and gloves with missing fingers.

The woman said, "The Dark Angels are trying to—"

Cassidy jumped to her feet.

"—kill me, but as long as I have my rosary, the Virgin Mary will—"

Before the woman could finish her sentence, a man in a Cubs jacket and cap grabbed her from behind and yanked her out of view.

"Oh shit! Oh shit! I couldn't see his face. Could you?"

"His face was never on camera."

Cassidy turned and stared at Zach. "You think that guy could be the killer?"

"Did you tell anyone who the witness was?"

She dropped into her chair, pressed the heels of her hands to her forehead, and tried to remember. "I talked to so many people." A pause. "Oh shit! I told Joan when I was sitting in the police car. Then I realized I'd made a big mistake and didn't tell anyone after that. But Joan probably told Tessa, and if Tessa and Andy are having an affair she would've told him, and from there it could've gone anywhere."

"Yeah, but even if the killer knew Delia was the witness, he wouldn't have had any way to find her. You didn't tell anyone she was schizo, did you?"

She frowned at his use of the word *schizo*. "Just the police."

"If the killer didn't know she was schizophrenic, he wouldn't have had any reason to be looking for a homeless woman." Zach stared into the middle distance. "Unless he hired a P.I. A good investigator could've found out she was schizophrenic, and given enough time, he probably would've been able to locate her."

"If the killer knew she was schizophrenic, why worry about her? She wouldn't have any credibility."

"If Delia got back on her meds, the police would listen to her."

"But she can't identify him."

"He doesn't know that. However, the odds are that the guy who dragged her away is a store security guard."

"Why would a security guard do that? Oh, I get it. He wouldn't want it to look like the parking lot is a haven for homeless people." Cassidy paced back and forth in front of the TV. "If the killer hired a P.I.," she said, talking to herself, "would he have told the P.I. to grab her? No, he wouldn't want the P.I. to know what he was up to. He would've found out where she was, then followed her until he had a chance to snatch her. God, I wish I'd been able to see his face."

"A friend of mine is a producer at the station. He could blow up some stills and email them to me. You won't be able to see the face, but maybe you can tell something from his build. While I'm doing that, you call the store. If the guy's a security guard, the manager'd know about it."

Zach used the landline in the computer room and Cassidy called on her cell. The Jewel operator transferred her to the night manager's answering machine. Cassidy left her name and number and said it was urgent that she speak to him.

Not long after Zach talked to his producer friend, he received an attachment with several pictures of the man who'd grabbed Delia. Cassidy couldn't determine his height or see his hair beneath the cap, but she could tell he was on the trim side.

She said, "There are only three male suspects I know of—Henry, Kenny, and Andy. I can rule out Henry right away—he's too thin and not agile enough to have grabbed Delia as fast as this guy did." She touched her fingernail to the man in the photo. "I'm pretty sure it isn't Kenny either. The Cubs jacket makes it a little hard to tell how big he is, but this guy's shoulders don't appear nearly as broad as Kenny's, and Kenny's hair would show beneath the cap. That leaves Andy, who's fairly lean but not as thin as Henry, has short hair, and keeps himself in shape."

"I hope you're not talking yourself into thinking Andy's the killer based on these pictures. Like I said before, the guy probably works for the store."

Wearing her fuzzy nightshirt and dingy slippers, which she never remembered to put in the wash, Cassidy hurried downstairs to refill her mug and grab a bite of breakfast. Since she seldom got up before eight, she had to really scurry on the days when she had nine o'clock clients. She went into the kitchen and glanced around, hoping to see Starshine, who often returned from her nocturnal visits about this time. Realizing that the cat hadn't made it home yet, Cassidy could feel her neck and shoulders stiffen.

Why can't she at least come home by the time I get downstairs? Here Zach and I have been pampering her for years but that's not good enough. She has to go find someone else to fawn over her as well.

Cassidy poured coffee, then impulsively reached for the bag of peanut butter cups in the cabinet. She'd devoured two before she realized what she was doing. *What's the matter with you? You came in here to eat yogurt, but instead you're wolfing down Reese's.* She consumed two more before she could force herself to put the bag away.

She emerged from her office at noon, certain that Starshine would be napping in one of her usual places by then. After checking all of the calico's favorite spots, she went through the house calling "kitty, kitty," but received no response.

She felt an urge to go into the computer room and vent her frustration to her husband but didn't give in to it. *Zach's got a career to save and you have no business distracting him.*

Chapter 30

At a little after two, Cassidy was filling out managed care forms when she heard the familiar sound of paws clomping on the stairs. She watched Starshine stroll into the room, hop onto the far side of the bed, pick her way across the nightstand, stop on the radiator cover to look out the window, then bounce over to Cassidy's desk. The calico flopped on her side on top of the form Cassidy was working on and presented her spotless white stomach for petting. A stomach, Cassidy noted, that was ballooning out just as it had before Cassidy put her on a diet.

She started to scratch the spot between Starshine's front legs, then reminded herself how angry she was. "Oh no you don't. You can't come waltzing in here after being out all night plus half the next day and expect me to be glad to see you." *Well, you are glad, but you're not going to let her know.* "This time you've gone too far. I've had all I can take and I'm going to put a stop to it."

Shouldn't make empty threats.

There's gotta be some way to keep her from going AWOL every night.

Starshine sat up, nipped Cassidy's finger, and left the room.

You could chain her to a bedpost, keep her in a cage, lock her in the attic. Or...you could buy a tracking device, follow her to the other house, and confront the weasel who's been luring her away from you.

Although Cassidy had watched plenty of nature shows where people clipped electronic gizmos on animals, then followed their movements across country, she had no idea how to obtain such a device.

Probably not sold at Radio Shack.

The vet was equally clueless.

She used Zach's laptop to Google "tracking device Chicagoland." The first four hits were websites that sold GPS tracking devices for cars. The fifth was a spy store that advertised a device for tracking housecats.

Cassidy parked and walked toward the store. She had expected it to be on the seedy side, the kind of place that catered to Peeping Toms or worse, but it wasn't. Instead it reminded her of a Sharper Image, the interior bright, chrome-filled, and impeccable. An attractive man, his thick black hair combed straight back, sat at a computer behind the counter.

She told him what she wanted and he brought out a box from the back. Inside was a four-piece set: a collar with a flexible antenna on the top and a plastic pouch on the bottom; a small gadget that looked like a radio; a large antenna; and earphones. He explained that the pouch on the collar held a transmitter and the radio-like gadget was a receiver. Then he placed the collar on one side of the room, took her to the opposite side, and showed her how to follow the beeps from the antenna back to the collar.

"It has a range of up to four miles," he said. "Farther than most cats go."

"How much?" Cassidy braced herself for the answer.

"Five hundred."

Even though she'd known it would be expensive, hearing him say the number out loud made her stomach twitch. "That's a little steep. I don't suppose you have a demo or a second-hand model?"

He shook his head.

Knowing it was useless, Cassidy plowed on. "I really need this, but I'll probably only use it once. Is there any chance you could rent it to me?"

"Sorry. It's against store policy." He began repacking the box.

"Well, thanks anyway." She trudged out to sit in her Toyota.

You should have bought it, then returned it after you found Starshine's other house.

A part of her was horrified that she'd even think such a thing. *That's practically stealing. You'd never do anything so sleazy.*

You think you can't afford it but that really isn't true. You and Zach together make a comfortable living.

It won't be comfortable if he gets fired.

She drew in air, then exhaled a long breath. *Starshine's behavior is driving you nuts and that tracking device is your only hope.*

She went back inside, plunked down her credit card, and returned to the car with the box in her hands.

When she got home, Starshine was asleep on the waterbed and Zach was on the phone in the computer room. Pushing aside the clutter on her desk, Cassidy set the box down and opened it.

One thing you don't have to worry about is Zach getting on your case for spending all that moolah.

Having grown up with wealth, he had a deeply engrained belief that there was always plenty of money, and he never felt a need to curb either his or Cassidy's spending. Since her experience was the opposite, she used to go into arrhythmia every time he brought home some new high-ticket item. Over the years she'd loosened up about his prodigal ways, even though some of his more extravagant expenditures still threw her into shock.

When she heard the phone call end, she carried her box into the computer room and set it on his work table.

"Ta da!" She spread her arms wide. "A tracking device. So we can find out where Starshine goes at night."

Zach got to his feet and examined each of the items in the box. "Sweet. I hope you don't intend to keep it all to yourself."

"You can have a turn. But first I need your help getting this collar on Starshine."

"It needs a battery."

In the bedroom, Zach took a box of batteries from a shelf above his desk and inserted one into the pouch on the collar. Then Cassidy held the calico on her lap while Zach removed the old collar. Taking off the magnet that operated her cat door, he attached it to the new collar and fastened it around her neck.

He stood back and Cassidy let Starshine go. Digging her hind claws through Cassidy's jeans and into her flesh, the cat launched herself off Cassidy's lap. After scratching at the new collar for a moment, the calico hunkered close to the floor and ran downstairs.

Zach said, "We can test this thing out by seeing if the receiver leads us to her now."

"I've only got fifteen minutes to get ready for my six o'clock client and I'd rather have you wait till I can do it with you."

Cassidy went upstairs to change clothes after her session with Julie was over. She glanced in the computer room and saw that Zach was reading something on the screen and listening to talk radio.

As she went into the bedroom, she checked the time. It was a few minutes past seven and the windows were black. She peeled off her therapist clothes and was standing in her panties and bra when the back doorbell rang.

A client you forgot to write in your calendar? Julie coming back for something?

Cassidy scrambled to put her pants and sweater back on.

"Who's that?" Zach asked, as she passed the computer room.

"Don't know. Maybe a client I overlooked."

She ran down the stairs, hastened from the front of the house to the back, and started to go around the room divider into the waiting room. But just as she stepped inside, she caught a whiff of motor oil. A large man stood with his back flattened against the divider wall. Fear surged through her.

Chapter 31

"Help! Zach! Help!" Screaming, she tried to run, but an arm snaked out and dragged her into the waiting room. A hand stuffed a dirty rag deep into her mouth.

The taste of oil was so strong she started to gag. *You can't throw up! It'll kill you.* Fighting off the nausea, she focused on the man's face. *Omigod! Kenny!*

He gripped her upper arms and jammed her back against the divider. "You dumb cunt! I told you not to go to the police! Now look what you made me do."

She tried to spit out the rag but it was too far back in her mouth. *Dammit, Zach, why'd you have to have that stupid radio on?* Using all her strength, she pulled her lower arms forward and pounded against his barrel chest, which had about as much effect as butterflies dive-bombing a concrete wall. She tried kicking his shins, but that proved just as useless.

He yanked her into the middle of the room and extended his leg behind her legs to trip her. She fell backward. Still holding her arms, he lowered her to the floor, her head touching the divider. She kicked at him and struggled to roll away, but he pressed his knee across her legs and his hands against her shoulders, nearly immobilizing her.

He removed one hand from her shoulder and pulled a white cord out of his jacket pocket. Straddling her stomach, he used both hands to draw the cord behind her head. She whipped her head from side to side in an effort to stop him, but he slapped her right cheek, then her left, hitting her so hard her teeth ached and her head went light and dizzy. Pulling the cord tight, he knotted it over the gag. Cassidy clenched her fists, ready to hit him again.

No, don't, he'll hurt you!

You can't give up!

She punched him in the soft spot just above his jaw, then hit him in the throat. Suddenly she remembered a self-defense move she'd seen on TV. She extended the first two fingers of her right hand and jabbed them into his eyes.

"Fuckin' bitch!" He jerked back away from her, shifting his weight just enough that she could slide out from under him.

She leapt to her feet, ran to the security system panel next to the door, and pressed the panic button, setting off a piercing whistle. *Oh, God, please let Zach hear it.* She stuck her thumb and forefinger as far back in her mouth as she could and wriggled the gag out from beneath the cord that was holding it. As Kenny grabbed her left arm and turned her around, she flung the gag over his shoulder and began screaming for Zach. The whistle kept ringing. Kenny punched her in the mouth, shutting her up, and tripped her again. This time she landed face down.

He sat on her lower back, caught her left wrist, and pulled it behind her. Realizing that he intended to tie her wrists together, she waved her right arm frantically. *If you can just hold out till the police get here.* He pushed her left arm higher, setting off a sharp pain in her shoulder.

"Ow! You're hurting me."

"This is just the beginning."

She stopped moving her right arm and Kenny grabbed her wrist, crossing one over the other. He tried to get a cord around both of them but she kept pulling them apart. Finally he tied the cord around her left wrist, held her left arm down with his knee, and tied her right wrist close to the left. He turned around, sat on her behind, and tied her ankles the same way.

Standing, he thrust his hands into her armpits and lifted her to her feet. He opened the back door and bent down to pull her head and torso over his right shoulder, her legs over his left. Then he stood erect, one hand holding her arms, the other her legs.

Cassidy gasped, her chest so tight she could barely breathe. *Has to kill you. There's no way he could let you go now.*

He went out the door and down the porch steps, then raced toward a big black sedan at the curb. Cassidy raised her head and stared west on Briar. She saw two police cars a block and a half away.

Kenny threw her in the backseat of his sedan and climbed behind the wheel. From the car's rumbly sound, she could tell he'd left the motor running. He stomped on the accelerator and sped toward the cul-de-sac that cut Briar off from Austin Boulevard.

Cassidy heard a siren start up behind him. *Thank God! The police saw him! They know it's a kidnapping.* She squirmed around until she was sitting on the torn vinyl of the car's bench seat. Through the back window she saw one squad in pursuit. Through the front window she saw a line of tall bushes marching across the width of the cul-de-sac. She expected Kenny to turn into the alley behind her house, but instead he shot straight ahead. Her eyes widened and her mouth went dry.

The car lurched as it went over the curb, throwing Cassidy down on the seat. A crash, bushes scraping the windows on both sides of the sedan. Kenny gunned the motor and the car plowed forward over the bush he'd knocked down. As the car bumped over the second curb, Cassidy went rolling to the floor.

She had just managed to drag herself back up on the seat when the sedan burst into the dense traffic on Austin Boulevard. Horns blared and tires squealed as vehicles came to a screeching halt, missing Kenny's car by inches. He charged into the left-turn lane at Chicago Avenue. The light was red but that didn't even slow him down as he sped into the intersection.

Watching two lanes of westbound traffic come rushing at them, Cassidy's heart seized with panic. Amidst a firestorm of horns, the westbound traffic skidded to a stop. It looked like Kenny's car would emerge unscathed. Then she heard a crunch of metal. Her head whipped around and she saw a van skidding away from the sedan's right rear fender. The sedan fishtailed to the left, then rocked violently. Within seconds Kenny had it under control again and was speeding eastward on Chicago Avenue. She looked at the backseat doors, noting that the handles had been removed.

Gotta get your hands out in front of you. He couldn't cross your wrists— that oughta make it easier. She drew her hands under her backside, bent double, and dragged them under her feet. She scrutinized the backseat in search of something she could use as a weapon, but the space was entirely empty. *You had to be kidnapped by someone whose car is much neater than yours.* She looked back again. The squad cars were losing ground. *Cops are under orders not to take risks so Kenny's got the advantage.*

He made an abrupt right turn, throwing her to the floor. She lay on the threadbare carpet facing the driver's seat. The smell of mold and dust made her nose itch. She erupted with three giant sneezes. A thin trickle of mucus began leaking from her nose. She pulled her tied hands up near her chin and extended her right fingers into the gap between the floor and the driver's seat. After feeling around for several seconds, she dragged out a plastic ice scraper attached to a wooden pole. A small bubble of hope rose in her chest.

She drew the pole out six inches but couldn't pull it any farther because her body took up most of the floor space. She tried again, this time drawing it out at an angle. When the scraper bumped into her stomach, she pulled the other end toward her. Once it was all the way out, she could see that she had a two-foot wooden pole with an ice scraper at one end and a sturdy snow brush at the other.

The car was moving at such a high speed the whole chassis bounced and swayed. It took several attempts to hoist herself back on the seat directly behind Kenny.

She reached down for the pole, braced her feet against the bottom of the seat in front of her, and pressed her spine against the backrest. Grasping the ice-scraper end of the pole with her right hand, she pulled it back, then swung the brush at Kenny's head. It hit him squarely in the temple. Blood burbled from the cut, and Kenny's hand flew to the side of his head to cover the wound. The sedan veered sharply to the left.

Cassidy dropped the pole and raised her arms to shield her face. The car jumped the curb and crashed into a wooden porch. She slammed into the back of the driver's seat, then crumpled to the floor. She wasn't exactly unconscious, but her head was swimming and she couldn't form a coherent thought. She didn't even try to move.

* * *

A beat cop opened the back door and touched the base of her neck with a white-gloved hand. "Got a pulse but it's weak."

Cassidy tried to say she was all right, but the only sound she could make was an indistinct mumble.

A second cop-voice came from the front seat. "The asshole's still with us."

From somewhere in the distance, she heard a familiar voice. "I'm her husband. Let me through."

Zach's here! Relief flowed through her. Gotta get yourself off the floor so he doesn't think you're dead. She raised her head and shoulders, dug the fingers of her right hand into a hole in the vinyl, and pulled herself up on her knees. From there she was able to crawl onto the seat.

A moment later he was leaning into the car. "Oh God!" He gently brushed her tangled hair back from her face.

Stretching out her wrists, she croaked, "Cut me loose."

"The police taken pictures yet?"

"No."

"Let me see what I can do." He disappeared into a group of cops, returning with a white photographer and a black plainclothes policeman. The photographer took several shots, then the policeman untied the cords and deposited them in plastic bags.

Two paramedics arrived, one considerably older than the other. The young guy took her pulse. The older guy said, "We need to take you to the hospital. The doc's gonna want to run some tests."

"There's nothing wrong with me except for a few bruises."

"You don't know that. There could be fractures, maybe even a broken bone or a cracked rib. You really need to be examined by a doctor."

"I won't go."

"They're right," Zach said. "You should let a doctor check you out."

Her eyes filled. "I want to go home."

"Then home it is." To the paramedics, Zach said, "As you fellows know, she's got the final say."

"Just a minute," the older paramedic said. He went into the cab of the bus and returned with a form on a clipboard. "If you refuse to go, you have to sign a release from treatment." While she signed, he continued. "If you start to feel dizzy, vomit, have vision changes, severe headaches, or can't walk straight, you should get yourself to a hospital as fast as possible."

"I'll make sure she does," Zach said.

The plainclothes cop stepped forward and introduced himself as Detective Freeman. "I need to take her in to the station for a statement. You can follow in your car if you want."

Zach hooked his thumbs in his jeans waistband. "I'm Zach Moran from the *Post*. We both know you can't make her do anything. Let me talk to her for a minute and then we'll tell you what she's decided."

The detective backed away and Zach leaned his head close to hers. "Could you keep going just a little longer? The sooner they get a statement, the better the chances of locking this asshole up for a good long time."

She desperately wanted to get home and climb into bed, but she knew Zach was right. She told him she'd go to the station.

"Half an hour," Zach said to the detective. "That's all you get. You can come to the house tomorrow and fill in the gaps."

Chapter 32

Clad in her nightshirt, Cassidy sat up in bed with three pillows behind her back. She'd just taken two Tylenol. Zach had offered to get her some Vicodin, and she was so not herself, she didn't even press him to explain why he had a stash of addictive painkillers.

"Anything else I can do?" he asked.

"Bring me some wine. Then I want you to sit here and comfort me and make me feel safe." She wouldn't have taken alcohol on top of Vicodin, but she was fairly certain mixing it with Tylenol would be safe.

He brought up two glasses of wine and sat with his back against the headboard, his knees bent. She wriggled around so she could lean against his knees while he massaged her neck, the least sore part of her body. She told him what she'd been through. When she finished, she was quiet for a while, then added, "I kept screaming and screaming. I was so mad at you for not coming down."

"If only I hadn't had that damn radio on. But even without the radio, I might not have heard you. The computer room's about as far as you can get from the back door."

"How'd you manage to show up at the crash?"

"Two cops answered the alarm. One went after Kenny, the other rang our back doorbell. *That* I was able to hear. He asked some questions, then joined the pursuit. I followed the squads." Zach took a long swallow of wine. "Before you came into my life, I didn't know the meaning of the word 'scared.' But if you keep messing around with thugs like Kenny, I'm headed for a premature heart attack."

A short silence. Then, "Remember when you asked me what I was trying to prove? And I said I didn't know?"

"Yeah."

"It's that I'm strong and tough and not afraid of anything."

"You think that makes you a better person? Acting impervious and invulnerable like I used to do?"

"Yes." A pause. "Well, no, not exactly. But I can't stand letting people scare me out of doing what's right."

"You know, if this act you put on was really convincing, I couldn't love you like I do."

She released a long sigh. "You're right. It is pretty obnoxious. And every time I get myself in trouble, I put you through hell."

"But I don't suppose you're likely to change."

She sighed again. "Probably not."

Awakening suddenly, Cassidy looked at the clock. Two-fifteen. She tried to figure out why she was awake. She didn't need to pee. Her body was sore, but that shouldn't have caused her to wake so abruptly.

A slight creak sounded from below. She turned to look at Zach's pillow and saw he wasn't there. *Probably got up to have a drink.* She didn't think he'd done that since starting his leave of absence. *But you can't blame him after what you put him through.*

She heard his steps on the stairs, then the door opened. He appeared in the doorway, backlit by the sconce on the wall behind him.

"What are you doing up?" she asked.

"I brought you something." He had Starshine in his arms.

"Where'd you find her?"

"In the basement." He put the calico down and she curled up in her usual place near Cassidy's head.

"I couldn't get to sleep," he said, "so I thought I'd try the tracking device. I started outside her cat door, but it led me back into the house and down to the basement. I found her in a box under the stairs."

"You think she's been hiding in the basement instead of visiting some other family?" *In which case you just blew five hundred bucks.*

"Beats me."

The cat purred boisterously.

"She's even going to stay." Cassidy smiled up at her husband. "Finding Starshine is the nicest thing you could have done for me."

Cassidy stood nude in front of a full-length mirror. Although moving exacerbated the pain, she had forced herself out of bed so she could see how bad she looked. Purple splotches were randomly distributed over her face and body. *Least it's winter so you can cover yourself from the neck down. And if you wear enough makeup, maybe nobody'll notice the bruises on your face. Or maybe they will and assume Zach beats you.*

"What're you doing up?" Zach said, coming into the bedroom.

"I know I look awful"—*and feel even worse*—"but there's no reason I can't sit in my chair and see clients."

"Don't you also need to think clearly—something most people can't do when they're in pain?"

"It's not that bad. Well, it is, but I'm sure I can manage three sessions."

"You just went through a severe trauma, and there's no way I'm going to let you act as if nothing happened. You have to rest up for at least one day. That isn't nearly long enough, but it's probably the best I can hope for."

"A few days ago, I was telling you what to do. Now you're telling me, and I don't like it any more than you did."

"If you don't cancel today's clients, I'm going to tie you up, carry you out to the car, and deliver you to the emergency room."

She looked him squarely in the face. From the set of his jaw, she thought he might actually do it. One part of her was pissed as hell, but another was secretly relieved that he wasn't going to let her jump right back into her facade of acting strong.

She spent the morning in bed trying to put thoughts of Renee out of her mind. *Really stupid. Like trying not to think of an elephant.*

It's your fault. If you hadn't gone to the police, Kenny wouldn't be in jail.

He belongs in jail! He's like a loaded gun ready to go off. At least now he'll be locked away for a few years.

Yes, but what about Renee?

"Well, that's about it." Detective Freeman, seated on Cassidy's blue paisley sofa, closed his notepad. He had a chunky build, shaved head, and hooded eyes, with an infectious grin that slipped out only rarely, transforming his face.

Cassidy sat in the small blue chair. Zach had said it would be okay to finish the interview in her robe, but she'd insisted on showering and getting dressed, despite the jolt of pain she felt every time she moved.

"Thanks for the time." The detective started to get to his feet.

"Wait! Did Kenny talk? I want to hear everything that led up to the attack."

Freeman sat back down. "Oh, he talked all right. Said he'd been watching your house ever since you reported him. He observed clients coming and going and figured out that you leave your door unlocked at least some of the time. Which reminds me, I was meaning to talk to you about that."

One more person to give you a hard time about your door.

"If I kept my door locked, clients would have to wait outside—sometimes in the snow or rain—until I could get downstairs and open it. If they arrived early and I was with another client, I'd have to interrupt my session to let them in."

"I hope you lock up when you don't have clients."

You should just lie so he won't think you're nuts.

"It's too hard to remember to unlock every time a client is due. So I don't keep the door locked when I'm home, although we always lock up at night and anytime we're both gone during the day."

His lips tightened into a thin line. "Do you realize how dangerous—"

"Of course I do! Look what just happened to me."

"I hope your recent experience will motivate you to rethink your open door policy."

What? Learn from experience? Not me.

Cassidy said, "You haven't told me why Kenny picked last night to make his move."

"He'd been waiting for the right opportunity. It had to be dark. And it had to be a few minutes after one client left with no other client coming in behind them. And your husband had to be gone. He figured that would be his best shot of catching you alone. He knew there was some risk of Zach showing up, but he thought he'd be in and out so fast the risk would be negligible."

"So why come in when Zach was home? He couldn't have known Zach wouldn't be able to hear me."

"He started watching the house from the other side of the intersection where he could see both the front and back doors. He watched for several days without seeing either of you use the front door, so he assumed you both used the back door exclusively. Then he moved his car closer to the back door so he could get a better look at your comings and goings, but that meant he couldn't see the front. So yesterday he saw your husband leave by the back door and he didn't know Zach had returned."

"The only time Zach uses the front door is when he's bringing in office supplies. So he can carry them straight upstairs. But it didn't matter anyway since Zach couldn't hear me."

"You were lucky." Freeman stood, and so did Cassidy. "No, you were scrappy. A real fighter. I wouldn't want to meet you in a dark alley myself."

After the detective left, Cassidy spent the rest of the afternoon making phone calls in search of an agency that would come to Renee's rescue.

Cassidy scooped up a second square of lasagna, her eyes glistening as she looked at Zach. *You're so lucky to have a husband who knows when you need comfort food and goes out and gets it without being asked.*

Starshine, who'd flattened herself in full stalking mode, had been creeping across the table since the beginning of the meal and now was only an inch from Cassidy's plate. Zach picked her up and deposited her on the floor.

"It never does any good," Cassidy said. "She just climbs back up and starts all over again."

"Eat fast."

"For two smart people, we're spectacularly unsuccessful at disciplining our cat."

"A disciplined cat is an oxymoron."

Starshine jumped onto the far end of the table. Cassidy finished eating, pushed her plate toward the cat, and let her polish it off.

Zach laid his unused napkin next to his plate. "I've been thinking about Kenny. About whether his assault on you makes him more or less of a suspect in Miles' murder."

"My first inclination was to think *more*. Before he attacked me, we had no evidence he'd go beyond stalking. Now we know he's able to escalate pretty quickly from being pissed to stalking to murder. But then I thought about the holes in his plan and I realized he wasn't all that swift."

"Yeah, that's what I was thinking. He should've continued to watch both doors. Duct tape would've been more effective than those cords he used. And he took a big risk leaving his car running in a neighborhood like ours."

Cassidy helped herself to a half-eaten piece of garlic bread on Zach's plate. Plunking her elbow on the table, she said, "The cops think Miles' murder was a professional hit, and Kenny's attempt on my life was definitely amateur. That leaves us with Henry, Tessa, and Andy." She took a bite of the bread. "I suppose any of those three could've hired a hit."

"It's a lot harder than you think. You almost have to be mob connected to get it right."

"So basically what we're saying is, we still don't have a clue."

Later that evening Cassidy was sitting up in bed with a closed book in her lap. She had tried to read, but her brain was so locked into the Marina City disappearances, it refused to take in any words off a page.

She thought about Joan. If she didn't report in promptly about the kidnapping attempt, Joan's anger, already at a high pitch over Cassidy's taking the card, would become even more intense.

You shouldn't have to talk to her now. You've been through this awful ordeal and your body hurts all over.

This is the best time to call. Once Joan hears that you're battered and bruised, she'll have to be nice.

Cassidy found the cordless on Zach's desk, sat back down on the bed, and punched in Joan's number.

"I suppose you're calling to tell me you've been up to more mischief."

"Yeah, I have," Cassidy replied, trying not to sound sarcastic. "I got myself beaten up, thrown in the backseat of a car, and nearly killed."

"What?"

Cassidy dropped her attitude and told Joan the whole story, including her belief that Kenny hadn't killed his father.

"You poor thing," Joan said in a sympathetic tone.

Cassidy cringed. She hated being called a poor thing.

Shifting one of the pillows behind her back, she said, "I don't suppose there's any news about Sandra?"

"The police interviewed her neighbor and me but they, of course, wouldn't answer any of my questions."

"I'm certain Sandra was killed."

"It's been three days since she disappeared and I'd be surprised as all get out if I ever saw her again."

Zach set Cassidy's mug on the nightstand. The aroma of coffee wafted into her nostrils, giving her a reason to try to sit up. But her muscles had stiffened during the night and the pain was even worse than the day before. She dragged her torso upright and lifted the mug with both hands. She needed to pee but wasn't sure her legs would carry her to the bathroom.

"I need a chamber pot," she said to Zach, who was reading the paper at his desk.

He helped her out of bed. "I'll walk you into the bathroom."

Once she was on her feet, it didn't seem so bad. "I'm all right. I just need to move around to get rid of this stiffness."

She took a long hot soak in the tub, then walked up and down stairs until her muscles regained some of their flexibility. By the time her first client arrived, she felt halfway normal.

Chapter 33

She saw her last client out at one, then went upstairs to call Renee.

"How you doing?" Cassidy asked.

"How do you think?" Renee's voice was as bitter as Cassidy had expected it to be.

"I guess you're pretty angry. And you must be devastated by Kenny's arrest."

"None of this would've happened if I hadn't let you in."

"I'm really sorry about the way things worked out. With Kenny gone, it's obvious you're going to have to find another place to live."

"A cardboard box is all I can sort of afford. My SSDI barely pays for a few groceries and my smokes. And don't you dare tell me to quit."

"I've located a woman who can get you into a wheelchair-accessible place."

"I don't need your help!"

That may be the single most ridiculous statement you ever heard.

"How 'bout I come over and bring some food and a couple of cartons of cigarettes. What brand do you smoke?"

"You think I'm gonna let you back in here?"

Cassidy drew an enraged cartoon face on an unopened gas bill envelope. "How many cigarettes do you have left?"

A long silence. "Marlboro."

"Give me a list of the things you need. I'll go shopping, then come to your place."

Renee was seated in her wheelchair next to the Formica table. A roll of toilet paper sat close at hand and wads of used tissue had piled around her chair as if a toilet paper blizzard had just blown through.

Several plastic bags dangled from Cassidy's hands. "Okay if I put these things away?"

"Leave them on the counter. Kenny had to kind of get things off the shelves for me."

After emptying the bags, Cassidy sat in the recliner and turned it to face Renee. "This woman I mentioned on the phone. She's a case manager for the mayor's office of disabilities. When I explained your situation, she said she could put you on emergency status and begin working with you right away." *As if she didn't have about a hundred other cases almost as bad.* Cassidy pictured a large woman dressed in blue tights and a red cape with a big red S on her bosom. *Super Social Worker to the rescue.*

"What's this wheelchair-accessible place you're talking about?"

"A shelter for the disabled. She said it's pretty decent. You'll have your own room and you can stay there until she's able to get you into subsidized housing. She'll also apply to Medicaid for an automated wheelchair." Cassidy fished a slip of paper out of her purse and placed it on the table, noticing that Renee had acquired a dank unwashed smell. "Here's her phone number."

Renee glowered at her out of red-rimmed blurry eyes. "Why did you have to go and lie to the police about Kenny?"

"What did he tell you?"

"You know what you did. When you were here before, you snuck into his room while I was on the phone and he sort of caught you. Naturally he was mad about it and told you where to go. Well, who wouldn't if they found you snooping in their bedroom? Then you lied to the cops and they came here with a search warrant. As if that weren't enough, your husband beat you up, and you lied again and told the police Kenny did it."

Cassidy opened her mouth to defend herself, then snapped it shut. *Renee needs to hold on to every shred of faith she has in her son. Don't you say one word to take it away from her.*

Cassidy stood in front of the sink eating peanut butter cups and gazing through her kitchen window into the kitchen of her neighbors to the south. She watched a couple of dark-skinned teenage boys start to scuffle, the smaller one head-butting his brother. A moment later Dorothy Stein came in and broke up the fight. She and her husband had adopted a large brood of children, their skin tones running from wheat to ebony. Cassidy, an only child, enjoyed sneak peeks of family life through her neighbor's window.

The sky surrounding the window was black. Cassidy took one more Reese's, then put the bag away. Zach was out talking to people in bars. Joan was mad at her for taking Tessa's card. The manager at the Jewel had not returned her call. Starshine was missing and Cassidy didn't want to use the tracking device until Zach was home to do it with her. Her body ached and none of the suspects seemed right.

Upstairs, Cassidy discovered the calico chasing a tiny pink mouse in the hallway.

"What are you doing here? I thought you were visiting your other family. Or hiding in the basement. Whatever it is you do when I can't find you."

Stayed home two nights in a row. Maybe she's over her wanderlust stage.

* * *

A short time later Zach came into the bedroom looking more buoyant than she'd seen him in a long time. "I've got a name," he announced.

"Who is it?"

He glanced at the clock. "Nine-thirty. Not too late to call."

"Can I listen in?"

"Sure. Why not?"

Zach sat at his desk with the cordless and Cassidy held the desk phone receiver to her ear.

A man's voice answered.

"Is this Simon Kulaski?"

"Who wants to know?" the man demanded in the tone people use when they're about to hang up on a telephone solicitor.

"I'm Zach Moran from the *Post.* I was having a beer with Joe Steger tonight and your name came up."

"I don't talk to reporters."

"This isn't about a story. In fact, I'm on a leave of absence right now."

"So why you calling me?"

"Seems like we might have a mutual enemy. According to Joe, you don't like Sam McCready any more than I do."

"Joe's blowing smoke."

"Let me tell you about my situation. I've been at the *Post* fifteen years doing a job I like. Then I get McCready for an editor and everything changes. He's got a grudge against me going way back, and now my job's turned to shit."

If even a whiff of this gets back to the Post, *Zach'll be outta there, like right now.*

"McCready's a shithead."

"Sounds like you and I are on the same page. Could be to our mutual benefit to sit down and talk."

"I don't know anything about you."

"You trust Joe, don't you? He'll vouch for me."

"I been burned by reporters before."

"What've you got to lose? You don't have to tell me anything you don't want to."

They agreed to meet for lunch on Saturday.

Zach clicked off the cordless and turned toward Cassidy. "Interesting comment about being burned by reporters before. His name hasn't appeared in any of the stories McCready wrote for the *Post,* and I don't recall his being mentioned in anybody else's stories either."

"Whatever his reason, he certainly doesn't like McCready."

"Doesn't mean McCready did anything wrong. Lots of people get pissed at journos for telling the truth."

"Joe give you any clue as to what Simon's problem is?"

"Told me he'd heard Simon go off on a rant against McCready more than once. When he tried to find out why Simon was so ticked, Simon shut up."

Cassidy straightened a pile of papers on her desk. "You know anything about Simon?"

"Joe gave me a little background. The guy's been retired for about a year, but before that he worked as a middle manager at Streets and San. A few years ago McCready wrote a series about bribery and cronyism in the department, but the people he exposed were at a much higher level than Simon. Although it's possible he was tight with the guys who got caught and so maybe he blames McCready for sending them to the joint."

"Here's hoping you get something you can use."

"I'm with you on that." Zach opened a magazine lying on his desk. Cassidy settled on the bed with a book.

Starshine ambled into the bedroom, jumped on Zach's desk, and stretched out on top of his magazine. He said to Cassidy, "I was counting on her to leave so we'd have a chance to use that new toy you bought."

"First I was upset at her for going away. Now I'm upset at her for staying home."

Chapter 34

Cassidy finished her coffee, got out of bed, and checked her calendar. *Two clients in the morning, two in the evening, a big gap in between. Way too much time for brooding about the Marina City murders.*

After seeing her morning clients, she tried to bend her mind to thinking about dinner, or filling out paperwork, or cleaning her house, but her mental faculties proved as unyielding as a concrete post. It drove her crazy to have so many unanswered questions. Which of the three suspects would be most likely to have a tie to the mob? Andy and Tessa had an obvious motive to kill Miles, but why would they kill Sandra? What was the meaning of "Our time is coming soon," the phrase Andy had scribbled on the bottom of Tessa's card? Was there any possible motive for Henry, who was, after all, the person whose call had drawn Miles out of his condo.

Even worse than the unanswered questions was the unfilled time. As long as she could run around talking to people, gathering information, filling in gaps, she could stave off the unresolved feeling that had settled over her as soon as her sessions were finished.

You aren't completely out of options. You could confront Andy and Tessa with the card. Unless Joan told them what you did and neither of them is speaking to you.

What good would that do? Even if they admit to having an affair, that doesn't mean they killed Miles, much less Sandra.

Yes, but it certainly would be interesting to see what they have to say. However, you shouldn't do anything until you find out whether Joan ratted you out to Tessa. And you also need to sweet talk Joan into giving you back the card.

Cassidy sat at her desk and dialed Joan's number.

"I've been meaning to see how you're doing," Joan said.

"I'm fine. Well, physically but not mentally. I can't stop thinking about the murders. It feels so unfinished."

"I've been having trouble with that too."

"I was curious what you did with the card."

"Why do you ask?" Joan wanted to know.

"It's the only piece of evidence I haven't followed up on."

"Followed up on how?"

"I was thinking of asking Andy about it."

"And what do you think that would accomplish?"

"Probably nothing." Cassidy piled up the stray paperclips scattered across her desk. "But it's the only loose end I haven't tied up."

"I should have given the card to Tessa and told her what you did."

"So Tessa and Andy don't know?"

"I hate to admit it, but I'm having doubts about Tessa myself. I can't understand why she kept her affair a secret from me. I was always so supportive. I thought she told me everything."

Joan has no idea how judgmental she is.

Cassidy said, "When people feel ashamed of themselves, they sometimes can't tell anybody."

"I checked out Andy's signature and the A's are the same."

"So how would you feel if I showed Andy the card? To see what he has to say about it."

"I wouldn't want Tessa to find out I knew about the card and didn't tell her."

"If you'll give it back to me so I can confront Andy, I won't let on that anybody else has seen it."

"I guess I could go along with that." Joan paused. "Actually, I don't even like having it here. Every time I see it, it makes me wonder what else Tessa is keeping from me."

"Remember me?" Cassidy asked the trim, ginger-haired man who stood in the doorway.

"Didn't you show up here with Joan to ask about the Lunch Bunchers?"

"Can I come in? There's something I'd like to go over with you."

The furrows between Andy's brows deepened. "We don't even know each other. How could you have something to go over with me?"

"If you let me in, I'll tell you."

"As a matter of fact, I'm in a real crunch with work. Maybe some other time."

What happened to that open friendly guy I talked to before? Maybe Tessa discovered the card was missing and told him I'd taken it. Or maybe he really is under pressure from work.

Cassidy moved a half step forward. "This won't take long."

"Oh, all right. But I have to get this project finished today. I can't give you more than five minutes."

He waved her into the living room. Cassidy sat on an easy chair. He perched on the edge of the sofa, looking as if he were ready to give her the old heave-ho the instant her time was up. The only thing he didn't do was stare at his watch.

Cassidy withdrew the card from her purse and held it in front of him.

He looked stunned for an instant, then his jaw clenched in anger. "How did you get hold of that?" he demanded.

"I found it when I was helping Tessa clean up after the cops searched her condo."

"And you just took it?"

"I thought the police might be interested," Cassidy said, refusing to let him put her on the defensive.

His entire demeanor suddenly shifted, as if a switch had gone off inside his head. The earnest expression he'd worn before returned, his brown eyes growing warm and liquid.

"That's the card I gave Tessa. I intended to get a sympathy card but I was in such a hurry I grabbed the wrong one by mistake. I suppose I should've gone back and gotten something more appropriate, but I didn't have time. So I gave her that one and explained the dumb mistake I'd made and we both got a good laugh out of it."

Cassidy's lips compressed. *Can't possibly think I'd fall for anything as lame as that.*

She opened the card, holding it so the inside faced her. "Do you remember what you wrote at the bottom?"

"Not really."

"'Our time is coming soon.' What did you mean by that?"

"Nothing. I don't even remember writing it. I've been under a lot of pressure...doing flaky things. Chalk it up to temporary insanity."

"You can do better than that."

"Look, I know it sounds like there was something going on between us, but there wasn't. We hardly knew each other. I felt sorry for her after Miles was killed and I wanted to make some sort of gesture but I screwed it up. I bought the wrong card and then I wrote that ridiculous message. I suppose I was trying to say something comforting, but whatever it was, it came out all wrong."

Amazing how he can look so sincere and tell such outrageous lies.

"If you and Tessa weren't involved, why would she tape this card to the underside of her desk drawer? You two are clearly having an affair. If you weren't, there'd be no reason for her to keep the card, much less hide it."

"I don't know why she kept it, but the reason for hiding it is obvious. She must've known the cops would search her condo, and she didn't want them jumping to the wrong conclusion."

"You mean the conclusion anyone in their right mind would jump to?"

His expression shifted again, this time to something akin to hostility. "I've told you everything I know. If you choose not to believe me, there's nothing I can do about it."

Jamming the card back in her purse, Cassidy followed the circular corridor to the elevators, then stood in front of them, not sure which button to push. She had intended to talk to both Andy and Tessa, but now she didn't see much point in continuing.

Andy's gotta be on the phone to Tessa right now. That means she'll either refuse to open the door or repeat Andy's story. You have no chance of getting the truth out of her, and she's bound to be pissed at you for taking the card.

Cassidy didn't like to face other people's anger. It made her feel guilty and defensive, even when their anger was unjustified. *Which in this case it isn't. Searching Tessa's desk was a definite breach of privacy.*

But she also had a hard time letting go until she'd seen a situation through to the end. And in this instance, that meant talking to Tessa. She pushed the up arrow.

"Cass. What a surprise. I didn't know you were going to be here today."

Tessa stood back so Cassidy could enter the condo.

Huh? Does this mean Andy didn't call her?

"So what brings you to Marina City?" Tessa closed the door and positioned herself in front of it, arms crossed, feet planted wide.

Cassidy stared. *What the hell is this about?*

"I asked what brings you here, but I already know. It's the card you found when you searched my desk. You realized what a betrayal that was so you came to give it back."

"I thought you might be able to explain what Andy meant when he wrote 'Our time is coming soon.'"

"I'm not going to *explain* anything." Tessa's voice rose in pitch. "Now you give me that card and I'll let you go."

"You can't possibly think you can keep me here by standing in front of the door."

"You're not leaving till I get that card back."

"Oh yes I am. All I have to do is call 9-1-1. Now you really don't want to have to tell the police why you wouldn't let me go, do you?"

"It's your word against mine." Tessa's cheeks were flushed and her large eyes glittered.

Cassidy suspected the younger woman was on the verge of hysteria. She started to reach for her cell, then hesitated. Tessa was taller and heavier than Cassidy, and possibly unstable enough to attack her. Cassidy's mouth went dry. She absolutely didn't want to get beaten up again. *But Tessa's not a street fighter. Probably as unnatural for her to get physical as it would be for you.*

She held her purse in front of her and reached inside for her cell. Tessa charged forward, grabbed Cassidy's purse, and tried to take it away from her. Wrapping both arms around it, Cassidy clutched it to her chest. Tessa yanked and yanked but couldn't loosen Cassidy's grip. After several seconds of struggling, she gave up, took a step backward, and sagged against the wall.

"How could you do this to me?" Tessa's eyes filled. "I thought you were my friend. You pretended you wanted to help, but you were just looking for a chance to sneak around behind my back."

"No, really, I did want to help. It never even occurred to me to look through your things until you went down to the store and I accidentally knocked everything off your desk. I just acted on impulse. I know I shouldn't have done it, but now that I've got the card, I can't just give it back."

"What are you going to do with it?"

"I haven't decided."

Tessa gave her a baleful look.

She knows you're going to give it to the police.

"The message Andy wrote. It's not what you think. He gave me the card after Miles was dead. He was just trying to say that with Miles gone, we can bring our relationship out into the open as soon as the police quit investigating."

Feeling shaky inside, Cassidy managed to hold herself together until she reached a curving padded bench in the underground lobby. She sank down, took deep breaths, and waited for her legs to stop quivering. Once she was calmer, she realized she ought to check in with Joan before she left the building. *What are you going to tell her? No need to embarrass Tessa by letting Joan know how out of control she was. Everybody's got a breaking point and Tessa's obviously hit hers.*

Cassidy called Joan and recounted the lies Andy had told her.

"Just because he's trying to cover up an affair doesn't mean he killed anybody. After all, a gentleman is never supposed to kiss and tell."

"I agree. The fact that they're having an affair doesn't necessarily mean anything." Cassidy paused. "Oh, by the way, have you talked to Henry?"

"I left a couple of messages on his machine and never heard back. But then Henry strikes me as the type who wouldn't bother unless he felt like it."

Chapter 35

When Cassidy got home, she wrote a note to Roloff explaining where she'd found the card, then put the note and the card in a brown envelope addressed to the detective. *Boy, will he be mad. Won't be able to order you down to the station, force you to give a statement, or yell at you for playing detective. Now all you have to do is screen your calls for the next year or so.*

She was just getting up from her desk when the phone rang. *But you don't have to start screening them yet.* She sat back down and picked up the receiver.

"It's me," a childlike voice said.

"Delia?" The caller ID displayed a name Cassidy didn't recognize. "Where are you?"

"I'm in a good place now. A safe place. The Dark Angels follow me wherever I go, but now that I'm safe it's easier to fight them off. Sometimes they quiet down enough I can almost hear my own thoughts. That's why I called you. I was feeling lonely and I remembered how nice you were. Except the time you brought the police to that abandoned building."

Cassidy started to protest, then remembered she wasn't supposed to argue with Delia's delusions. "You're lonely?" She read the name on the screen. "But aren't you staying at the Kapp's house?"

"Nobody knows the trouble I've seen," Delia sang in a mournful voice. "Nobody knows but Jesus."

"Tell me how I can help."

"There isn't any help. The Dark Angels are everywhere. The whole world is doomed. But Mom told me the Virgin Mary would protect me as long as I have my rosary. And she'll protect you, too, because you have white magic."

"Since I have white magic, maybe I could visit you. Then you wouldn't be alone."

Silence on the other end.

"Delia? Are you there?"

The schizophrenic woman didn't answer, but Cassidy could hear the sound of breathing. She made several more attempts to engage Delia, but after a minute passed with no response, she wrote down the name and number displayed on the caller I.D. and disconnected.

Cassidy went into the computer room to talk to Zach, who was jotting down names on a notepad.

"Whatcha doing?" She planted her posterior in the chair beside his.

"Trying to think of people I can trust to keep their mouths shut. I'm running a little low on buddies I can count on."

"You're seeing Simon tomorrow. Maybe he'll dish the dirt you need."

"And maybe he won't. I need plans B, C, and D."

"How'd you like to take a break and work on my Delia problem?"

Zach set his pad aside and swiveled to face her. "I heard the phone. Was that her?"

"Yep. According to our caller ID, she was at the house of somebody named Kapp."

"Any idea how she managed that?"

"Um...she broke into Kapp's place and is holding him or her hostage?... Kapp took pity on Delia and invited her to move in?...I really can't imagine."

"Let's see the phone number."

Cassidy laid the paper with the name and number on it in front of Zach.

He rolled his chair closer to his monitor and Cassidy stood to look over his shoulder. He pulled a reverse directory website out of his favorites and typed in Kapp's number. *Lynn Kapp*, followed by her address, popped up on the screen. Next he Googled her name. A Chicago law firm topped the list of hits. Lynn appeared as a partner on the firm's website. Her name did not show up on any of the other links.

Leaning back, Zach folded his hands on his chest. "We could drive over and see what's going on."

Cassidy looked at her watch. Five-thirty, and the windows were already dark. She never quite got used to how early night fell during the winter.

"I think we should try to talk to Lynn Kapp first. I'd much rather know what the situation is than go in cold."

"Partners in law firms usually don't get home this early."

"I'll leave a message for her to call me—that is, unless Delia picks up, in which case I don't know what I'll do. If we don't hear back by eight, I think we should go to her house."

Cassidy got Lynn Kapp's answering machine: "My name is Cass McCabe. I've been trying to locate Delia Schiff, and according to my caller ID she phoned me today from your house. Please get back to me and let me know if she's staying with you."

The phone rang at seven-thirty.

"This is Lynn Kapp. I haven't seen Delia in almost twenty years and I'm at a complete loss as to how she could have gotten into my house and used my phone."

"Are you Delia's cousin?"

"What's your connection to Delia? How'd you know she has a cousin?"

"My husband and I own a condo at Marina City. Last summer, when she was stabilized on medication, she rented our condo and she and I got to know each other. Then, a few weeks ago, she went off her meds and had a psychotic break. She called me to come help her, then ran away, leaving all her possessions in our condo. As far as I know she's been homeless ever since. From time to time she's called me and I've tried to get her into a hospital, but she's always slipped away. The reason I guessed you're her cousin is that her therapist told me you're the only family she has."

"Did her therapist mention that I threw her out of my house and told her I never wanted to see her again?"

"She did say something about that." Cassidy jiggled a pen between her fingers.

"Delia's parents were wonderful people. Saints to endure all the misery she put them through. After they died, I felt I owed it to them to take her in. I did my best but she was impossible to live with. The day she came after me with a knife was the day I gave up on her. But now you're telling me she's somehow intruded into my life again."

"You have any idea how she could've gotten into your house?"

"There's no sign of a break-in, so she must've found the key I hide near the back door. Once she was gone, I had the locks changed and stopped keeping a key outside. But after several years with no contact, I thought it'd be okay to leave one out again."

"When she called today, she told me she was in a safe place."

"What are you saying? That she didn't just use the phone and leave? That she's still here in my house? That's impossible."

"Are you sure? Is there any place she might be able to hide?"

"Omigod! The attic! It's such a jumble up there, I don't know how she'd even find room....but now that I think about it, there've been several times when food was missing from my refrigerator. I assumed I'd eaten it and couldn't remember, and then I started to worry that my memory was going...and that old sweater I wear around the house. It simply disappeared from my closet."

"So there's a good chance she's in your attic."

"Oh God, she may've been there for weeks and I didn't know about it. She could've murdered me in my bed. I'll call 9-1-1 right away."

"I hate to think of her being dragged off by the police. My husband and I were planning to come get her and take her to the hospital. She trusts me. I think I can convince her to come with us." *Oh yeah? Like you convinced her the other two times?*

"It's too risky. You don't know how violent she can be."

"Please let me try to talk her down first. After all, it isn't her fault she acts this way. It's the illness. She's the real victim here."

"What about me? I don't care if she's a victim. I don't want her coming after me again and I don't want her trashing my house."

"Please. She's been through so much already."

"You're trying to guilt me into doing what you want. Oh hell, I guess I can hold off on calling the police until you've had your chance at her."

Cassidy found Zach in the kitchen preparing a plate of cheese and crackers for an early evening snack. Starshine stood nearby scarfing down the crumbles of cheese he'd sprinkled on the counter as a bribe to keep her away from his plate.

"I just talked to Lynn Kapp. Turns out she's Delia's cousin and Delia's been hiding in her attic. Apparently she comes out when Lynn's at work and helps herself to food and the phone." Cassidy told him everything Lynn had said.

"An attic, huh? Should be easy for the cops to subdue her there." Zach put the wedge of cheddar in the fridge and the box of crackers in the cupboard, ignoring the mess he'd made on the counter.

Now you have to explain the dumb thing you just did. "You're probably going to think I'm nuts, but I persuaded Lynn to let us take a shot at getting Delia out of the attic before she calls the cops. It'd be so much easier on her if we could take her to the hospital instead of having to be hauled in by the police."

"You're right. I do think you're nuts." He popped a cracker with a slice of cheese on it into her mouth. "You tried to get her to go with you twice before and both times she took off like a cat with its tail on fire."

"Yes, but now she's in an attic. If you block the bottom of the stairs, she won't be able to leave. That'll give me time to convince her that you and I are the White Angels her mother sent to whisk her away from the Dark Angels."

Skepticism spread over Zach's face. "Do you have any idea how strong schizophrenics can be? I know a big brawny cop who tried to take one in and she punched him out along with two other officers."

"Yeah, I know. I've heard the same stories."

He took some time consuming a couple of cheese-and-crackers. "So what's the real reason you want us to go up against a schizophrenic instead of calling the cops? Is it that proving-yourself thing again?"

Cassidy grimaced. "You're starting to sound like a therapist."

"Occupational hazard of living with one."

She searched inside her head. "I think I'm trying to make up for the fact that I screwed up so badly at the beginning. Before Delia moved into the attic, she had to live on the streets in below-freezing weather because I was more interested in looking for evidence than getting her into a hospital. I didn't do any of the things her therapist told me to do."

"So this is all your fault?"

"Are you in or out?"

"What do you think?"

Chapter 36

"We'll need flashlights." Zach removed two from the hall cabinet, which was stuffed beyond capacity with a wide variety of items they had nowhere else to put. One was a mag light, the kind cops carry; the other a regular household size. Zach handed the mag light to Cassidy.

"This is heavy enough to use as a weapon. If Delia attacks, aim for her head."

"She isn't going to attack," Cassidy said, refusing to listen to the voice in her head that told her she had no idea what Delia might do.

Zach's lips pressed into a thin line. "You know, I think I'll call 9-1-1 myself and send the cops to get Delia."

"What?"

"Lynn told you Delia came after her with a knife. I just finished telling you about a schizophrenic who inflicted serious damage on three cops. You're obviously in complete denial about how dangerous this gig could get."

"She's always run away. She's never tried to hurt me. I have white magic, don't forget."

"Look, I know all about denial. Believe me, I've done my share of it. This is not a situation you can afford to go into with your eyes shut. Unless you snap out of it, I'm not letting you leave the house."

"You think you can stop me?"

"You bet I can."

Cassidy nearly gaped at her husband. Zach had never before tried to physically stop her from doing anything. *Which means you probably are in denial.* She suddenly remembered how Delia had come at her the first time she'd mentioned hospitalization.

"Okay, I'll use the flashlight to protect myself if I have to."

"We're also taking duct tape."

"Yeah, I suppose we should."

They drove to Albany Park, a neighborhood on the northwest side of the city. The housing was mixed: bungalows, two-flats, and large well-kept homes that smacked of wealth. Zach parked in front of a large Queen Anne. The snow had melted except for a dirty mound along the fence to the south of the yard.

Lynn Kapp stepped aside so they could come into her quarry-tiled foyer. A soft light emanating from an antique brass fixture filled the spacious entryway. An Oriental vase stood in an arched niche on one wall.

Cassidy introduced Zach to the lawyer.

"Nice to meet you." He extended his hand.

Lynn, clad in a dark red pantsuit, gave it a firm shake. Her hair was pulled back in a tight roll, her eyes were steely, her mouth was pinched. Cassidy couldn't imagine her loosening up enough to enjoy a hearty laugh.

Lynn shook her head. "I shouldn't have let you talk me into this."

"Just think how nice it'll be if we can convince Delia to come with us," Cassidy replied. "So much better than having squad cars with flashing lights and sirens converge on your house."

Cassidy took off her coat. *This woman's so programmed to follow the rules, she'd never be so rude as to refuse to take our coats. And once our coats are in her closet, she's not going to tell us to leave.*

Reaching for Cassidy's coat, Lynn asked Zach if he'd like her to take his as well.

"No thanks, I'll keep it on. In case I have to grab the duct tape out of my pocket."

Lynn looked at Cassidy. "I thought you said you could get her to go quietly."

"We don't know what's going to happen," Zach replied. "If you show us your attic stairs, we'll take it from there."

"I hate for anybody to see my attic. It's really a mess. I keep thinking I need to hire someone to help me clean it out, but I'm always so busy."

"Don't worry about it," Cassidy said. "My house is a mess too."

"I never should have put those boxes up there, but it's so hard to throw away things that've been handed down through the generations."

"I can understand why you wouldn't want us to see it, but it's the only way to get Delia out of there."

"All right. I'll take you to the stairs."

They went up a staircase with an oak railing. When they reached the top, they were in the middle of a long hall that ran the length of the house. Turning to the left, Lynn led them past two open doors, then stopped at a closed door located about twelve feet from the east end of the house.

"This is it," she told them.

Cassidy said to Zach, "I need to go upstairs and try to coax Delia down, and you need to stop her from getting away."

"I'll pull the door all the way open and stand against it. That way if she comes busting out of the attic and runs down the hall, I'll be behind her. Much better to be to the rear of a raging bull than in front of it."

Lynn said, "I'll just stand back out of the way." She crossed her arms and leaned against the east wall.

"Now before you go up there," Zach said to Cassidy, "you've got to promise you'll yell for help if she even looks like she might attack you."

Cassidy frowned briefly, then nodded. She never liked anyone laying down the law to her but she knew he was right.

Carrying the large flashlight, she flipped the switch and went up the narrow, dimly lit stairway. As she neared the top, she could see tall piles of boxes extending in all directions. She stepped onto the bare floorboards and studied the layout. Two diagonal paths branched out from the stairway. A single bulb hung from the center of the steeply pitched roof.

On the outside, Lynn's this slick, totally in control professional. On the inside, she's a packrat.

Taking a deep breath, Cassidy called out softly, "Delia, it's me, Cassidy. I've come to visit so you won't be alone."

She listened for several beats but there was no response.

"You don't have to come out. Just say something and I'll find you."

All she could hear was the sound of her own breathing.

Cassidy shivered from the cold air in the attic. Not being able to see over the tops of the boxes made her feel trapped and claustrophobic. She absolutely didn't want to leave the safety of the stairway.

The pathway to the left led toward the east end of the house. The pathway to the right led toward the center of the room where the bulb was hanging. Cassidy headed toward the light. As she moved forward, she glimpsed an open area in front of her, which turned out to be a circular area containing old pieces of furniture: a floor lamp with a torn silk shade; a wooden rocker; a couple of trunks; two easy chairs with missing seat cushions. On the opposite side of the circle were two more pathways, one leading toward the back of the house, the other toward the west end.

"I thought you could use some of my white magic," Cassidy said to the invisible Delia. "If you just let me know where you are, I'll share it with you."

Again, no answer.

Cassidy started down the path that took her toward the back of the house, a shadowy area beneath the steep pitch of the roof. She had gone only a short distance when she began to notice an unpleasant odor. She stopped and sniffed the air, but the smell was too faint to identify. She took a few more steps and stopped again. This time she could detect the smell of body odor, urine and feces. She examined the boxes on both sides of the aisle. Gradually she was able to discern that the boxes to her right were arranged in such a way that a medium-sized one on the floor could be removed without the others falling down. Her scalp prickled.

"Delia, I'm right outside your door. My magic led me to you. Would it be all right if I come in?"

The removable box inched its way out into the path. *Does this mean she wants me to join her? But if I crawl through that hole, I'll be completely at her mercy.* Swallowing, Cassidy shifted her weight from one foot to the other. *Just do it. There's no backing down now.*

She pushed the box out of the way, got down on all fours, the mag light in her hand, and crawled halfway into an open space behind the boxes. The darkness was so thick she felt as if she'd been transported to the other side of the moon.

"Is it okay if I come in?" she asked, repeating herself.

"Can you really give me some of your magic?"

"Didn't I say so?" Cassidy emerged into Delia's house. The floor felt soft and spongy. She guessed that Delia had feathered her nest with blankets and quilts she'd found by treasure hunting through the boxes. The air was so fetid Cassidy had to breathe through her mouth for the first few moments.

"Would you mind if I turned on my flashlight?"

"No, wait."

There was a rustling sound, then the space was illuminated by a boudoir lamp on a small wooden table with curved legs. Delia sat next to the table, the missing chair cushions beneath her derriere and behind her back. They were in a rectangular area about four by six feet, a couple of flat boxes covering the top. Cassidy was sitting on a large pile of quilts that lay against one of the six- foot walls, an ancient bed pillow on top of the quilts. Two coffee cans, which she assumed were the source of the stench, occupied one corner. Directly opposite the opening she'd crawled through was another opening about the same size.

"How are you going to give me your magic?" Delia asked.

Cassidy crawled into position in front of Delia, sat Indian fashion on the floor, and reached out toward the other woman. "Put your hands in mine."

Delia grasped Cassidy's hands.

"Squeeze tight, close your eyes, and just feel the magic flow like an electric current from my body to yours."

Cassidy made a humming sound for about a minute, then let go of Delia's hands. "Now you have the same white magic I do."

"I don't feel any different."

"You can't actually feel the magic, but it's like an invisible shield. It'll keep the Dark Angels from hurting you."

Delia offered a wobbly smile. Her greasy hair hung in jagged points and her gray-tinged face looked puffy. Cassidy noted a scattering of small red bumps on her face and hands and wondered if they were flea bites.

"This is your cousin's house, isn't it?"

A suspicious look came over Delia's face. "How'd you know that?"

"People with white magic know things. This is a wonderful place you've built for yourself. So much better than where you were before."

Delia began rocking back and forth. "Nobody knows the trouble I've seen," she sang again.

"One of the reasons I came is, I thought you might want to go somewhere even better than this. A place that's bigger and warmer."

Delia tensed, her eyes narrowing, her back going ramrod straight.

Cassidy held her breath for a moment, then let it out slowly. "Your cousin found out you're living here. She's going to call the cops unless you leave. The only way to save yourself is by coming with me."

"No! You can't make me!" Lunging forward, Delia scuttled toward the square hole opposite the one Cassidy had come through. She dove into the aperture.

Oh shit! There's no way I'm going in there.

Oh yes you are. You can't let her get away when you've come so close.

Cassidy sat frozen for a beat. Then, switching on the flashlight and gripping it in her right hand, she followed Delia into the hole, which turned out to be a tunnel. Shining the light ahead, she caught a glimpse of Delia making a sharp right turn.

What if she comes out the other end and hides among the boxes?

Cassidy tried to crawl faster but the mag light slowed her down. The wooden floor jarred her knees and a splinter embedded itself in her palm. Her head bumped the top of the tunnel, her elbows rubbed the sides.

She made another turn and the end of the tunnel came into sight. Dragging herself out of it, she realized she was in one of the paths leading to the stairs. At the end of the path, Delia was disappearing into the stairwell.

"Zach!" Cassidy yelled. "She's coming toward you." Cassidy followed in Delia's wake. By the time she reached the bottom of the stairs, there was no sign of either Delia or Zach. Cassidy raced after them, arriving at the second staircase in time to see her husband running toward the open front door.

Chapter 37

Cassidy dashed downstairs and out onto the porch, catching a glimpse of Zach as he rounded the corner of the house. Doing her best to keep up, she aimed her flashlight at Zach's moving body. He was now only a short distance behind Delia.

He threw himself onto Delia's back, pushing her to the ground. Cassidy sprinted toward the thrashing bodies, hoping Zach would be able to hold Delia down, but the woman rose onto her hands and knees and dislodged him. He jumped to his feet and pushed her over onto her back. She kicked, threw punches, and screamed. One of her fists landed in his eye.

Standing in back of her head, Zach grabbed at her wrists. First he caught her right wrist, then her left. He twisted one arm over the other and rolled her onto her stomach.

"Get the duct tape out of my pocket," he yelled at Cassidy.

Dropping her flashlight, she yanked it out.

"Now sit on her ass."

Delia squirmed and struggled as Cassidy plunked down on top of her.

Even in the faint light Cassidy could see a sheen of sweat on Zach's forehead as he forced a still screaming Delia to bend her right arm behind her back. Cassidy wrapped tape around her wrist, then waited as Zach pressed the second wrist up close to the first. She twisted the tape around and through and over until the wrists were tightly bound together. Then she stood and put the tape back in Zach's pocket.

He leaned over, hands on his knees, head down, and huffed and puffed for several seconds. Then he pulled himself upright and blew out a cloud of white air. "Next time I get a new tenant I'm not letting you near her."

Grasping Delia's upper arms, he hauled her to her feet. He stood behind her and lifted her arms as a way to steer her.

"You dickhead...you prick...you mother fucker," Delia shrieked at him.

"Let's put her in the car," Cassidy said. "Then I need to get my coat and talk to Lynn." Now that her adrenaline was draining away, she could feel the cold biting into her flesh.

As they started toward the street, a short, corpulent woman with frizzy hair stepped out in front of them. "You stay right where you are."

Cassidy's gaze zoomed in on the gun the woman was holding in both hands, nice and steady, as if she knew how to use it.

"They're trying to kill me," Delia wailed.

"Now don't you worry, hon. The police are on their way."

"This woman is schizophrenic," Cassidy said. "I'm a friend of hers and I've been trying to get her into a hospital for weeks."

"We'll just let the police sort this out," replied the gun-toting neighbor.

"It's okay, Babs," Lynn said, approaching from the front. "Delia's my cousin and she really is psychotic. She's been living in my attic for I don't know how long, and Cass and her husband came to take her to the hospital. When she gets violent like this, she has to be restrained."

"Well...if you say so." The neighbor lowered her pistol.

Lynn handed Cassidy her coat. "I never thought you'd be able to get her out of there. But you did, and I'm glad I didn't have to deal with the police."

"I'm sorry to have to tell you this," Babs said, "but the cops will be here any minute."

Cassidy and Zach put Delia, who was now talking to the Dark Angels, into the back seat of the Subaru. He clicked the child-proof locks.

"Where to?" He turned on the engine.

"Northwestern Hospital."

They heard sirens as they pulled away from the curb.

"Since she doesn't have an insurance card, won't Northwestern ship her off to a state hospital?"

"Given how rich she is, I'm sure she has insurance. She may not know the name of her carrier, but her therapist will. I'll give the intake worker Sue Bolas's number, and Sue should be able to straighten it out."

Zach drove for several blocks. Then, "I'm sure Delia appreciates the fact that we didn't let the cops manhandle her."

Saturday afternoon Cassidy sat at the dining room table trying to decide what to cook for dinner. She was sorting through a pile of recipes she'd clipped from the *Post,* all chosen because they appeared under the heading "quick and easy." She scanned a honey-ginger-chicken recipe, accompanied by an enticing photo of pieces of chicken surrounded by colorful vegetables. Ten ingredients were listed, most of which had to be chopped. Fifteen minutes was cited as the prep time.

It'd take fifteen minutes to get out the utensils and ingredients, not to mention the hour or so of shopping. She skimmed through the rest of the pile, discovering that all the recipes required more time than she wanted to put into a simple dinner.

So what now? Spaghetti for the third week in a row?

Hearing the back door close, she went into the kitchen, eager to find out what Zach had learned from his lunch with Simon, the guy who disliked McCready as much as Zach did.

She scrutinized her husband's face, ignoring the raw red crescent beneath his left eye, the shiner Delia had given him. His eyes were bright, his mouth spread in his trademark easygoing smile.

"What did he say?" she probed.

"Looks like McCready may be on his way out."

"Don't play with me. I want details."

"You need to learn a little patience."

"No, I don't. I just need for the world not to make me wait."

"Let me get a beer, then we can sit in the living room and I'll tell you the whole story."

"From the way you smell, I'd say you had a few already."

What's that? Bitchiness for bitchiness's sake? You can see he's perfectly okay.

"Three. Simon needed a little lubrication before he was willing to talk." Zach grabbed a Heineken's out of the refrigerator and pried off the cap.

They went into the living room. A cold draft leaked in around the edges of the west-facing picture window. A thin layer of snow, already blemished by muddy footprints, had fallen earlier in the day. Cassidy glimpsed a glowing orange ball through the bare tree tops on the opposite side of the street.

Zach said, "Remember I told you McCready wrote a series exposing corruption in Streets and San? And that Simon was a middle manager whose name didn't come up? Well, in the course of researching his story, McCready discovered that

Simon, a married man, was sleeping with a coworker. Now something like this would never be considered newsworthy, but it did make excellent blackmail material. McCready demanded fifty K to keep quiet and Simon had to take out a loan on his house to pay the asshole off."

"I knew he was scum. It was obvious from the way he treated his best reporter. But if Simon was willing to pay that much to keep his affair a secret, why tell you?"

"Because everything's different now. The reason he paid McCready off was to protect his wife. She died a while back and he married the coworker. So now he doesn't have anything to hide."

"Protect his wife? I'd say it was more about protecting himself. His pension and his assets."

"The really good part is, he taped his phone conversations with McCready. He always hoped that someday he'd be able to use those tapes to bust the bastard, but the statute of limitations has run out, so Simon won't be able to bring any legal action. However, there's no doubt he'll be able to get McCready's ass canned."

"That's wonderful!" Elation bubbled up inside her. "You set out to find a way to get rid of that lowlife McCready and you succeeded. Now you can get back to doing the job you love."

"Things are definitely looking up. That is, if Simon's able to tell his story without letting my name slip."

"Did he say anything about the black eye?"

"First thing he asked was if I'd been in a barroom brawl. I said I'd tangled with a schizophrenic and that seemed to satisfy him."

"I don't understand why Simon didn't press charges before the statute ran out."

Zach smiled a sardonic smile. "Maleness. Guys hate to admit they fucked up. It was only after I got down on myself for letting McCready walk all over me that Simon told me what he did. All these years he's been blaming himself for getting drunk and blabbing about his girlfriend to some guys from work."

"If Simon has such a hard time talking about it, how do you know he won't back out?"

"I think he feels a connection with me and won't want to let me down. But to be absolutely sure, I told him I'd go to his house Monday morning, give him the name of the Public Information guy—that's the person who takes complaints—and stand there while he calls and explains why he needs an appointment. After the first guy hears what Simon has to say, he'll kick it upstairs and then the Public Editor will schedule an appointment. Once the appointment's nailed down, Simon's the kind who'll follow through."

"So we might be able to get our normal lives back fairly soon? What an idea."

Zach leaned forward, his arms resting on his legs. "I think I should tell you about Simon's wife." He gazed at the floor, letting the silence stretch out. "During the first part of their marriage, they were pretty happy. A lot like us. Then she got depressed. Simon never could figure out what brought it on, but he could see her sinking into a black hole. She cried a lot, wasn't interested in sex, didn't want to talk to anybody. About all she did was sleep and sit in a dark room watching TV."

Taking a deep breath, Zach let it out slowly. "Simon tried to get her to talk to her doctor or see a therapist, but she refused, and after that he didn't know what to do. He went through all these emotional swings—angry, scared, lonely, guilty.

After a while, he started blaming his wife and then he got to feeling like he deserved some happiness for himself. That's when he hooked up with this woman at work. But he told me that even after he started sleeping with her, he still loved his wife. So when McCready threatened to tell her about the affair, Simon was afraid she couldn't handle it. He really *was* trying to protect her."

"I'm absolutely blown away that this guy who didn't want to tell you anything opened up so much about his feelings."

"It's my job to get people to say more than they intended."

"How'd his wife die?"

"Single car accident."

A short silence.

Zach gave himself a shake and turned to Cassidy. "You have anything planned for the next couple hours?"

"Just cooking dinner."

"What're you talking about? It's date night. Plus we have something to celebrate. We're going to the nicest restaurant that'll take us without reservations."

She smiled, not the least bit sorry to forgo choosing a menu, shopping, and preparing. It occurred to her that learning to cook had been a bad idea.

Zach stood, reached for her hands, and pulled her to her feet. As she leaned against him, he wrapped his arms around her.

They went upstairs, put on a Ray Charles CD, threw off the bedcovers, and dropped their clothing to the floor. Zach came up behind her and fondled her breasts. Turning around, she put her arms around his neck and brought his open mouth down against hers. As his tongue probed the inner lining of her mouth, she felt a mounting sense of urgency.

After they made love, they lay exhausted, her body spooned against his. A long time passed, then Cassidy opened her eyes and moved a few inches away from him. It was always hard to pull back into her own skin once they had melded into each other.

"You ready to get up?" Zach asked.

"Uh huh."

"I'd like for us to sit in bed and talk a little."

"Okay."

A few minutes later they were sitting with pillows behind their backs, a glass of wine in their hands. Zach wore his robe. Cassidy had slipped on her nightshirt.

He took a large swallow. "When I was in that funk, did you feel like Simon did?"

"He pretty much nailed it."

"During all those weeks, we didn't have sex." Zach ran a hand over his face. "It never occurred to me how much I was depriving you."

"You mean because we didn't have sex?"

"Yeah."

He already feels bad about it. Don't rub it in.

She laid her hand on his thigh. "Not having sex was the least of it. I missed your energy, your vitality. The kind of talking we do. The way you make me feel loved. And I was scared to death you wouldn't come out of it. But that wasn't the worst. The worst was how pissed I was that you wouldn't get help."

"If I ever get that way again, I want you to hire a couple of big lugs and have them drag me in to see a psychiatrist."

Chapter 38

They ate at Philander's, then stopped at a movie rental place. As Cassidy came through the back door, Starshine jumped down from one of the waiting room chairs and rolled on the floor to greet her. Cassidy sat on her heels to scratch the cat's cheek, then stood and gazed at the seat cushion Starshine had just vacated. It sported three muddy paw prints and an accumulation of cat hair. Cassidy doubted that any client would be willing to lower their tush onto that seat. She knew she ought to wash the cushions more often but had trouble holding onto the thought.

Starshine ran through the kitchen and jumped onto the counter next to her bowl. *Mwat,* she said in a wheedling tone.

Cassidy dished up food from a freshly opened can. The calico took one sniff and walked away.

"You drive me nuts! Yesterday you loved this stuff and today you won't touch it. There's no way to ever know what you want."

After Cassidy and Zach watched the movie, she went through the house searching for Starshine. Failing to find her, she returned to the bedroom and said to Zach, "She's either in the basement or visiting her other family. This seems like a perfect time to get out the tracking device."

Zach retrieved the box from the computer room and set it on his desk. "Since I already had a chance to use it, you should have the honor this time."

She assembled the gear, went out in the hall, and turned the antenna in a slow circle. The beeps were loudest when she faced the stairs. With Zach at her heels, she followed the sounds to the cat door. As she moved away from it, the beeps grew fainter.

"Starshine's outside," Cassidy said. "I bet she's going to lead us to her sneak-thief other family."

They put on their coats and went outside. The tracking device took them from the cat door to a stucco two-flat three houses down from theirs on the opposite side of Hazel. A dull light seeped through the blinds covering the large front window. They stopped at the foot of the steps leading to a low concrete porch.

Cassidy pulled off her earphones and let them dangle around her neck. "This must be where our darling little vagabond has been spending her nights."

"Didn't we meet the people who live here at the block party last summer?"

"I think so. I seem to remember a woman on the first floor and two gay guys on the second."

"Since the lights are on, she's probably still up. Let's go read her the riot act for stealing our cat."

Cassidy pressed the doorbell, pressed again, and then pressed a third time. "She either isn't home or isn't answering."

"She'll answer. You just keep punching that bell till she can't stand it a minute longer."

After two more rings, Cassidy heard the scritchy sound of the lock unlocking, then the door moved inward an inch.

"Don't you ever give up?" a woman's voice asked in a surprisingly good-natured tone.

"We need to talk," Zach replied.

The woman opened the door a few more inches and stood in the crack. "Talk about what?"

"Our cat," Zach said.

"And why you've been luring her away from us," Cassidy added, still holding the tracking device.

"Oh shoot. I didn't think you'd be able to find me. And I never imagined you'd go to such high-tech lengths to do it."

She was not much taller than Cassidy, with loose straggly hair dyed an unrelenting black. The hair looked harsh and unnatural next to her jovial, softly wrinkled face. She wore a scruffy robe over faded pajamas.

"Can we come in?" Cassidy asked. "We really do need to talk about what's been going on here."

"How 'bout I just give you back your cat and we don't talk?"

"I want to know why you did it."

"Oh, all right. You can come in." The woman opened the door wide and stood against the wall so they could file past her. "Just go on into the living room."

Cassidy and Zach seated themselves on a shabby brocade sofa, Cassidy depositing the tracking device next to her feet. The woman took a chair on the opposite side of a scarred wooden coffee table. She picked up a blanket from the table and spread it across her lap. "You might want to keep your coats on. I turn the thermostat down pretty low."

Cassidy glimpsed movement out of the corner of her eye. Starshine was emerging from behind a shelving unit against the wall to their right. The calico wandered around the perimeter of the room, hid behind the blanket on the woman's lap, then came over to sniff Cassidy's shoes. Looking up out of moist green eyes, she hopped onto Cassidy's lap and purred ardently.

Thank goodness she picked me. If Straggly Hair had won, I'd be the scorned woman that hell hath no fury like.

"Okay," the older woman said, "you caught me catnapping your cat. So sue me."

Cassidy said, "Let's start at the beginning. I'm Cass McCabe and this is my husband, Zach Moran."

"Ida Russell."

"How'd you get Starshine to come into your house? She usually won't go near strangers."

"I was watching out the window one day and she came into my yard to sniff the bushes. I thought she was just about the prettiest cat I'd ever seen and maybe she was a stray. So I went outside and called her, but she just looked at me, then headed back toward your house. I'd seen her a few other times, so it seemed likely she'd be back." Ida pulled the blanket up over her shoulders. "If you're moving around it's not so bad, but after you've been sitting awhile the cold gets into your bones."

Zach said, "You were telling us about Starshine."

"Don't worry. Now you got me talking, you'll never shut me up." She gave them a jaunty smile. "So what I did was, I bought one of those itsy bitsy cans of food that send you into orbit when you see the price. Then I waited for her to come sniffing around again. When she did, I put that fancy cat food out on the walk and called her, and this time she came over and ate it. After I fed her a few more times, she let me pick her up and take her into the house."

Cassidy said, "You were standing outside waiting to grab her at nine o'clock at night?"

"I started doing it in the afternoon. Then, when she got really used to me, I put the food out at night. All I had to do was stand in the doorway and call and she'd come in for seconds."

"Why did you want to keep her overnight?" Cassidy asked.

The woman shrugged. "I don't know. I just did."

Cassidy waited.

"I had a cat for eighteen years and she slept with me every night. I lost her about ten months ago." Ida swallowed and turned her head away. "I miss her so much."

Cassidy felt her own throat constrict. "Why didn't you get another cat instead of stealing ours?"

"I thought of it as borrowing. I mean, I let her go every morning, didn't I? At first, when I started taking her into the house, she'd stand at the door and howl. But after a while, she didn't seem to mind so much, and she was always happy to sleep with me. The reason she kept coming back was, she never could resist that fancy food."

Zach said, "You still haven't explained why you didn't get a cat of your own."

Ida stood up. "I'm going to make a cup of tea. How about you? Wouldn't you like a nice warm mug to wrap your hands around?"

"We're fine," Zach said, speaking for both of them.

Starshine jumped down and stretched, raising her rump and extending her front legs. Snatching up a cloth mouse, she shook it vigorously, threw it a few feet, pounced on it, and threw it again.

Ida returned, clutching a mug that gave off a sweet cinnamony aroma. "I'm afraid it's past my bedtime," she said pleasantly. "You folks will have to take your cat and go home."

"Ida," Cassidy said, "why don't you go to the Animal Care League and adopt a cat? There are so many that need good homes."

"I can't afford another cat."

"But you had one until ten months ago."

"I live on a fixed income. As long as Lucy was healthy, I could manage her food and litter. But when she stopped eating, I had to take her to the vet in a cab. The vet couldn't seem to diagnose her, so there were blood draws and an ultrasound and exploratory surgery. A few days after the surgery"—Ida sucked in air through her mouth—"she was in so much pain I had to have her put to sleep."

"What an awful ordeal," Cassidy said, trying not to think what it would be like when Starshine died. "Those vet bills must have taken a huge bite out of your income."

"Hey, what are credit cards for?" The woman shrugged in an attempt at nonchalance.

Zach said, "So you don't want another cat because you're afraid of more vet bills."

"There'll always be vet bills. People shouldn't have animals if they can't take care of them."

He folded his hands on his chest. "We'll take you to the ACL, pay the adoption fee, and have all the vet bills sent to us."

A look of dismay washed over Ida's face. "Oh no! I didn't tell you that to make you feel sorry for me. I may not have much money, but I still have my pride."

Not so much pride she wouldn't steal other people's cats.

Cassidy said, "Couldn't you take some pride in giving an abandoned cat a home? The animals at the shelter may have food and a roof over their heads, but they don't have anyone to love them. If you refuse to let us help you, you'll be dooming some poor cat to live out its life in a cage."

"Oh." Clasping her hands together, she held them against her mouth, her slender body folding in on itself.

A short time passed, then Ida dropped her hands and drew herself up straight. "If you really want to do it, I guess I ought to let you."

They left soon after that, Zach carrying the tracking devise, Cassidy holding Starshine against her shoulder as if she were a baby.

He said, "Since she likes that fancy food so much, maybe we ought to start getting it for her."

"Oh no you don't. She's staying on her low-cal diet." They walked a little farther, then Cassidy added, "I'm so glad you offered to pay her vet bills. It took me completely by surprise. I'm the one who usually jumps in and tries to fix things. You're the one who usually stays detached."

"I was sure you'd want Ida to have a cat and I know how you hate to spend money, so I figured if I made the offer, you wouldn't have to agonize."

Chapter 39

Cassidy held the receiver to her ear, listening to one ring after another, so many rings it was obvious the machine wasn't going to kick in. *Might as well hang up.* But she waited a little longer on the off chance he was in the bathroom or just now coming through the condo door.

A mechanical voice said, "Memory is full. No more messages will be recorded."

A feeling of dread rose inside her. *Oh no! Not Henry too! You said somebody might be after all three Lunch Bunchers but the last thing you wanted was for it to be true.*

Now don't go getting ahead of yourself. I'm sure there are other logical explanations, even if you can't think of any at the moment.

She absently picked up a sealed envelope and sliced it open but did not remove the contents. She lined up her stapler and her tape dispenser. Then she called Joan and reported that Henry's answering machine was full.

"Oh dear!" Joan didn't speak for several seconds. "You know, he is getting old. Maybe he's been forgetting to delete messages."

"I'm coming to Marina City," Cassidy said. "I think we ought to take a look inside his condo. Can you get his key?"

"I have a friend in the management company who owes me. But the fact that his answering machine is full doesn't give us much in the way of justification for entering his unit."

"We could turn it over to the police. Although I have to admit, I'd much rather have a chance to go through his condo first."

"It's not likely to do us any good. If somebody picked him up off the street like we think they did with Sandra, his condo will look just the same as before and we won't be able to tell whether he's out for the afternoon or gone for good."

"I know you're right but I still want to do it. There are times I've turned up some good leads looking through people's houses." *Like the card taped to the underside of Tessa's drawer.*

"Why don't we start by talking to his neighbors? Maybe one of them has seen him lately."

Before leaving, Cassidy went down to the basement to tell Zach where she was going. Now that he was finished with McCready, Zach had decided to use his remaining time at home to clean out the subterranean space beneath their house. Cassidy couldn't be happier. Their basement wasn't as bad as Lynn's attic, but if they continued putting things in without taking things out, it soon would be.

She explained why she was going to the twin towers.

"That does sound a little ominous." Zach set a box of old textbooks on her laundry table. "But I still think your Agatha Christie plot about somebody bumping off all the Lunch Bunchers is pretty absurd. It's more likely his machine's busted or he's off traveling somewhere."

She wrinkled her nose. "You're probably right. In fact, I hope it's nothing worse than a broken machine. But I'm still going to check it out."

"Of course you are."

The elevator doors opened and Cassidy and Joan stepped out onto Henry's floor. "Did he ever return any of your calls?" Cassidy asked.

"Nary a one. But I just chalked it up to his not being a call-returning type."

They walked a quarter of the way around the corridor and pushed Henry's doorbell twice. There was no response. "Just what we expected," Cassidy said.

"That neighbor over there." Joan pointed her chin toward the door to the left of Henry's. "She's one of the residents I couldn't get anywhere with. Far as I can tell, she hardly speaks to anybody."

"Let's try anyway."

They rang her bell, then listened as footsteps approached the door, paused, and left.

Joan said, "Guess she looked at us through the peephole and didn't like what she saw."

Next they rang the bell at the door on the other side of Henry's condo. A middle-aged couple came out into the hallway to talk.

"Have you seen Henry lately?" Joan asked. "Or heard any sounds from his condo?"

"That Henry," the woman replied, a venomous look on her face. "Thinks he's better than everybody else. After he had that cancer a few years back, I was hoping he'd move to a retirement home."

"When was the last time you saw him?" Joan persisted.

"Not sure. A few weeks ago. He never even acknowledges our existence, you know."

Three doors down, an attractive black woman said, "It's been a while. I used to bump into him fairly often. He'd go out for his morning walk about the same time I left for work, but lately we've been missing each other. I love that old-fashioned courtly charm of his. Wish I could find a boyfriend who had at least a clue about what it means to be a gentleman."

Most doors didn't open but Cassidy and Joan continued to make their way around the circle. They were close to the halfway point when a heavyset woman in her fifties answered the bell. She had a jowly toad-like face and was dressed as if she'd just returned from church, her rotund body bedecked with necklaces, bracelets and rings.

"Joan, what a surprise. Haven't seen you in ages."

"I'm trying to track down Henry Lucas. You know who I'm talking about? The elderly man who lives on the other side of the corridor."

"Met him when he first moved in. Said he was looking for a maid so I gave him the name of my girl. She isn't as thorough as I'd like, but she speaks good English and she's very reliable."

"When was the last time you saw Henry?"

The woman shrugged. "We don't run into each other very often. But you know, an odd thing happened. My maid was here Thursday and she told me she'd been at Henry's the day before and he hadn't put out any instructions or money. First time that's ever happened. And what's even stranger, she found some rotten bananas in a bowl. Carmen was really surprised. According to her, he's very particular—never a thing out of place. But I suppose he must've gone out of town and forgotten to take care of things."

Cassidy asked, "Do you know if he travels often?"

Stroking her chin, the woman gazed into space for a moment. "Hmm...I believe Carmen mentioned that he's gone a lot. Sometimes for several weeks."

Joan gave the woman her best hardball stare. "Why didn't you tell anybody that Henry might be missing?"

"Missing? I just thought he forgot."

"You know two people have disappeared from this building, don't you?"

"I heard about it," the woman said, her voice defensive. "It crossed my mind that something might be wrong. But what happens to Henry or anybody else is none of my business."

The door slammed shut.

Definitely not her brother's keeper. But you have any gossip about him, she'll be happy to listen.

"Dang!" Joan said. "I knew there was something about that woman I didn't like."

"Looks like we're going to need a key."

Joan shook her head. "I don't think we'll find anything."

"I wouldn't bet against you, but I still want to take a look. I hate leaving things unfinished."

"So do I. Okay, I'll get the key."

As Cassidy crossed the threshold, she picked up a faint odor of spoiled bananas, but when she looked in the kitchen, there was no sign of the offending fruit.

Maid must've thrown them away.

Cassidy and Joan followed separate paths through each of the rooms, making sure they checked all the closets. Finishing first, Cassidy returned to the living room and stood in front of the glass case she'd noticed earlier. Inside were half a dozen small shelves, each displaying its own piece of gray-green pottery.

Joan joined her in the living room. "Why are you staring at that fancy case? You see a clue in there?"

"I have this vague feeling something's different but I can't put my finger on it."

"I think you're just trying to come up with an excuse for our being here when we really don't have one."

"Yes we do. I did find something. Or rather, something missing. I didn't see a single piece of luggage. Which seems to indicate he really is away on a trip."

Joan perched on the arm of one of his enormous chairs. "Either that, or he keeps his luggage in his storage unit like I do."

"Oh. I forgot about the storage units."

"Let's go look at Henry's."

The units were on the twentieth floor in a locked room next to the laundry area. Each was a four-by-five cage labeled with its condo number. Henry's unit contained four expensive-looking pieces of matched luggage.

They stared at the suitcases for a couple of beats.

"I guess he isn't traveling," Cassidy said.

Joan tugged at the pendant she always wore. "Roloff must be sick of hearing from me. I suppose you'd like me to forget you were here."

"I can't get away with it this time. The cops will talk to that woman and she'll tell them you had someone with you."

They returned to Joan's condo to make the call. While they were waiting for the detectives to arrive, Cassidy reflected on Tessa's bizarre attempt to take Andy's card away from her. At the time she'd attributed it to stress, but the more she thought about it, the more it seemed like Tessa's actions might be an indication of something more serious.

Cassidy said, "I'm concerned about Tessa. I know she's been through a lot, but even taking that into account, some of her behavior seems extreme."

Joan frowned. "What are you talking about?"

"Remember when I showed Andy the card? And I told you I decided not to talk to Tessa?" Cassidy moistened her upper lip. "Well, I lied because I didn't want to embarrass her. The truth is, I went inside her condo and the first thing she did was try to block the door and not let me out, and after that she started grabbing at my purse. I suppose it could just be a response to her feeling that I'd betrayed her, but she seemed really strange, not like the Tessa I've seen before at all."

"Look how much she's been through. Wouldn't that make anybody a little strange?"

"I'm hoping it's just the stress. But then there's the panic and hysteria. What was she like before Miles disappeared? Did she seem pretty anxious?"

Joan tilted her head, resting her cheekbone against her fingertips. "She was generally good-natured. Let things roll off. But you're saying it might be more than just a normal reaction to her husband's murder. So what do you think it is?"

"It could just be stress. Or it could be Posttraumatic Stress Disorder, which I'm sure you know is a lot more serious. It'd be good if you could keep an eye on her. If she gets unreasonably angry or aggressive, if she panics over little things, she ought to see a therapist."

"You think I could get her to see one? I can lean on her for little things, but getting her into a therapist's office—."

The doorbell rang. Rollof came inside and took their statements.

He gave Cassidy a stony cop stare. "I see you didn't listen. So what do I have to do? Charge you with obstruction?"

"Why don't you start by telling me what I've obstructed?"

Chapter 40

It was two P.M. Thursday and Cassidy had just returned from visiting Delia in the hospital. She was hanging her coat in the closet when the phone rang. She scurried to the far end of the kitchen and picked up.

Joan said, "The last time you and I talked, you said I should let you know if Tessa's anger is out of proportion, or if she doesn't seem like herself."

Joan should let me know? Not how I remember it. I was trying to dump Tessa into Joan's lap. I certainly didn't want Joan dumping her back into mine.

Cassidy stretched the phone cord across the kitchen so she could wash out Starshine's bowl. "What kind of behavior are you seeing?"

"She's so much angrier than before. She just finished screaming at me for forgetting Amy's birthday. When Amy was two, I attended a party for her. At the time, I told Tessa I was no good at remembering birthdays, but I'd appreciate it if she'd remind me ahead of time so I could get Amy something every year. Last year was fine. Tessa told me, I gave Amy a present, everybody was happy. This year Tessa didn't say a word and I completely forgot. And now, just a few minutes ago, Tessa comes storming up to my door and yells at me because I didn't do anything for Amy's birthday. She didn't even come in, just stood out in the hall screaming. The old Tessa would never do anything like that."

"Have there been other incidents?"

"Nothing I've witnessed first-hand, but she told me about a panic attack she had, and two residents mentioned that she'd gotten into fights with them."

"So you think she needs professional help?"

"Isn't that what I just said?"

No, it's what she avoided saying. She wanted me to say it first so she doesn't have to take responsibility.

"What would you like me to do?" Turning away from the sink, Cassidy headed back toward the doorway, went into the dining room, and sat at the table. She gazed out the window at a heavy charcoal sky. Water dripped slowly from icicles overhead.

"I'd like for us to sit down together and strategize a way to get Tessa in to see a therapist. You're the professional. Your words will carry more weight than mine."

You couldn't even get your own husband in to see a therapist.

Cassidy said, "Aren't you forgetting that she hates me?"

"She doesn't like me much better at the moment. But Tessa's my friend and she's in trouble and we have to figure out a way to get her the help she needs. You and I are alike. We both believe problems can be solved if you just try hard enough."

Manipulating you. Trying to get you to be in charge of Tessa's mental health. You don't *believe all problems can be solved. There are some people you could take a blowtorch to their butt and they still wouldn't go to therapy. But I guess I have to try.*

"All right," Cassidy said, "I'll come to Marina City and we can put our heads together. This isn't going to be easy so let's just do it now and get it over with."

As Cassidy donned her coat and boots, another thought hit her. *Maybe Tessa doesn't have PTSD. Maybe it's guilt that's pushed her over the edge. Like the insomniac hand-washing Lady Macbeth.*

Large gloppy snowflakes began to fall as Cassidy drove east on the Eisenhower Expressway. *You should turn around. Tell Joan you'll do it some other day. It'll be rush hour by the time you're ready to leave and with snow like this, you'll have a long crawl home.*

She knew the smart thing would be to head back to Oak Park, but there was some part of her that refused to retreat. She switched on a radio station and listened for the weather report. Before long, an effervescent voice announced, "One to two inches of snow in Chicago, but look out Indiana. The wind is out of the north and as it travels over four hundred miles of open water in Lake Michigan, it picks up moisture and then dumps it in the form of snow in northern Indiana."

Cassidy was well aware that a couple of inches in the city could create gridlock.

Turning north onto Dearborn, she drove the length of the Loop, stop-and-go all the way. When she reached the twin towers, she spotted a parked car with its taillights on, ready to pull out into traffic. *Well, something's going right. The parking gods just saved you eleven dollars.* Maneuvering into the right lane, she waited for the car to vacate its precious space at the curb.

Pedestrians walked with their heads lowered, watching where they put their feet. As Cassidy pushed coins into the meter, she saw that the SUV in front of her was parked next to a fireplug. *Given the cost of city parking tickets, that driver must not mind throwing big bucks down a rat hole.* She plodded uphill toward the Marina City entrance, her eyes downward to avoid patches of ice.

A few feet ahead she noticed legs moving toward her. She looked up to see a man in a parka, the hood pulled low over his forehead, a medium-sized box in his hands. Suddenly his feet went out from under him and he fell backward, catching himself with one hand. She bent down and took hold of his arm to help him up. He slowly got to his feet, then stood looking at her. With a scarf around the lower part of his face, all she could see were a classic nose and deep-set eyes surrounded by age lines. A spark of recognition showed in them. She glimpsed movement, his arm swinging toward her. A blow to the side of her head creating a vivid burst of color. Then nothing.

Cassidy became aware of a throbbing pain in her head, then crackling noises and a mild smell of burning wood. A murmur of internal voices started up, indistinct at first, then gradually becoming clearer.

Don't wake up. You don't want to know what's happening.

Can't just lie here and be a victim. Have to find out what that man in the parka is up to.

She moved her legs and heard a crinkly sound. Feeling the surface beneath her, she concluded she was lying on plastic. She resisted opening her eyes for several seconds, but curiosity got the better of her. As she glanced around, everything appeared blurry, nothing but pools of darkness and light. Then forms began to emerge, and finally she was able to distinguish her surroundings.

Still wearing her coat and boots, she was stretched out on a sofa with a plastic sheet beneath her. The sofa right-angled a large stone fireplace framed in wood, flames consuming a huge pile of logs inside it. Several feet back from the fireplace, an oriental rug lay on a polished wood floor. Behind the rug, two enormous armchairs faced the fire, a round antique table between them, a floor lamp beside each chair, the lamps casting subdued circles of light. A man sat in one of the chairs but the room was so shadowy she couldn't see his face.

Cassidy swung her feet down to the floor and sat up.

"I didn't say you could do that," the man remarked in a genial tone.

Henry! Henry's dead. No he isn't. He's right here in this room with you.

She stared at him for several seconds. He continued to gaze at the fire, paying no attention to her.

"I didn't recognize you on the street. You didn't have to do this."

"Couldn't take chances. Besides, what difference does it make? Everybody has to die sometime."

"So why am I still alive?"

"Do you know what the weather's like?"

"Snow?"

"This is northern Indiana. We have blizzards here. I can't get the backhoe out until it clears."

"Backhoe? You mean...for digging a grave?" Her mouth went dry. Her voice came out in a rasp.

"Of course, there are other possibilities. I could kill you now and bury you later. I've never killed anybody in my house before but there isn't any reason not to do it." He leaned forward. "I have to admit, our surprise encounter caught me off guard."

"But there isn't any hurry, is there?"

He's old, probably not very strong. Maybe you could fight him off.

This guy's an expert at killing. If he considered you any kind of risk at all, you'd be tied up so tight you couldn't move an eyelash.

As her eyes continued to adjust to the darker areas of the room, they lit on a gray-green piece of pottery. It sat in a place of honor at the center of the mantle, surrounded by primitive wood carvings.

"That bowl on your mantle. It used to be in the glass case in your living room."

"Very perceptive of you."

"Why take this particular piece?"

"Everything in the case is from the Koryo Dynasty in Korea. It's called Celadon, which refers to the kind of glaze. I didn't think anyone would notice if one piece was missing. I picked that bowl because the glaze is exceptionally translucent." He looked at her. "I'm sure that's more than you ever wanted to know about Celadon. Now if you'll excuse me, I'm going to get something to drink."

The lamps flickered and the gleaming hardwood floor creaked as he walked through a doorway in the wall behind the sofa. He returned with a brandy snifter containing a couple of inches of amber liquid. Cassidy—head pounding, body cold, muscles stiff and achy—gazed greedily at his glass.

"Could I possibly have some of that?"

He gave her a contemptuous look. "You're a problem to be dealt with, not a guest."

Feelings of self-pity welled up inside her. Her eyes filled, and it took every ounce of effort she could muster to hold back the tears.

Distract him. Divert him. Don't give him time to decide when and how to kill you.

"You did such a good job of faking your disappearance, why take the risk of coming back?

Oh, wait, I understand. You came back to get that box you were carrying."

"Very good."

Cassidy noted a slight shift in his tone. She'd said something intelligent, and he'd moved from regarding her with contempt to displaying a small degree of respect. *Liked Miles because he considered Miles an equal. Now if you can just avoid clichés and stupidity, may decide he likes you as well. Not that that would stop him from killing you.*

"Why's the box important to you?"

"I didn't think it would be. When I left Marina City, I didn't give it a second thought. The box contains old photos and memorabilia, and I've never had the slightest interest in that sort of thing. The only reason I kept it was...well, I'm not sure why I kept it."

He set his glass on the table, got up, and pulled a footstool closer so he could rest his feet on it. "You see, I'm a sociopath. I know, they've changed the label to Antisocial Personality Disorder, but I prefer sociopath. Can't see any reason for changing the names of things. So—since I'm a sociopath—I've never experienced any feelings of nostalgia or sentimentality. However, after I moved here, I began to think about the box. I hadn't opened it in so long I didn't know what was in it. But now that I'm about to die, I found myself wanting to go through it. I have no memory of my mother's face, and I thought it might be interesting to view the photos."

You didn't think sociopaths had feelings like that either. But of course nobody fits neatly into any one diagnostic category.

"You said you're dying. Did the cancer come back?"

He turned his head in her direction, his face approving. "Lymphoma. When it first appeared, they knocked it out with chemo." Henry got up and went to stand in front of one of the two windows flanking the door. Moments later, he returned to his chair.

"I recently started having symptoms again, and this time it's metastasized to my lungs and liver. It was important to get rid of Miles and Sandra before I got too weak to handle their bodies. I took care of them, had all my affairs in order, and was ready to settle in here, then I run into you on the street and a blizzard makes it impossible to dispose of you properly. But that's all right. The weather will clear and you're so small I won't have any difficulty carrying you to the barn."

Chapter 40

"Why kill Miles and Sandra?"

Henry chuckled. "They know where the bodies are buried. Literally."

"What?"

"It's a long story." He swallowed the remainder of his brandy, then looked down into his lap and began muttering to himself. "You should kill her now. Then you could get some sleep."

Cassidy noticed the slump in his shoulders. *Maybe it isn't hopeless. He's tired from driving through the storm, getting sicker by the day. Maybe you can get away from him. But have to start flexing your muscles or you won't be able to run.*

She rose and stood with her back to the fire, bending one knee up, then the other, to get rid of the stiffness.

"I'd really like to hear why you needed to kill the other two Lunch Bunchers."

"What you'd like doesn't interest me."

The windows rattled and the lights flickered again. Now that she was on her feet, she had a better view of the round table. It held a thick book, a telephone, a plastic candle-lighter, and a contemporary oil lamp. Cassidy liked the design of the lamp, which was short and angular, with a bright yellow design on one side.

She said, "But maybe you'd enjoy telling somebody what you did before everyone is dead." *Sociopaths are grandiose. They like to brag.*

Henry stood, rolled his shoulders, then headed toward an entertainment center on the wall opposite the sofa. He put on a CD and classical music filled the room. Sinking back into his chair, he said, "Sit down. You're blocking my view."

She did as she was told. "I'd like to hear about Miles and Sandra."

"You have a taste for the macabre, do you? All right, the first thing you need to know is that I'm a professional killer."

Oh really? What a surprise.

"I command high fees because of my expertise at making people disappear. Not one of my bodies has ever been found. Miles—who had some small connection to the mob—hired me years ago on behalf of his sister Sandra, who wanted her mother disposed of. After I fulfilled my contract, we went our separate ways. Then, about nine years ago, Miles and I bumped into each other. I mentioned that I was looking for a place with a lake view and he suggested Marina City. Once I moved in, I discovered he was a kindred spirit."

"A sociopath?"

"More of a narcissist, but we had a lot in common. Then I developed lymphoma, and while I was undergoing chemo, I was too weak to handle the physical aspects of my work. Just before I started treatment, Miles went out on his own and discovered that clients were harder to come by than he'd expected. He needed money, I needed somebody with a strong back. Somebody I could trust. So we reached an agreement. I planned and supervised, he performed the labor."

"Then you recovered and didn't need him anymore?" Cassidy remembered the notebook Tessa had found documenting mysterious payments to Miles over a period of about three years.

"He got busy with his consulting business and wasn't interested in the side jobs anymore. And I was doing well enough I could have continued on my own. But I was in my sixties and preferred not to have to do the physical work myself. By then,

Miles had talked Sandra into joining us at Marina City, and he convinced me she could do the job as well as he could. So I took her on, and since she had an insatiable need for money, it worked out to everyone's advantage."

"And then the cancer returned and you thought you had to kill them?" Cassidy could hear the incredulity in her voice. None of it made sense to her.

He went to stand over her. "Of course you wouldn't understand. Things like this are beyond you."

The floor lamps suddenly went out.

"Damn! I should've had the candles lit." He picked up the candle-lighter and applied it to the oil lamp's wick. An orange flame blossomed inside the elegant glass container. Then he began taking fat round candles out of a credenza next to the entertainment center.

Has his back to you on the other side of the room. This is your chance.

To do what? Run into the kitchen? Maybe go outside and get lost in the storm? Henry's legs are twice as long as yours. If he wasn't sure he could outrun you, he wouldn't be so nonchalant.

Henry distributed lighted candles around the room, then sat down again. "One reason I'm at the top of my profession is that I have the ability to make bodies disappear for good. I take great pride in my workmanship, and I intend for those bodies to remain hidden for the next thousand years. If I left either Miles or Sandra alive, my secret would inevitably get out."

"But they're as guilty as you are. Don't they have the same investment in keeping it quiet?"

"If more than one person knows a secret, it eventually gets divulged. Just look around you.

People drink too much. They indulge in pillow talk. They can't resist telling what they know."

Not even Henry, who is right now giving in to his urge to tell you about his world-class status as a hit man.

The lights came back on. They sat in silence gazing at the hypnotic flames until Cassidy asked, "Would it be all right if I went over and looked out the window? I'd like to see if the storm's letting up."

"Eager for the next stage, are you?" He got up from his chair and let the fire warm his backside. "The blizzard's irrelevant. I could do you any time I want."

"I'm not in any hurry." She got up and walked slowly across the room, taking note of everything she could see, searching for something she could use to protect herself. Stopping in front of the window, she stared out at snow swirling thickly around a yard light.

She returned to the sofa. "Okay, I understand why you had to kill Miles and Sandra. I even understand why you have to kill me. But after you die, this property will go to someone else and won't that person find the bodies?"

A self-satisfied smile appeared on his face. "I own a big piece of land here, and a lot of it's wetlands. Bought it over forty years ago. When I'm in Hanleyville, everybody knows me as Frank Madison, a rich guy from Chicago who retreats to his farm whenever he wants a little peace and quiet. I even had a girlfriend here for a while, a young lady who works at the post office. And I've got every piece of ID you could ask for to prove I'm Frank Madison."

Clasping his hands behind his back, he rocked on the balls of his feet. "When I die, my property will go to the Nature Conservancy. They've contracted to hold this land as a wildlife preserve in perpetuity. So you see, no one will ever have the right to dig up my bone yard."

"Well, I'm impressed. It seems like you've thought of everything." *Except nobody ever does. The best laid plans of man and sociopath.*

Henry glanced around the room. "No point letting the candles burn down. I might need them several more times before the end." He went to the credenza, took out a candle snuffer, and began extinguishing the flames.

A bad feeling came over her. *Doesn't make sense. The power could go out again any minute. So what's he up to, anyway?*

Starting from the wall opposite the sofa, he moved around the perimeter of the room in her direction. The bad feeling grew stronger. He walked over to a shelving unit about two feet behind the sofa, put out the candle, then stood a moment longer, doing something she couldn't see.

She heard a small rustling sound. Twisting toward the back of the sofa, she saw his arms above her head, his hands holding a piece of twine. As she threw herself down on the seat, he let out a startled grunt and lunged at her.

She rolled off the sofa, ran to the table, grabbed the oil lamp, and spun around to face the fireplace. Out of the corner of her eye, she could see that Henry's lunge had taken him head first over the back of the sofa and he was still trying to pick himself up. Holding the lamp high, she hesitated, not sure where the oil would do the most good.

Just throw it or he'll be on top of you. She smashed the lamp against the wood trim on the left side of the fireplace, the section farthest from the sofa. She knew she needed to escape as fast as possible but couldn't get her legs to move until she found out whether her attempt at fire starting had worked. As soon as flames began licking the wood, she raced toward the doorway into the kitchen. Reaching the threshold, she looked back. Henry was trying to smother the flames with the oriental rug, a stream of curses issuing from his mouth.

Bad idea. Rug's likely to catch fire.

She darted into the kitchen and switched on the light. A square room, Corian counters, cooking implements hanging over a butcher block island. *Henry a gourmet cook on top of being a Celadon collector and a world class hit man?*

Cassidy sprinted toward the door on the opposite side of the kitchen and looked through its window into another room that resembled an enclosed porch. She dredged up the term mudroom from many strata down in her memory, a word she didn't know she knew. Stepping into the unheated space, she flipped on the light, buttoned her coat, and pulled her collar up around her ears. Henry's parka hung on a peg near the exterior door, his boots standing nearby. A bag of salt leaned against the wall, a broom and shovel stood in the corner, a trash can sat off to the side. Rough hewn shelves covered one wall.

She crossed to the door and peered through its multipaned window. A diffuse light coming from somewhere else made it possible for her to see the SUV in the carport. The driver's side door was about three yards from where she stood. *Keys. Where would they be? In the ignition? He's a city boy, has a lifelong habit of never leaving keys in the car.* She knew that in rural areas people often hung keys near the door. There were three hooks close at hand but all of them were empty. Next she inspected the shelves, which also did not have keys.

Anxiety sluiced through her as she realized that if Henry had them with him she was trapped.

What does Zach do with his? A light bulb went off. *Coat pocket.*

She hauled the front of Henry's parka away from the wall and thrust her hand into one of its pockets. Her fingers touched cold metal. She pulled out his car keys. As she was opening the door, she heard a noise behind her. She looked over her shoulder and saw Henry coming though the doorway into the mud room.

She carefully negotiated the three snow-covered steps down to the concrete driveway. The wind nearly knocked her over. She was relieved to discover that the white stuff on the ground was light and powdery with no ice underneath. The rear end of the SUV was thickly covered with snow, but the layer on the windshield and the driver's side window was only about an inch thick. She brushed the snow off the side window and mirror with her bare hands, then reached for the handle. *Oh God, let it be unlocked!*   Her prayer was answered. She climbed inside, closed the door, and pushed the button to set the locks. A satisfying click told her that Henry could not get in without a key, which she was sure he didn't have with him. She moved the seat forward so she could reach the pedals.

She glanced at the mud room door and saw Henry coming down the steps in his parka and boots. As she turned on the engine, the driver's side door rattled. Henry looked at her through the window. His face was flushed, his forehead sweaty, his beautiful white hair stuck out in all directions. He walked away from the car and began tromping through the snow toward the barn, which was set back from the house about fifty feet.

Cassidy punched on an interior light above her head, her nerves stretched so tight she moved in jerky little spurts. She examined the two rods sticking out from the base of the steering wheel, searching for a way to turn on the headlights and the windshield wipers. Discovering the icon for the windshield wipers, she watched as two fan-shaped areas streaked with white appeared on the glass in front of her. She could see snowflakes whipping in circles around the car.

She gazed at the confusing array of lights on the dashboard, locating three icons that depicted the rear window wiper. She pressed all three, gave up on the headlights, and began backing the car out of the carport.

She couldn't see a thing behind her. The rear window wiper was inadequate to the task of clearing off the heavy snow and the side mirror was covered in white again. She opened the door and stuck her head out into the wind and snow. A dense line of evergreens and bushes stood about thirty feet to the rear of the car, but it looked like she had plenty of room to maneuver. She backed up several feet, then came to a dead stop, unable to move in either direction. Peering through the windshield, she saw Henry coming out of the barn carrying something over his shoulder.

She began rocking the car in an effort to get unstuck. She tried to concentrate on what she was doing, but it was hard to keep her eyes off Henry, who was plodding through knee-deep snow in her direction.

The SUV was rocking forward when Henry trotted up close to the car. She could not tear her eyes away from the object in his hands. An axe. He took up a stance on the passenger side, gripped the handle in both hands, and swung the blade.

She lowered her face and threw her arms up in front of it. A deafening crunch shook the car. It took her an instant to realize there was no falling glass. When she got up the nerve to look, she saw that the axe was stuck in the windshield, and a spider web of cracks had spread out from the point of impact. As Henry jerked the axe free, she pressed the accelerator and rocked forward.

When she saw him prepare to swing again, she closed her eyes and turned her head away. The axe hit the side window, an explosion of glass pellets assaulting her. Her eyes popped open and she watched in horror as Henry thrust his arm inside the broken window.

She rolled the car backward, then forward, doing her best not to lose traction. This time she kept moving. She heard a click from the passenger side. Henry had reached inside and opened the door.

She gunned the motor, hoping to force him to withdraw his arm. Looking again, she saw that his head was no longer visible but his arm was still hooked over the edge of the window, his hand clutching the inner door handle. *Good God, you're dragging him.*

She drove to the front of the carport, then jerked the car into reverse and sped a good distance backward, careful to avoid the place she'd gotten stuck before.   The door swung open. She couldn't tell if Henry was still hanging on or not. She jammed on the brakes and the door slammed shut. Henry's arm was still attached. *Could be unconscious. Maybe too far gone to hurt you. But you can't take chances.*

She sucked in air and tried to get her bearings. The yard lights were hazy from the snow and it was difficult to see. She opened the glove compartment, found a flashlight, and shone it on the area around the SUV. In back of her was the line of trees and bushes. It appeared to mark the right hand edge of the driveway.

Another sound from the passenger side. Shining her light through the window, she saw that Henry was trying to open the door again. Her heart pounded, blood rushed in her ears.

Turning the car sharply to the right, she plowed through a hillock of snow, mentally crossing her fingers that she wouldn't get stuck again. Then she veered diagonally toward the line of trees. When her right fender hit the underbrush, she turned and drove forward, the right side of her car scraping the branches. She kept her eyes straight ahead, not able to bear the thought of seeing Henry's arm hooked through the window. She crawled ten feet or more,   then the SUV bumped down into a ditch and came to a stop. She tried to get the car moving again, but it refused to go either forward or backward.

She forced herself to look at the passenger door. Henry was gone. Laying her arms across the steering wheel, she rested her forehead on them and sat like that for a minute or so.

Have to get back to the house.

Too hard. You'll never make it.

Have to do it. For Zach and Gran and everyone who loves you.

She stepped down into waist-deep snow. Slogging through it, she made her way to the driveway where the snow was only a few inches deep. She shone her light along the line of trees but could not see Henry's body.

By the time she opened the mud room door, she was shivering all over. She ransacked the kitchen for the brandy bottle, found it, and poured herself half a tumbler full. She clutched the glass with both hands and went into the living room, which smelled strongly of burnt wood. Ignoring the fire marks and crumpled rug, she crouched in front of the embers, drank brandy, and soaked up heat.

A short time later, she heard a crash in the kitchen. Too numb to be afraid, she went to see if Henry had returned. His body lay spread out on the kitchen floor. Although she didn't care whether he was alive or dead, she went upstairs, operating on automatic pilot, and brought down a blanket to throw over him.

Time to make phone calls. Zach first, then 9-1-1

Chapter 41

"I have a bottle of champagne," Delia told Zach. "I don't know how to open it but Cass said you could do it."

"I'm an expert," he replied.

"I'll just go get it." Delia went into her kitchen and brought out a bottle of Dom Perignon.

"Wow!" Cassidy said. "I keep forgetting how rich you are."

"I'd trade all the money in the world not to have this illness."

"Living with schizophrenia has to be just awful," Cassidy said.

"I'm one of the lucky ones. Most schizophrenics are never able to function half as well as I do."

"People with schizophrenia," Zach corrected. He took the bottle from Delia, aimed it at the ceiling, and worked the cork loose. It made a satisfying pop as it flew out of the bottle, ricocheted off white plaster, and banged against the sofa. Shafts of early April sunlight angled through the glass wall. Delia had opened the door to the balcony to let in the fresh spring air. Along with the air came raucous city noises from the streets below. She had been out of the hospital for a month, and during that time she'd had the condo cleaned and repainted.

"Why don't you sit down while I mix the Mimosas?"

Cassidy and Zach settled into upholstered chairs at the square wooden table in front of the glass wall. Before long, Delia carried a pitcher to the table and filled their glasses. She sat down and passed a cheesy brunch casserole, a bowl of fresh fruit, a mixed green salad, and muffins.

Zach sipped his Mimosa. "This champagne's so good you shouldn't contaminate it with orange juice."

Delia stood up. "I can get you a glass of straight champagne if you like."

"Thanks anyway, but I have to demonstrate to Cass on a daily basis that I don't drink too much."

"Not that you always succeed."

Delia hastened to change the subject. "I invited you here to thank you for letting me stay. I was sure you wouldn't want anything more to do with me after all the trouble I caused. I was planning on giving you permission to break the lease."

"We wanted you to stay," Cassidy replied. "Zach and I talked it over and he said you'd been through enough already and shouldn't have to look for another place to live."

"You did?" Delia's face exhibited shock. She said to Zach, "I thought you were against having me here from the beginning."

"I was at first." He heaped more casserole on his plate. "But I don't think anybody's life should be as hard as yours."

"Maybe mine won't be so hard anymore. I have a new doctor who listens to me. And some new friends too."

"Who are they?" Cassidy already knew that Joan had taken Delia under her wing, but she didn't want Delia to think they'd been talking about her behind her back.

"Joan Frasier appeared at my door and introduced herself just a few days after I got back. We started chatting on the phone, then she invited me to her place for lunch. That's where I met Tessa, so now I've got two friends here in the building. At first I didn't trust them. I was sure they were trying to get their hands on my money. But I talked about it with my therapist and she convinced me it was just my paranoia."

"Joan's a good person to have as a friend. You can always go to her if you need help. And Tessa has a lot to offer as well." Cassidy was aware that Joan had succeeded in getting Tessa into therapy, but she wasn't about to pass that piece of information along.

Delia pushed her light brown hair back from her face. She now wore it in long loose curls, which made her look younger, and she appeared a couple of sizes thinner than when Cassidy first saw her. "After I had lunch at Joan's, I got the idea of having you two over. But it was kind of scary, because I've never done anything like this before. I was going to have it catered, but Joan convinced me I could do it on my own."

Bullying's not all bad. A person as insecure as Delia will probably thrive on it. In fact, you've had good results yourself using it on Zach.

He said, "The food is great. I hope you noticed I took seconds."

Delia smiled shyly.

The sound of a horn blasting repeatedly was so loud Cassidy could barely hear what the other two were saying. She gritted her teeth, suppressing the urge to go out on the balcony and yell obscenities down at the knuckle dragger who was honking.

"Now that you're back on your meds," Zach continued, "are you symptom free?"

Cassidy examined Delia's face, trying to determine if she was uncomfortable talking about her illness. She appeared not to be bothered by Zach's question.

"The voices never disappear completely, but when I take my meds they get quieter and I can tell they're coming from my brain, not being beamed into me from someplace else. I always have a little paranoia, but I can keep it under control. The symptoms are something I can live with, just like people live with all kinds of other illnesses." Looking down, she picked up muffin crumbs from her placemat and dropped them on her plate. "I've been talking too much, haven't I?"

"Not at all," Zach responded. "I was interested in everything you had to say."

Delia twisted a lock of hair around her finger, then said to Zach, "I'd love to hear what you're working on."

"A series on bad judges. I don't mean corrupt, I mean judges who act like little tyrants in their courtrooms. There was one who refused to let a defendant go to the bathroom, made her stay where she was till she wet herself. This is my kind of story. Gets my juices flowing."

Delia said, "There's something I've been wondering about but I'm not sure if I should bring it up at the table."

"Sure you should." Cassidy scooped up the last bite of her salad and held it in the air. "There's nothing we like better than the gruesome and bizarre."

"It's about those bodies buried on Henry's land. Do you think the police were able to find all of them? If they don't have the victims' DNA on file, how can they identify them?"

"They've got the remains of one hundred and three victims," Zach said. "Cadaver dogs went over every inch of dry land, so they probably didn't miss anybody. The FBI's taken over the identification process, and hundreds of people have come forward looking for missing relatives. One guy was identified when his wife recognized his wedding ring. But there are a lot of old bones that'll remain anonymous."

Fortunately Ann's mother isn't among them. They found her body early on.

Delia caught her bottom lip between her teeth. "It's a shame Henry never regained consciousness. He probably knew the names of most, if not all, the victims."

"It's a shame he got off so easy," Cassidy retorted. "Justice would've been better served if he'd died a long lingering painful death. And even if he had lived, he wouldn't have given up a single name."

Delia appeared surprised at what Cassidy had said.

Everybody expects me to be so nice, but a lot of the time I'm not.

Later, as they were standing in the entryway to say good-bye, Zach said to Delia, "You're very pretty, you know. Now I want to go on record that I'm not hitting on you or committing sexual harassment. I just get the sense that you don't have any idea how attractive you are."

She covered her face with her hands. "No I'm not!"

"You don't see yourself the way others do. Especially guys. I bet there are a lot of guys who'd like to ask you out if you didn't keep yourself so hidden away."

"Don't say things like that! It confuses me. I don't know what to do with it."

"Take it to your therapist."

As soon as they were in the car, Cassidy said to Zach, "Who is this person that's taken over my husband's body?"

"You mean because I said she was pretty?"

"You shouldn't have said that. The last thing she needs to think about is relationships. But it was obvious you were trying to be kind and build up her confidence. Me compassionate, you detached. You're encroaching on my territory."

"Look, you don't own the copyright on sympathy. She's a decent person. She deserves better than the life she's got."

"You're stealing my lines. I'm the one who's supposed to care about people and you're supposed to balance me off by being indifferent."

"I have to be objective when it comes to the people I write about. But Delia's so fragile and self-effacing. She kind of got to me."

Cassidy reached over and put her hand on Zach's thigh. "Okay, I guess it wouldn't be that bad to have a husband who's nicer than I am—as long as it doesn't happen more than once a decade."

Printed in the United States
134487LV00003B/121/P